Almost

Amy Booker

Amy Booker
Almost

ISBN-13: 978-0-578-36773-6

To everyone with an Almost.

CONTENTS

1

From Afar

RYAN

I didn't expect to run into her so soon. When I suggested the band come to my hometown of Chandler, Ohio, to work on our next album, I knew I would see her at some point. Statistically, it was inevitable. It's a small damned town. That it's happening within the first hour of arriving back was not the plan. Recognizing her long chocolate brown hair, I know her the instant my eyes catch sight of her. Sarah Lawrence. Watching her from inside the gas station, and basically blocking the door for all incoming and outgoing traffic, not that I care, takes my breath away. She's standing by the back of her car while filling it up, her eyes are closed, and I can tell she's in her own little world, humming a song to herself as she always does.

The early evening slanting sun shines on her hair, casting a copper glow on her beautiful, suntanned face. Sarah is simply stunning, and my breath catches a little as I take her in. Her curves still curve in a way that drives me nuts, and a new dragonfly tattoo forms part of a half sleeve on her right arm. We'd talked about her wanting to add that particular one, and I'm happy she followed through. It suits her perfectly. Quiet. Peaceful. Beautiful. That's my Sarah. Well, not *my* Sarah.

"Excuse me," an older woman says impatiently as she pushes me aside in a hurry to return to her car. She glances back and gives me a vicious glare while shaking her head like she's got any clue what's happening in mine. She has no idea I suddenly spotted the unrequited love of my life, and at that moment, my heart left my body and dropped to the grimy store floor. Metaphorically, of course, but this lady doesn't realize that. Not letting her distract me, my focus is strictly on Sarah, who is still oblivious that I'm only around thirty feet away from her, watching her like some stalker.

Shit, I think, abruptly aware of how horrifyingly creepy I must appear to everyone around me. I glance down at the power drink in my right hand and the car keys in my left, as if they'll give me some clue as to what I'm supposed to do with myself. *Right. I stopped to buy a bottle of water on my way to my band's hotel. No big deal. Did I pay for this already? I did, right? Fuck, Ryan, get your shit together.*

Shifting back to the doors, I'm unsure if I should make myself known to Sarah or slink out with my head and face obscured somehow. My baseball cap mostly does the trick, and I'm pretty good about going incognito to escape getting recognized, but I didn't foresee hiding in my own town. Not that I'm super famous, but our band's popularity is picking up a little, and I can't always guess what to expect from people. This moment caught me completely off guard, even though I envisioned my reunion with Sarah a million times in my head. To be fair, our meeting again did not happen at the corner gas station whenever I dared to picture it, but here we are. I need to figure a way out of this. I am not prepared to face her yet.

Acting on impulse, I duck my head deeper into my hat and speed walk to my car without flat out running to avoid being inconspicuous. I probably look like a complete idiot to anyone paying me any mind. My feet slide a little on the greasy concrete as I move past Sarah, whose eyes are still shut, and I can hear a snippet of the tune she is singing to herself. The sound of her sweet voice carrying on the wind sends a tingling down the skin of my arms. One of the hardest things I'll ever do is go past her; without acknowledging her, calling to her, being in her presence without her detecting that I'm here. My heart lurches a little, and I have to take a deep breath.

This isn't the time or place for a reunion. The band still needs to settle in at their hotel, and I want to get myself situated at my mom's house and hang out with her at least for a little while. I haven't seen her in person for almost a year, and even then, she had to come visit me while I was on the road. Close to three years have gone by since my last time here in town, and this is the exact reason why. I knew as soon as I saw Sarah, I would lose all control. All the bricks in the wall I built around me and my heart would instantly crumble, and I was right. The dust and ash of those bricks and mortar are falling all around, getting ready to choke me.

Jumping into my car, I slump down behind the wheel as

much as my 6'2" frame can, quietly thanking our manager Vanessa in my head for renting one with tinted windows. At least if Sarah looks around, she won't see me. I don't start the car but continue to stare silently as Sarah finishes filling her tank, her eyes popping open when the pump automatically stops. I could watch her when she gets in her musical reveries all day. Her singing is the purest form of happiness I know on the planet. She grabs her receipt, frowning at it briefly before getting into her car. It hits me then she's driving her mother's Honda. The sedan must be pretty old by now, and it's odd she's not using the new car she bought a few years ago when she graduated from college. It makes me wonder if she's been in an accident or something since I saw her last. This thought makes my mind go dark, imagining her hurt or worse. I shake my head to clear those thoughts and look on as she carefully pulls onto the road, heading further out of town in the direction of her house on the lake. Maybe she just filled up her mom's car for her. It would be like her to do that for someone else.

I'm so tempted to follow her. To go to her house and tell her I never stopped thinking about her. I never stopped loving her. Of course, I'd never told her I loved her in the first place, so that would probably freak her out. I let that chance slip through my fingers long ago, so I can't do that. I need to play it cool. I feel enough like a damned stalker already from just watching her here. Sighing loudly, I push the air out of my chest, which is suddenly heavy with a weight I've not felt in a long time. The significance of my feelings for Sarah could drown me if I let them. I can't let them. Not now that I almost learned how to live with them. *Almost* being the keyword.

Come Home

SARAH

The front door hinges squeak in protest as I push it shut. The constant humid air from Lake Erie only a few hundred feet away makes itself heard in the groan of the old metal. There are too many things needing repairs and never enough time, energy, or money to fix them. One of these days, I'll have that door fixed.

"Is that you, Sarah?" my younger brother Benji calls from the kitchen, sounding distracted. I sigh inwardly. *Who else could it possibly be?*

"Nope," I yell back, a sarcastic smile growing. "The ghost of Christmas Future just appeared from nowhere, and dude, we need to talk." As I turn into the kitchen, I find Benji at the counter, his face buried in one of his textbooks and a sandwich Dagwood himself would be proud of in one hand.

"Very funny," he mumbles, covering his mouth trying not to spray ham and lettuce all over his new book.

He's starting college in a week, and I'm still shocked at how time has flown. My chest tightens at the thought of him leaving so soon to go hundreds of miles away and me living in this massive house all by myself. Our mom would have wanted it this way; I need to remind myself. Fighting back the tears burning the back of my throat, I ask, "What's up? How are your books looking? Think you're going to be able to handle it?" I cringe a little when the last question comes out, but I need to be sure he will be in the right head space. I won't be there for him if he should need me.

His jaw tenses, but he rolls his eyes at me. "I'll be fine. These books aren't too bad. I think there will be some overlap to my senior term. And besides, Joe will be with me."

Joe has been Benji's boyfriend for the past eighteen months or so, and the two of them together are beyond adorable. Meeting at a grief support group, starting as friends, and gradually becoming more, they are the definition of relationship goals. Joe understands Benji's emotional complexities in a way few people can, and since our mother's death two years ago, he has been a comfort to him.

"Good," I sigh a little too loudly. I don't want to show I'm relieved, but I am. I worry about Benji so much and always will. He went through a scary, rough patch when Mom passed away and went to a dark place I didn't think he'd ever come back from. He couldn't start college when he first graduated from high school because of how he handled her death, or, *didn't* handle it more like it. I'm so proud of how far he's come in two years. Joe showing up in his life when he did probably saved him more than anything else could.

The five year age difference between us can sometimes feel like an entire generation gap, and other times we act like twins. How we each dealt with our grief brought us together as siblings in a way I don't think anything else could have. Now that he's twenty-one, and leaving to attend college, I'm about to become a super young empty nester.

Benji closes his book and wipes his hands together to get rid of the sandwich crumbs. He glances up at me, a severe worry taking over his sharp features. His brown eyes that match mine soften as he speaks hesitantly, his voice barely audible, "So, did you see him?"

I stare at my brother, utterly confused. "Who?" I have no idea what he's talking about, and the concerned expression on his face is beginning to freak me out. "Who was I supposed to see?" His eyes drop to the floor where our shepherd mix dog, Gunner, is hungrily gobbling up fallen crumbs. Benji is avoiding my question. You can't throw a loaded question at me like that. "Benji?" I ask again, more forcefully this time. "Who was I supposed to see? Talk to me, dude."

He glances nervously out the back sliding doors leading to the deck and then further out to the lake before slowly dragging his eyes back to me. "Ryan Crawford."

Time halts, the waves on the lake outside stop crashing, and the world pauses spinning for a second when I hear his name. The name I've tried so hard to forget the last three years but failed miserably. It haunts me both day and night, no matter how hard I try to forget him.

"Are you alright?" Anxiety takes over his face. "Are you going to be sick?"

"I'm fine," I lie, flashing a brief fake smile at my brother. "No, I haven't seen Ryan." My voice catches a little on his name as I say it aloud for the first time in forever. The reverb sound of it vibrates in my chest like an echo chamber. Busying myself, I pick up his plate and turn to wash it, desperate to hide my face I'm sure is betraying my every emotion. "Is he back in town?" I ask, trying to sound uninterested. I am obviously *highly* interested.

"Yeah, I guess he and his band are in town to record a new album. Since you work at Lakeshore Studio, I figured you would have known about it."

The plate slips from my soapy hands and clatters to the sink, luckily not breaking. I whip around to face my brother, "*His* band is the one recording at Lakeshore?" I knew the studio was booked and blocked for two whole months, but I didn't know it was Indigo King, Ryan's band that are taking it over. I've been upset that myself and the other studio musicians and producers, who depend on the income from working there, would be shut out for so long. My stomach feels sucker-punched, and a million thoughts fly through my mind in seconds. *Why didn't anyone tell me Ryan would be at Lakeshore? Does he know I work there?* I'm getting way ahead of myself in my downward spiral into Crazy Town and am jolted harshly back into the present with the sound of a light knock on the front door. I hadn't noticed anyone pull into the driveway. Water drips from my hands, forming little puddles on the kitchen floor around me as I freeze in place.

Benji and I gawk at each other, and our eyes lock the way

siblings do when they're thinking the same thing. "It couldn't be, right?" he asks. Not pulling his eyes away from me, he gets up carefully and walks to the foyer to check who it is. My breath is still caught in my windpipe where it stalled. *There's no way Ryan could be here. Why would he be here?* We haven't seen each other in three years.

I'm still frozen in place when Benji calls from the hallway, "It's only Joe with his hands full of too much food for dinner." Seconds later, Joe strolls into the kitchen, looking fabulous as usual. His jet black hair is slicked back and gleaming, he's wearing his billion-dollar smile, and his arms are heavily laden with groceries.

"Hi darling," he purrs, looking over the frames of his designer sunglasses at me quizzically, and leaning over to air kiss each of my cheeks. "You look like you've seen a ghost. Am I that pale? I am, aren't I? If I didn't wear two gazillion SPF, I might have some color." The bags slide to the ground in a graceful tumble only Joe could pull off.

My mind finally snaps back into place, and I let my breath out in a long whoosh, damp hands going to my heart to calm down the racing, leaving a wet hand print on my faded tank top. "I'm fine," I fib, flashing another fake smile. The heat grows rosy on my cheeks, betraying my nerves. "You just gave us a scare, that's all."

"I'm so, so, sorry," Joe slaps his palms together, begging for forgiveness. "You know my little Prius is the complete opposite of my boisterous self and doesn't like to draw attention. She does like to sneak up on people, though, the little electric sorceress."

"I wasn't scared," Benji chimes in, bending to help Joe unpack the groceries. He gives Joe a sly sideways grin, his voice conspiratorial, "She's bugging out because her ex-boyfriend is back in town."

Joe's eyebrows fly higher on his face than nature should allow. "Boyfriend? Sarah? Since when? Do tell. I want all the juicy details." He leans forward with his elbows on the island, chin propped up on his folded hands, eagerly awaiting any upcoming gossip. "What's his name? Is he hot? Is he taller than you? Please tell me he's taller than you."

I roll my eyes at Benji and point at Joe with a 'see-what-you-started' expression. "He was never my boyfriend," I say matter-of-factly. *I just wanted him to be*, I think to myself.

"Well, you wanted him to be," Benji says, reading my mind out loud, expertly juggling a few apples Joe brought without missing a beat.

"I did not," I lie again, giving him a dirty look. I grab a piece of fruit out of the air and, taking a big bite, head to the sliding doors. "Call me when dinner is ready, peasants," I call snarkily over my shoulder. "I need to get to the bar early tonight for the party." I've decorated the Stout Hideout Pub, where I luckily also bartend, this afternoon for my best friend Jenny's engagement party tonight. I'm determined to make sure everything goes without a hitch, but this news about Ryan has thrown me. I'll have to set aside my current shock about Ryan's arrival in town and reschedule the nervous breakdown I was just about to have for a later date. Jenny would kill me if I even tried to bail on her or not show up, and I wouldn't do that. This party is so crucial for her and Luke.

Jenny's father Marty owns Lakeshore Studio, which now makes me wonder if she knew Ryan's band would be here. Jenny's the only other person in the world that knows how I really felt about Ryan. Shit, how I *still* feel about him. All these years later, and just hearing his name makes my heart skip a beat. It's crazy.

Gunner trails on my heels as I escape any further inquisition by Joe, stepping onto the deck, across our small back yard, and down the stairs to the rocky beach below. The sounds of Benji and Joe's laughter and chatting as they prepare our dinner follow me through the late summer air as I walk away.

Gorgeous bright oranges and pinks streak across the horizon as the sun sets on the lake. I find my usual spot on one of the larger driftwood branches offering the best view of the nearby lighthouse in Nightingale Harbor, down the shore from our house. Gunner splashes joyfully in and out of the tide, chasing imaginary friends I assume he can detect, but I can't. Ghosts seem to be everywhere today, some more real than others.

Once I settle in to watch the sunset, I can't help but lift my knees and hug them tightly, digging my chin in as this latest news settles over me like a heavy blanket. Ryan Crawford is back in Chandler. *Does he even know I'm still living here? That I work at Lakeshore? About my mom?* I have so many questions, and no answers. I really need to talk to Jenny tonight.

When Ryan left to go to LA three years ago, we never talked or even texted again, and it hadn't ended on the best terms. I made sure of that. *Does he somehow know I lied back then?*

11

3

From Where You Are

RYAN

When I pull into the driveway of my childhood home a few hours later for the first time in three years, waves of nostalgia wash over me. But I don't have time to reminisce since my mom is already rushing out the front door waving what looks like a dishtowel. Her five-foot-nothing frame barrels into me as I get out, slamming me into the driver's side door. She could be an all-star linebacker if she wants to; she's so damn strong.

"My boy!" she cries, tears streaking her cheeks as she squeezes me tighter. "My boy, the rock star is finally home!"

"Mom..." I gasp, trying to drag some air back into my lungs and becoming a little embarrassed, as the neighbors who happen to be outside are getting quite the show. "Ma, I'm happy to be back." Kissing the top of her head lightly, I peel her off me and hold her by the shoulders at arm's length to take her in. Her youthful face never seems to age, but there are hints of dark circles under her bright eyes. She's obviously tired. A touch of pine cleaner lingers around her, and I can tell she most likely stayed up all night and day cleaning the house in preparation for my arrival. It's just how she is. Her dark hair is in its usual tight bun piled on top of her head, and I notice a few new silver strands sparkling in the glow of the streetlights. "You're looking lovely as ever," I smile, looking down at her.

"Oof. El timador," she blushes as she swats the towel playfully at my chest, wiping tears from her eyes. Her Spanish always comes out when she's overly emotional. Unfortunately, it isn't something I learned much of, and she never pushed me to, wanting me to be thoroughly American. She thought I would have a better life than her if I spoke only English. I never forced it either. I didn't want to be different from my peers or picked on like any kid. A pang of guilt flows through me at the thought, as it often does when I think of how her heritage is lost on me. "Hustler, or trickster to you, Yankee," she nods and winks at me.

"I get the gist Ma," I croak, stuffing my emotions down as I always do. The long day of traveling and the emotional roller coaster of seeing Sarah earlier are mixing with my excitement at being home. The combination is now hitting me like a truck and making me exhausted.

"Good," she says, walking around to the car's trunk and rapping on it with her hand. "Let's get you settled and fed. You look like an esqueleto." She quirks an eyebrow at me, and her examination of me is disapproving as only a mother can be. "Doesn't Vanessa feed you? I send her recipes."

My mother and our manager are now like sisters in the sorority of Indigo King, whose entire mission in life is to make sure we eat, sleep, and exercise properly. Our music and careers are only secondary, which I guess isn't a wrong way to think in the whole scheme of things, but that's not productive or conducive to success in the music business.

"I'm not a wilting flower, believe me," I say, as I nudge her jokingly out of the way with my hip, and pull out my duffel bag and guitar case. She reaches to grab one, and I lightly slap her hand to stop her. "Nope, I'll get these. Why don't you finish cooking whatever delicious meal I can almost taste from here? My mouth is watering, I haven't had food to eat in days, and I'm starving." I whine and clutch my stomach, giving her my best fake pitiful expression. I'm not lying, though, I am hungry, and it does smell delicious.

"Oof," she sighs again, grinning. She turns on her heel and leads me into the house.

Returning to the childhood home you grew up in is always strange. It feels smaller for some reason that doesn't make any sense to my brain. Nothing has changed. The furniture is the same and hasn't been moved in decades. The decor and paint aren't any different. Frames hang on the same spots on the walls. The familiar aroma of the house, with its spices and cleaners wafting in the air, triggers memories of growing up here. The quintessential essence of home; there's nothing else like it in the world.

Once in my old bedroom, which hasn't changed either

since the day I left home, I toss the duffel bag on the floor at the foot of the bed. A twin bed. I groan inwardly as I imagine myself trying to cram into this thing for the next few months. *How did I sleep here before?* I've not grown taller since leaving. Picturing our cramped van and the bunks on our occasional tour bus if we're lucky, I shrug and mutter, "slept in worse spots, I guess."

I look around at the surrounding posters, all my music idols, and bands I admired and wanted to emulate. High school talent show ribbons still hang from hooks by the door, swaying softly from the breeze of the ceiling fan above. My old vinyl record collection still takes up half of one wall, with the other half crammed with battered paperback books, and I absently run my finger along the spines of the covers. So much of my life is showcased here--so much inspiration.

My eye catches on the bulletin board above my old desk, full of photos and notebook pages of lyrics. I unpin one of the papers and read it, my thumb tracing the ink as I recognize Sarah's neat handwriting. Its sharp points and smooth curves form words I hoped her heart meant, but of course it didn't.

Someday you'll see me
You'll see how much I love you
And someday you'll love me too

Somewhere, with a love like that, I always knew
There were chances, just a chance for something more
Somewhere, with a love like that, I always knew
There were chances, just a chance for something more

My hand starts to crumble the page instinctively, but I stop myself, noticing for the first time that there is something different about my room. Every picture of Sarah is missing. Gone. Group photos that included her have disappeared too. My heart clenches as I pin the lyrics back to the corkboard, smoothing out the wrinkles, knowing that my mom is only trying to protect me by taking those down. She only ever wants the best for me and will do anything for me, including trying to rewrite history. She saw how devastated I was when I left for LA without Sarah. I'm sure she thought, 'out of sight, out of mind,' when taking them away, but life doesn't work that way. I can't think of Chandler, let alone breathe its air without thinking about her. *How could I not?* When I was here, she *was* the air I breathed.

This entire room reminds me of Sarah, even without the visual cues of pictures. We spent so much time inside these four walls, talking about books we've read, laughing and joking, writing songs, and being comfortable in each other's company while she quietly studied, and I played my guitar. And of course, the last day we were ever together, when I asked her to go with me out to Los Angeles, and she refused. Not only did she turn me down, but she shattered my hopes for us as a couple once and for all. It was a side of her I'd never seen before, or even know she possessed. She made it seem like asking her to go with me was the most offensive thing I could have ever done. I didn't think she had a mean bone in her body. I thought I knew Sarah, but it turned out I didn't know her at all.

I had dared to start opening my soul to her, something

I was scared to death to do as I knew it could devastate our friendship, and I had been right. It *did* ruin everything. Even though I didn't tell her about how deeply I felt for her at the time, I still wonder how things would be between us if I hadn't started. She stopped me well before I got too deep into my feelings. Maybe things would be different, but probably not. She was crystal clear how little I meant to her.

I run my hand through my hair and then shake out my fingers, as I often do when anxious. The chains and leather bands around my wrist rattle together faintly in the quiet of the empty room. Coming here to record might not be such a great idea after all. I thought I could handle being home again, and it would make for good songwriting to return to my roots. If this keeps up, though, the only thing I'll be writing about is heartbreak and heartache. Sure, they're standard song fare, but how long can wallowing in self-pity be the motivation for my music? I need to find a new muse before I make myself crazy. History can't be rewritten, no matter how much I want it to be.

Traitor

Sarah

Chandler isn't exactly a popular live music destination compared to Cleveland to the east, but it is a hidden gem for the local community. With a renowned performing arts college nearby, the area is bustling with budding artists of all kinds, especially musicians. The Stout Hideout Pub is part bar, part event space, with enough room for smaller intimate concerts but is mainly used for Open Mic Nights, and a terrace in the back leading to the beach only used in the summer.

The sound of the band warming up on the patio behind the bar carries out to the parking lot as I shut my car door. I hired the other house musicians from Lakeshore Studio to play tonight's party. It helps that the bride-to-be, Jenny, is also their boss's daughter. As I round the corner to the back, I'm met with a soft glow from the string lights stretching on posts and connecting the umbrellas centered in the tables. The clear bulbs reflect softly on the white roses I intertwined with them earlier this afternoon when I set up, and the effect is lovely. It's like something out of a fairy tale. Well, a fairy tale taking place on a pub patio, at least. The fragrance from the flowers in the air is fantastic, and I bet Jenny will swoon when she gets here.

She and I talked about and planned our respective weddings ever since we were girls in grade school, and Jenny's colors were always white and gold. And here we are, about to celebrate the beginning of her wedding preparations with her engagement party decked out in white and gold. She's always been particular about what she wants for her wedding and its festivities. I love that she trusts me enough to capture her vision with this party. I hope everything meets her expectations.

I smile and wave my hellos to the band as I make my way inside to check on the catering and drinks. Mark, the bartender working tonight, catches my eye and calls me over. Since the beginning of summer, he's new to the bar and cute in his way, but a perpetual flirt. Even when he's not flirting, he's flirting; he can't help himself. He exudes confidence. Mark is definitely not my type, so I don't ever take him or his innuendos too seriously. The overt flirting is a running gag between us at this point. We both know nothing will come of it.

"Hey there, Sarah," he smiles at me, giving me an overly obvious once over. Heat prickles my cheeks and neck in response to the attention. "You're looking mighty fine this evening." A twinkle in his eye that is always there sparkles.

"Thanks, Mark," I say, ignoring his impishness and trying to keep my tone professional. Tonight's not a night to joke around. This is too important to Jenny. "How are things looking for tonight? Got everything you need to set up outside?"

"I think so." He's catching on to my seriousness and putting a final bottle of white wine in a box to take to the patio. "The instructions you left this afternoon were pretty clear. Sorry I couldn't be here to help you set up earlier." He gives me a sheepish grin and puppy dog eyes I'm sure other women can't resist. But resist them, I do. When someone says they'll "try" to do something, I never count on it. Relying on other people isn't one of my strong suits.

"No problem," I mutter, trying my best to brush him off and scanning for a sign of Jenny and her fiancé Luke's arrival. I need to talk to her about what I heard today about Ryan before the party goes into full swing. My calls earlier went straight to voicemail, and a rock settles in the pit of my stomach. *Is she ignoring me to avoid the conversation?* The possibility Jenny knew Ryan was coming back and didn't tell me bothers the crap out of me. *Is it possible Marty hadn't told her about Ryan's band recording at Lakeshore?* I guess it could be. Maybe I should give her the benefit of the doubt and assume she wasn't aware, or was too preoccupied with her engagement to pay attention to the Ryan situation. Jenny can be a little scattered at times, and important things can slip her mind. She'd once made it to the airport for a vacation when she realized her suitcases still sat in the foyer at home. I love her to death, but she can be frustrating as hell. I'll be heartbroken if she did know about Ryan but kept it from me, but I'll cross that bridge if and when we come to it.

Lorelai, the owner of the Stout Hideout, comes out of the kitchen with her hands full of hors d'oeuvres. Her fiery hair frames her round and happy face. Everything about Lorelai is round and happy. She exudes positive energy from her pores. "Well, aren't you a sight for sore eyes," she beams at me, her lilting voice sounding like a song. "Your friends should get engaged more often," she winks.

"Thank you," I blush. "And thanks again for letting us have the party here. It means a lot." And it truly does. She's letting us use the place for free and only charging us the cost for the drinks and food.

"Pssshh," she scoffs at me, waving her free hand. "Think nothing of it. I'm a big softy for a good love story." As she leaves through the patio doors, I hear Jenny and Luke's laughter coming from that direction and head back outside.

The late summer air on the lake is perfect for a night under the stars. The rising moon isn't quite full, but it shines rays of cool light down on everything, giving the party an even more ethereal aura. I spot Jenny and Luke walking hand in hand among a large group of other new arrivals. She glows in her white and gold dress, and Luke appears dumbfounded when he gazes down at her like he can't believe how lucky he is. The two of them are perfect for each other, and I'm glad he finally got the nerve to pop the question. With Jenny already done planning her entire wedding when she was twelve, I'm not surprised he was a little intimidated.

"Sarah!" Jenny squeals when she sees me. She runs over and wraps me into a huge hug, rocking me from side to side and almost throwing us off balance. "It's perfect," she whispers, digging her chin into my shoulder. "Just perfect." She leans back and dabs at the corners of her eyes with the back of her hands, not wanting her makeup to run. "I knew you would knock this out of the park. Everything is amazing."

I let out a long breath of air, relieved she's happy with all the work I put into making her night special. "Well, of course." I laugh, bumping her with my arm, "I've envisioned what this party would be like since we were kids. It would be hard for me to get it wrong at this point."

She giggles along with me and nods, "You're so right. I manifested this whole thing."

More people arrive and head towards us, so I touch Jenny's arm lightly, "Find me later when you have a chance," I say. "There's something I need to talk to you about." She raises an eyebrow at me, but nods her head before getting pulled into another hug by someone else. Talking to Jenny about Ryan can wait until we both have a few dances and a little wine in our systems.

# # #

The party goes without a hitch, and everyone seems to enjoy themselves. About halfway through, I joined the band and sang a song I had written for the couple, making Jenny ugly cry. Luckily pictures had been taken before I took the stage, so the engagement photos aren't ruined along with her mascara.

As people begin leaving and things are winding down, Jenny finds me on the steps of the patio leading to the beach beyond. The band breaks down their equipment, and soft acoustic guitar music is playing on the speaker system. The moonlight on the waves is hypnotizing, and I appreciate the wine a little too much.

"Hey." She quietly takes a seat on the step below me, peels off her strappy sandals, and wiggles her toes in the sand with a relieved sigh. "Ah, that's better." She leans back onto the step behind her, and looks at me with her brow furrowing in concern. "Are you okay? You look a little upset."

I search her face briefly for any sign she might understand why I'd be upset, but don't see any hint that she does. "Did you know Ryan's back in town?" I hold my breath a little as I watch her reaction. Her eyes widen and then close, and she lets out a long sigh.

"Shiiiiiiiit," she draws out, and slowly opens her eyes to gaze back at me. She's known he was coming back and didn't tell me. It hits me like a bullet to the heart.

"Why didn't you tell me, Jenny?" I ask, disappointment dripping from my words. "And he's recording at the studio? Did you know that too?"

"I was going to tell you," she nods, reaching out and grabbing my hand. "I swear I was going to tell you last week..."

"Last week? An entire week?"

"Actually..."

"Longer than a week? Jenny, how could you keep that from me?" My voice strains as I try to keep my composure. The betrayal stabs at my heart. I pull my hand roughly out of hers. I'm acting immature, but I'm so hurt right now I can't seem to control my emotions. Jenny knows what Ryan means to me. Well, what he meant to me years ago. She's also aware I haven't gotten over him completely, and probably never will. She knows what his being back will do to me.

"I'm so sorry. We've both been so busy with this party and the wedding planning. To be honest, I didn't know how to tell you," Jenny explains. Her eyes are glistening with un-fallen tears, and I feel like shit for getting mad at her. I can never stay mad at her for too long. She has a heart of gold, and she wouldn't do anything to hurt me purposely. "Really. You knew the studio was booked, so it didn't matter who booked it, right? Plus, the anniversary of your mom is coming up, and I didn't want to pile more stress onto you."

I nod, agreeing that it isn't an excellent time for this, but there wouldn't ever be a good time either. "I understand," I croak, fighting back the burn of my tears in my throat. "And I'm really sorry for freaking out. I know I'm acting like a child, and it's stupid. With Benji leaving, the anniversary of my mom like you said, the studio closing for two months, and now Ryan being back, I'm a fucking emotional train wreck. I didn't mean to take it out on you. Especially not at your en-gagement party where everything is supposed to be happy."

She scoots up to my step and puts an arm around me, giving me a tight squeeze. "Don't even worry about it. Now that you know it's Ryan's band at the studio, what are you going to do?"

I stare up at the moon, the glowing halo around it, and think of my mom. I think about all the nights we would sit outside during her chemotherapy and gaze at this same moon. This moon that witnessed me lie to her about Ryan's leaving for LA, knowing in my heart the lies I told to both of them was the right thing to do. I finally shake my head, "I have zero clue. I need to talk to your dad on Monday about a few things, and grab my guitar. I need to know if I'll still be able to sneak free recording time for my own stuff that I'm working on. Or if that's off the table for two months now too."

"You'll be okay. No matter how dire you think things are right now," she says, giving me a slight squeeze. "I'm surprised my Dad didn't tell you it was Ryan's band, to be honest." She shrugs. "Maybe Ryan will want you to work with them? Producing? Vocals? You *can* do it all. Not that I'm jealous or anything." She laughs, but then a tentative flash of fear crosses her face. "Would you be alright working with Ryan like that?"

I swallow hard. *Would I be okay with that? Can I be professional enough to work with Ryan?* I flashback to writing songs with him what feels like forever ago. He was so easy to write with. We were always on the same wavelength. *Would that be different now?* "Surely, your Dad would have mentioned that by now. I guess we'll have to wait and see."

I Fall to Pieces

RYAN

I pull into Lakeshore Studio, and park next to a car I swear is the same one Sarah was driving the other day. *What would she be doing here?* Grabbing my guitar case, I head toward the entrance when she walks straight towards me. She's carrying her own guitar, and her head is down, her face reddening with, *what is that? Anger? Sadness? Both?* I can't tell. My heart skips as I stop on the walkway in front of her. It is impossible to avoid it this time; neither of us has anywhere else to go. My palms are already starting to sweat.

She glances up and our eyes meet, and a thrill goes straight through me. But I can tell now that it *is* anger. She's even beautiful when she's angry. Her features sharpen somehow when she's mad that always drove me crazy. Now is no different, but what could make her so mad?

"Hey," I say lamely. *Great opening line, dipshit. Such a lady killer.* I try to smile, but god only knows what my face is doing; I can't feel it. Everything has been numb and tingly since our eyes met.

She glances around almost frantically as if trying to find an escape route to run to, but then five different emotions go through her at once. She lands on neutral and pushes her shoulders back. "Hey," she says, equally awkward. She can't meet my eyes and stares somewhere around my chin area. *Why is she so nervous?* I can't tell if she's happy to see me or not. Probably not, but this isn't how I expected this to go. I'm not sure what I expected, but not this angsty teenage bullshit. *Smile or something, you idiot.*

I lean in a little and catch her eyes. Smiling to show her how happy I am to see her, I ask, "How are you? You look mad. Did something happen inside?" I wave at the studio behind her.

She comes to, realizing where she is, and lets out a long breath. "Yes, I'm mad." She glares at me. *Why would she be mad at me?* I would be dead, buried, and forgotten if looks could kill. *What the fuck did I do?*

"Did I . . . do something?"

"Are you being serious?" She stares at me with disbelief all over her face. As if it's obvious what atrocities I've committed. She puts her free hand on her hip, making me notice her curves again, and my mouth goes dry.

If I ever wondered if I still have feelings for this woman, there's absolutely no doubt in my mind now. Everything rushes back to me instantly, and I have to restrain myself from falling to my knees in front of her. I've only been back in town for a few days; that's not enough time to get into any trouble. And I certainly wouldn't have done something intentionally to piss her off.

"What did I do?" I ask again, trying not to sound too defensive. Apparently, I did something truly awful, and I'm dying to know what it is so I can fix it. I can't stand her being mad at me like this.

She examines me again, and her face changes when it dawns on her that I have no clue what she's talking about. "You didn't know I worked here, did you?" Her tone has softened some, but her eyes are still wary of me, like a cornered animal afraid of being rescued.

"You work here?" I ask, surprised. "Of course I didn't know that." No one has said a thing to me about Sarah. Since coming home, everyone has gone out of their way to avoid talking about her to me.

"Yeah, well, thanks to you and your band, I'm now out of work *and* free recording time while you guys are here, for what, two whole months?"

I'm taken aback by how distraught she is. The only thing I had heard about Sarah was that she was basically running the Stout Hideout since Lorelai was winding down her time there. I had hoped to 'run into her' at the bar once I'd worked up the nerve to go. "Aren't you running Lorelai's place now?"

The glare that had softened some is now back in full force. Her eyes are piercing right through me. "Yes, but the money's not enough to cover Benji's college tuition -"

"Tuition?" I don't understand what's going on. None of

this is making any sense. "Why are you paying for Benji's tuition? Why isn't your mom paying?"

She steps back from me like she's been hit in the gut, her eyes suddenly filling with tears, and now I'm even more confused. *What did I say?* Her mom worked two jobs once her father died years ago to be able to put Sarah through college, and she said she would do the same for Benji. *What has changed?* I glance around desperately for something around this studio that can give me an answer, and my gaze stops on her car. Her *mother's* car. Chills run down my spine as I turn back to her. Dread flows through my veins like ice. *No....*

"Sarah," I can barely get her name out of my mouth. I don't want to say it. I don't want to know this, but I have to. I need to hear it from her. "What happened to your mom?"

She drops her guitar case, and her bravado crumbles. Her hands fly to cover her face to hide her tears as her entire body shakes with grief. I drop my case too, not caring if everything inside it shatters to pieces, and instinctively step toward her. I want to pull her to me, wrap her in my arms and let her cry as long as she needs to, but she senses me and steps further away. I'm fighting back my own tears, remembering her mom. She would do anything for her kids and did, working so hard to make life easier. That grace extended to their friends, and I was always welcomed like part of the family when I was at their home, which was pretty often. I can't believe my mother didn't tell me this news, and I'm sick that I'm only learning about it now.

"I'm so sorry," I croak, my throat constricting with emotion. I can't think of anything else I can say to ease her pain like I so desperately want to. There isn't any comforting some-one on the loss of a close parent. There just isn't. She and I both know that, having each lost our fathers when we were young. "I'm so sorry, Sarah. I didn't know. I had no idea."

She gathers herself and is only sniffling now. She wipes the tears from her face, and again my body aches to reach out to her, to try to make her better somehow, to take her pain away, but I can tell she wouldn't want that.

"I'm sorry. This isn't exactly how I thought seeing you again would go." Her cheeks redden under her tear-swollen eyes that she keeps wiping with the heels of her hands, making it worse. Even through all of that her dark eyes are intoxicat-ing, and I could get lost in them. "I figured your mom would have told you or something. The anniversary…. nevermind. Anyway, so that happened. And, I didn't know it was your band that reserved the entire studio until the other day. Not that it makes a difference, but for some reason I expected you to know these things about me. No clue why. I'm rambling…."

"Oh," I say, nodding with as much awkwardness as a per-son can put into a fucking nod. *What the fuck am I doing?* I want us to talk like we used to. I want to catch up on every-thing that she's done the last three years. I want to take all the pain she's gone through away. I just want to spend time with her again, even though it would be insanity. Any time with Sarah would be dangerous for my heart.

She suddenly grabs her guitar and rushes past me to her car, muttering, "I have to go…"

"Wait, Sarah-" I call out to her, but she's already backing out by the time I realize what's happening. One second ago, she was talking to me for the first time in years, and now she's driving away, and somewhere in between, I learned the worst news I could. I should have said something more than fucking 'Oh.' That response was truly inspired. Done more than just stand there like a fucking idiot with nothing to say. It probably looked like I didn't give a shit, when that's the furthest thing from the truth. I was so in my own head, I let her slip away.

This has been the most intense five minutes of my life, next to the last time I saw Sarah three years ago when she basically told me to fuck off and have a nice life. She ran away from me then, too, before we could talk about it. Just disappeared from my life like a ghost. The same empty feeling I had then returns and completely hollows me out like a rotted tree trunk. The numbness running through me only moments ago with the joy I had at seeing Sarah again takes on a different tone. One with an edge of pain to it. One I should be used to by now.

Shadows Of My Name

SARAH

Fuck! I can't believe what just happened. I can't believe I ran into Ryan Fucking Crawford. He was not on my list of all the people to let loose a nervous breakdown in front of today. Since finding out he was back in Chandler, I planned to avoid him. Lie low until he left again, so I wouldn't have to face him and potentially lose my shit as I did. He did look amazing, though. *Fuck! I'm such an idiot.* I cannot let myself start to think of him like that. Going down that path in my thoughts is dangerous and will only lead to heartache. *My* heartache. Something I've had enough of, thank you very much.

How had he not known about my mom? Doesn't he talk to anyone from Chandler anymore? How could his mother not tell him? She had to realize how important my mom was to him, despite whatever happened between the two of us. I can't believe she could be so cold. I guess it explains why neither of them came to the funeral or reached out. All this time, I thought he was just being an asshole. That he didn't care. Their absence had hurt at the time and hurts again now. *What did I expect?* When I told him I didn't want to ever see or talk to him again, I ended our intense friendship of three years. I made it more than clear not to contact me, and he's followed that rule this entire time. His mom must have taken the exile from my life upon herself as well.

About a mile down the road from the studio, I need to pull off into Edgewood Park. I'm still crying, and driving isn't the best idea. I almost plowed over a poor cyclist a few blocks back because I didn't notice him through my tears - and he was wearing neon bike shorts. Better to be safe than sorry.

Even after I park in a shady spot and take a deep breath to calm my nerves, my mind won't stop racing. Everything in my body feels heavy, and every limb weighs a million pounds. I know it's mental weight, but it suffocates. Emotional burdens can be equally as heavy as physical ones, if not heavier. Sometimes they can completely flatten you.

Remembering how cruel I had been to Ryan three years ago, makes my stomach curdle still today. It was one of the hardest things I've ever done. We were almost inseparable best friends, on the brink of something more. Well, at least I was. I always wondered if Ryan felt the same way, and suspected he did. I had to make him go to LA without me, and with zero strings. So I had to be a bitch to him. Someone needs to be the supportive push others need, and that's me. Always has been.

It has been my job in every relationship. I might sometimes go about it in a really fucked up way, but I make sure it gets done somehow. Like when I pushed Ryan away.

Ryan. Oh my god, he is still so hot. His ripped jeans, shaggy hair always needing a cut but looking great anyway, and his piercing eyes. Those eyes are able to cleave right into my soul no matter what's going on, and I could tell he saw me today like always. The way his face fell and his entire demeanor sagged when he realized about my mom almost crushed me. The way he reached for me when I started balling like an idiot makes me think he didn't care about himself right then; he only cared about me. *That would be nice, huh?*

If only I wasn't ugly crying like I'm still doing. *Pull your shit together, Lawrence.* None of it means anything to him. Of course, it doesn't. Three years have passed, so there's no way he has any feelings for me. Not for friendship, and definitely not for anything more. We are not the same people we were three years ago. Too much has happened since. He most likely has a girlfriend back in LA. Or he brought her here for all I know. Maybe he's got several girlfriends since his band is getting popular. He's probably got groupies all over the country; shit, all over the world. He was only feeling sorry for me. Nothing more.

This thought sobers me up, and I grab some tissue from my purse to clean up my face. Now is not the time to fall apart. Now is the time to strategize. I still need to figure out how to finish paying Benji's tuition now that I can't rely on the studio income. I take another deep breath and let the air out slowly; my eyes closed. *Think, Sarah. Think.* While I'm sitting here, my mind empty of any solution, my phone buzzes. I pull it out of my bag, glance at it, and freeze. A message from Ryan flashes on the screen. *He still has my number?*

RYAN: Are you okay?

Am I okay? Did I seem okay? He and his band are why I'm now in a financial mess in the first place. If they weren't hogging up the entire studio for two whole months, I wouldn't be scrambling for alternative ways to make money to help Benji. And, damn him for coming back here and dredging up old feelings that should be long forgotten. And damn him for making me cry today. Just damn him! I'm a strong person. I can and have handled a lot of emotional shit, but ever since I heard his name from Benji the other day, I've been a total mess. It's so unlike me to not have control of my feelings like this. It's like my wires are crossed, causing me to think backwards. I can't respond. I'll say something I regret.

I glance back down at the screen and seriously debate with myself about sending a snarky reply to tell Ryan off, but shove my phone back into my purse. I can't deal with him right now. I can't. It buzzes again, and I reach in and shut it off entirely without looking at the new message, and toss my bag to the floorboard where I can't reach it. My mind is going on tangents, and my emotions are riding a roller coaster. *Fuck you, Ryan. And your stupid band.*

He hadn't shown an inkling of concern for my being out of work for two months. Not even blinked an eye at that. Only questioned why I cared so much about my job. *Duh, who doesn't care about their jobs, Ryan?* Not everyone in Chandler is a big rock star now and can take over a fucking studio for two whole god-damned months. Not everyone is an only child with zero responsibilities. *Did LA and the music business do this to him?* Probably. Over time, my brain most likely created a fantasy version of him for me to think of that isn't based on reality - but what I want him to be instead. *Brains do that, right?* Our imaginations have one job - to plug the holes pain makes in your heart.

But absolutely *none* of that is right either, and deep down I know it. My imagination is working overtime. He *did* look concerned for me. And he *did* seem upset about my mother's death. I'm just making shit up in my brain so I can deal with seeing him again, and not facing the truth of how I put myself in this position in the first place. I'm not being fair to Ryan at all, and I should have given him the benefit of the doubt. If he'd known about my mom's death, he would have been here in a heartbeat. It's part of why I pushed him away to begin with. I know that.

I have to try to remember that he was a really good friend to me at one time. Regardless of how I ruined it for both of us, it wasn't his fault, or anything he did. He should be the one mad at me, not the other way around. Even if I think I had good reasons for what I did, I have no right to be angry with him or his band.

As I watch the few park-goers enjoying this sunny summer morning, I refocus my thoughts. I need to organize and mobilize. Plans must be made and executed. Benji and I are running out of time to get him financially situated at school, and I refuse for him to take out student loans. I swore to our mother I wouldn't do that, and I'll keep that promise no matter what. Insanely enough, the interest rates on those loans are higher than the mortgage on the house. The accountant who helped with my mom's estate advised me to focus on paying for Benji's school first. It would be better in the long run. I'll figure something out. I always do.

Now that I think I'm done with my mini mental breakdown, I push my shoulders back and jut my chin out a little, trying to gather some confidence I don't possess at all. It doesn't work, but I put the car in gear and head home. Once again, I have more important things to think about than my so-called love life.

A Concert Six Months From Now

RYAN

What feels like a million hours later, Vanessa is droning on about our 'goals' for the recording sessions while avoiding any 'pain points' if we can. I swear if she pulls out a slide presentation, I'm going to throw something against the fucking wall. I can't focus on what she's saying to save my life anyway. The only thing I can think about is Sarah. I did not expect to run into her today. Finding out about her mom and seeing her so upset really got to me. My mother and I will have a long talk later to find out why she didn't tell me about Mrs. Lawrence. I don't know how long ago it happened or what happened. *How could absolutely nobody tell me? Was there an accident or something? Is Benji okay? Is that why Sarah is driving her mom's car?*

I keep fidgeting and glancing down at my phone. Sarah's

not responding to the texts I send asking if she's alright, and it's starting to irk me. It's been years, but I know Sarah. We used to reply almost instantly to any text we would send to each other, no matter the subject or the time of day. It was something we could count on between us. Shit, at this point, if she sent a stupid thumbs-up emoji, my mind would be at ease. She left in such a hurry and while still in tears. That can't be safe. *Any reply is common courtesy, right? The nice thing to do? Is that not who Sarah is anymore? Has she changed that much?*

I've followed her rules the past three years and didn't reach out once to her even though it nearly killed me not to. When I told her I was moving to LA, and wanted her to come with me, she basically said she wanted nothing more to do with me. So I gave her precisely what she wanted. No texts. No calls. No showing up on her doorstep like I wanted to so badly. No, I ran to LA with my heart broken and my tail between my legs.

"...Sarah-"

My ears catch her name like a radar ping, and my head snaps up as if it wants to give me whiplash, "What about Sarah?"

Vanessa glares at me, fully aware that I've not been paying attention and not too happy. "Sarah, is the person we need to talk to at..." she checks her laptop, "the Stout Hideout? About the test shows to try out the new material. We should do one right away before we start recording to receive some initial feedback, and then another one when we're close to wrapping up. I spoke to the owner earlier on break, and I have an appointment this evening to talk to this Sarah about setting those up."

"I'm cool with that," Matt, our drummer, says, tapping out a random beat on his thighs like he always does when forced to sit still. He's the high-energy one of the bunch. Everyone seems to be in agreement, and they look at me expectantly to go along with them. They are all oblivious to what this means for me. What Sarah means to me. What torture this is going to put me through.

"Do you know this Sarah person?" Vanessa asks, raising an eyebrow at me while shutting her laptop. She must see the pained look on my face, though I'm trying desperately to hide it.

"Me?" I stall, trying to think of how to answer that. "Do I know Sarah?" *Why, yes, I've been in love with her for years but never got the nerve to tell her, and oh, by the way, she still wants nothing to do with me.* That would be a great response. *Not.* "I used to," is all I can think to say that is accurate, and my voice sounds alien to my own ears.

"How do you stop knowing somebody?" Jude, our bassist, asks. He's the sarcastic one, and our accidental philosopher. "Either you know someone, or you don't."

I glance at him, then down at my phone, still with no response from Sarah, and consider his question. I guess I really don't know Sarah. I thought I did once. "You'd be surprised, dude."

Vanessa sighs, looking down at her own phone, suddenly worried. "Well, shit," she mutters.

"What is it?" I ask. Maybe the text is from the Stout

Hideout, and we don't have to do the shows after all. Wishful thinking on my part.

"It looks like I need to head home to Virginia," her shoulders slump, and her eyes are misting over. "My dad needs emergency surgery, and I need to go home to take care of my mother while he's in the hospital."

Nobody says anything right away. Everyone glances around like idiots trying to figure out what to do next. Their gazes finally land on me, as if somehow my call. *Really, people? This isn't hard.*

"Then get out of here," I say, standing up and motioning her to gather her things and leave. I glare at the rest of the band, trying to convey what idiots they are being right now to hesitate about this. "Family first. You know that."

"But the shows..." She's getting frantic as I escort her gently to the exit.

"We can take care of it."

"And the recording session goals..."

"Vanessa," I say, turning her to face me and putting my hands on her shoulders, trying to put her at ease. "Believe it or not, we're adult men who can take care of things occasionally. Go be with your family. We got this."

"But-"

"No buts," I turn her toward the door. "You know we don't discuss butts with you. Go take care of your mother. I'll call you tomorrow to check in. I promise."

She nods silently with a grateful smile. "Thank you, Ryan." She softly touches my arm and gives it a slight squeeze before leaving. Vanessa is one of the most caring people I know, and we lucked out getting her to manage us. We would be so lost without her, especially on the road. She takes care of everything for us, but we never let her know that for some reason. We need to work on that once she's back from taking care of her parents.

I head back to the rest of the band, in a huddle together and whispering with their voices low. "What's up?" I ask, retaking my seat, ready to wrap up our planning session.

"We just voted for you to go talk to this Sarah person about the test shows since, well...," Jude waves toward the door that Vanessa left through, "that just happened."

"You voted, huh?" I ask, glaring at them. A distinct knot is twisting and turning in my stomach, thinking about facing Sarah again. Considering how perfectly our first reunion went a few hours ago, this should go swimmingly. "I don't know, guys..." I hedge. They have no idea what they're asking of me, and I can't bring myself to tell them either.

"You got some sort of history with this chick or something?" Matt finally joins the conversation and decides to start with interrogation. *Lovely.* "You said you used to know her. Did you guys date or something?" He's always been the intuitive one of the group.

It's an innocent and valid question, but my mind stutters for a response. I stare at them with my mouth hanging open like a tool. The blood drains from my face, and I can feel myself grow pale. *I need to find a fucking grip.*

"They totally did," Jude chuckles. "I bet that's why we never play Cleveland."

They're both staring at me, waiting for me to respond, but

I still don't know what the fuck to say to these guys. When I get cornered like this, I tend to shut down and shut everyone else out. "Fuck you, Jude," is the best I can come up with as I turn to leave. I flip him the bird for good measure, like the grown adult man I am. I'm seriously becoming unraveled. I don't like it. At all.

"But what about that appointment to set up those shows Vanessa wants us to do?" Jude calls after me, zero remorse in his voice. Not that I expect any from him.

"I'll handle it," I bark at him as I slam through the exit door and head to my car. The sun is lower than I anticipated, and I check my watch to see the day has flown by. If the next two months pass by like today, I can slide out of this reasonably unscathed. I glance briefly at the spot where I saw Sarah standing only a few hours ago, and the wind off the nearby lake whips at my hair, blurring my vision. My thoughts swirl with never-ending questions. *Can we have a strictly business conversation without emotions boiling over? Will she be receptive?* The big question is, *will she let us have shows there? What will we do if she doesn't?* I check my phone one last time to see if she's texted me back. Nothing. Zero. Zilch. This is going to be more challenging than I thought. All of this is.

Set Fire To The Third Bar

SARAH

My day just keeps getting worse by the hour. I fell asleep when I got home earlier. I cried myself to sleep, and I woke up with the light outside slanting on the horizon, so I'm late for work at the bar. I don't have any time to shower or glance in the mirror. I can only grab my purse and keys and drive there as fast as possible. Lorelai is going to kill me. A glance in the rear view once I arrive forces a groan, and I quickly wipe at the smeared eyeliner and mascara under my eyes. I look like something out of a bad horror movie. My hair is a lost cause, and I have no choice but to wait until I get inside, and get the bar officially opened to do anything about it. The bar is usually slow until after dinner when the regulars come in, and tonight isn't an open mic night, thank goodness. I couldn't deal with that headache today.

As soon as I step into the bar, I freeze. This can't be happening, not twice in one day. Ryan is sitting at the bar and chatting with Lorelai like he doesn't possess a care in the world. *Fucking hell.* I dart back into the shadows of the doorway for a second to eavesdrop on them since they didn't spot me come in. Lorelai is pouring the charm on thick, and Ryan seems like he's being polite about it. He keeps sneaking glances at his phone but tries to appear like he's paying attention. I know that move. The socially multitasking mask we all wear at some point. *Sure, I'm listening to you and care about every word you're saying, but I'm more interested in what's happening, or not happening, with my phone.* Maybe he has completely changed in three years after all. He was never this rude before he left.

The fact he's acting like that with Lorelai, who is a downright saint, propels me into action. "Hey Lorelai," I say casually and purposely ignore Ryan. I throw my purse into the cabinet under the register and turn to face the bottles on the shelves, giving Ryan my back.

"Oh, hello, sweetie," Lorelai sings. "Nice of you to join us, love." She's giving me the stink eye once over only she can give in what is really a caring way. Not judgmental at all, but concerned things aren't going well.

"Sorry I'm late," I mutter, picking up a clipboard with this week's beer order and pretending to study it. "I've had a... day."

"Well, you're here now," she chirps, "and we care about

nothing else. This handsome young man here is Ryan Crawford. He's with the band Indigo King." I shrug a noncommittal shoulder in his general direction, and keep pretending to be highly focused on the beer order, which I already handled yesterday but left the paperwork on the back counter. Neither of them can know that, though. As cheerful as ever, Lorelai is nonplussed by my silence and goes on, "They want to play some test shows here in our humble establishment to try out some new songs. He's here to arrange that with you since you handle all the live events and internet web stuff to get the word out."

I almost drop the clipboard but can lie it gently back on the counter and slowly turn around. "Oh?" I ask, forcing a smile, my voice between bitter sarcasm, hot anger, and mild curiosity. You need to know me to know which one it is. Ryan *does* know me, and he clears his throat hard, grabs the beer Lorelai probably gave him, and takes a long draw. He's avoiding looking at me; his eyes travel from his beer to the ceiling, back to the bar, and eventually land on his phone. *Of course. His phone. Where something or someone more critical obviously resides.*

"You don't expect us to pay you, do you? For the privilege of letting your band play here?" I ask angrily, placing a hand on my hip for emphasis. We couldn't afford them. I'm sure of that. So, I hope for Lorelai's sake it's not a part of this deal. I'm more panicked than I am angry, so it's all coming out wrong. I don't know why the hell I'm being this hostile towards him again. He doesn't deserve it. I'm dealing with my own shit, and he's the one bringing it all back up, making him a convenient target.

"Of...course not," he stammers, shaking his head and raising his hands in self-defense. "You're doing us a favor here, not the other way around."

Lorelai alternates her gaze between us, unsure of what's going on with the weird energy in the room, and claps her hands together. "Right." She shakes her head. "I'll leave you two to straighten this all out."

Ryan's eyes finally meet mine, and our gazes lock into an intense stare. We don't flinch when Lorelai backs herself stealthily into the office and out of the line of fire, but we don't give anything away to each other. Neither of us wants to be the first to break away or speak. Memories of this afternoon's mess of a reunion hit me with fresh awkwardness, and embarrassment for falling apart in front of him like I did. *And now he wants to play here? And for me to arrange it all for him?* I really don't know how I feel about any of this. Having to work with Ryan is really going to force me to deal with my feelings for him all over again. I don't know if I want to go through that.

He pulls his eyes away first, examining his beer bottle as if he's holding the most important bottle of beer ever. And speaking of his hands, I notice now that his are trembling. He catches me looking at them, and he grabs the bottle tighter with both hands, his knuckles growing whiter the harder he presses. I'm half anticipating the bottle to shatter in his grip from the force. *Is he nervous about being here?* That can't be true. *But why else would his hands be shaking?*

The thought softens my mood, considering he might be

uncomfortable around me. Just because we're not friends any-more doesn't mean we can't be civil when interacting. It's the professional thing to do. This is my only place of employment, for the time being, after all. I'm also being a complete and total ass. I need to make sure I keep the one job I have. So be it if that means putting on my big girl panties and working with Ryan Crawford, no matter how much it hurts my heart.

"So," I start, not knowing what else to say to break the ice. We've got to get past this somehow.

"Hey," his tone is apologetic, "Vanessa wanted to do all this, but she had to leave town suddenly for a family emergency."

"Vanessa?" A twinge of jealousy spikes in my chest even though I've no business being jealous of anything to do with Ryan. I gave up that right years ago. *Shit, I've never had that right.*

He rakes a hand through his hair, a nervous habit I note he hasn't gotten rid of. And it's still hot as hell to watch the taut muscles of his forearm flex and smooth with the motion. It's very distracting.

"She's our manager." He glances up at me, his eyes meeting mine in a challenge. Like I shouldn't question who she is or don't have the right to ask it. *Bingo. He can still read my thoughts.* But he's not wrong. "She had the appointment to meet with you, but I got nominated since we have a...history." The last word is forced out with disdain. Like, he hates the fact we even know each other, and he's being coerced into dealing with me now against his will.

The repulsion in his tone at him dealing with me cuts me

deep, and I forcefully compose myself to not lose it again in front of him. I keep a strict one nervous breakdown per day rule, and if I'm not careful, I'm about to break it. Sure enough, I break that rule completely. The abrupt burning behind my eyes of threatening tears makes me turn around quickly, so he can't see me wipe them away rapidly as they fall. *Why the hell am I crying? Why am I caring about this? About him? About how he feels about me?* I shouldn't care at all. It shouldn't affect me that he hates me now. For all he knows, I deserve it.

I lean down and start rummaging through the bottom cabinets, as if looking for something to keep my back turned from him, while tears stream freely down my face. I can't stop the torrent, and if I sniffle now, he'll know I'm crying again. With my back still to him, I start to head toward the door to the office that Lorelai retreated through. "I'll be right back," I croak, my voice full of my tears. *Damnit.*

"Sarah," his voice is husky with emotion. "Please stop." *That voice.*

I do, but I don't turn around to face him. I can't. If I turn now, then everything I worked on to live without him for the last three years will come undone. I'll be back at square one with him. I stand completely still, unable to move. I'm barely able to breathe as I wait for him to speak again. When he does, it surprises me to hear him directly behind me. I didn't notice him getting up or walking over. I almost jump out of my skin.

"I really am sorry for all of this." The remorse in his voice is genuine, and the gruffness gives me goosebumps on my skin. He has a *fantastic* voice. A *let-me-take-all-my-clothes-off-f-for-you* kind of voice. I don't know how I resisted it for so long, but I have. And I need to keep fighting it. "I'm sorry about the studio job. And I'm sorry you have to deal with me for this stuff. I know I'm your least favorite person, but I'll do my best to keep it professional. Business only, I swear."

Least favorite person? Is that what he thinks? Maybe that's a good thing. While I am upset about his band hogging the studio for two months, I know he had nothing to do with my being temporarily out of work because of it. He didn't know a lot of things before coming back to town. I shouldn't hold that ignorance against him.

"Give me a sec," I say, holding a hand behind me to ward him off, still hiding my face. I push through the swinging door to the back kitchen area without waiting for his response. My feet start pacing the length of the kitchen as I grab paper towels to try to clean up my face. "Get it together, Sarah," I chant under my breath. I lean down and try to see my reflection on the steel prep table in the center of the room, but it sucks as a mirror, and there's nothing but a shadowy blob looking back at me. "Shit. Shit. Shit."

"What's with all the shits, love? And why are you keeping such a handsome gentleman waiting out there by his lonesome?" Lorelai asks from the office doorway. When I straighten, she can see my red, puffy eyes from all the crying and god knows what else on my face. I'm sure I'm atrocious right now. "Oh no, no, no," she says, walking over and pulling me into a big mama bear hug she's famous for. Lorelai gives the best hugs in the world; probably the universe. Her strong arms just make you believe you are safe and cared for. Like everything will be okay, even if it probably isn't. She'll make you feel that way for a little while at least, which is almost as good as it being true. "We've had enough of that," she coos, stroking my hair. "Did that boy do something wrong to you? He broke your heart, didn't he? You know he looks like a heart breaker. I thought so as soon as I laid eyes on him."

"No," I half laugh, half sob at her faulty observation. "He didn't do anything. I did. It was a long time ago, so I'm stupid for going through all this again now."

"Stuff and nonsense," she waves my words away. "I'm sure you had your reasons."

I nod, "I thought I did."

"Well then, there you go." She takes the damp paper towel from my hands and wipes gently under my eyes. "Everything is in the past now, love. He seems to have moved on perfectly fine, no? So now take your turn to pull yourself together and do the same."

"He thinks I hate him." *And he has every right to,* I think.

She gives me a knowing look I can't quite read and pats my shoulder, easing me towards the door leading back to the bar. "Well, dear, go show him you don't."

True

RYAN

I slide back onto my bar stool and take a long draw off my beer, emptying it. *What the fuck? Why does everything I do or say make Sarah cry?* I reexamine everything I've said to her since coming back. *All what, five words in total?* I mean, I understand that she'd be upset, but shit, I didn't even know about any of it. And ending our friendship was all her doing. She's the one that pushed me away before I left. Not the other way around. I should be the aggrieved party, not her. *Fuck. That's not right either, you moron.*

The door to the kitchen swings open, and the whiplash is back as Sarah walks in. She's avoiding looking at me, but she appears to have calmed down from whatever just happened. I'm afraid to ask her if she's okay for fear she'll start crying again. My mere existence appears to do the trick. I don't comment on her puffy and bloodshot eyes but instead, raise a curious eyebrow at her. That may be innocuous enough to stave off tears and provoke a reply.

This gets a small apologetic smile from her, and I'm again captivated by her lips. Her full bottom lip is always a little chapped from her chewing on it when she concentrates. My thoughts start jumping down rabbit holes, chasing ideas about those lips and what they could do. I haven't seen any of her live and in-person for years until today, but my memory was bang on while away. I memorized every inch of her I could before I left for LA, and thoughts of her were never far from my mind, so I'd revisit her memory often.

There are girls on the road, sure. There's always hangers-on with a band. That's part of the rock 'n roll deal. Plus, the road gets lonely. Anyone who says otherwise is lying. And, I happen to be a hot-blooded male, so shoot me. But none of the girls I've been with - and there aren't like, a lot of them - none of them mean anything close to what Sarah means to me. *Fuck, it is still, isn't it?* I'm under a curse for life to love this woman with nothing in return. *Just fucking great.*

"Sorry." She pulls a book out from under the bar, a sheepish small smile playing on her gorgeous lips. I want to kiss those lips so badly it hurts. "I was looking for this; the scheduling calendar."

"No worries."

We both ignore the blatant lie, and she presses on, opening the book on the bar between us. As she leans over it with her long hair brushing the pages, being only a few inches from me, I can't help but catch her fruity and floral perfume. The scent screams, *Sarah*. It's the perfume that she's always worn, and it's unmistakable and undeniable what it does to me. Heightening all of my other senses instantly as it hits me, I'm overloaded. I need to lean back and catch my breath before I do something stupid like jump over the bar and pull her into a rapturous kiss. Shockingly, I find some self-control and only reach out and grab one of her hands. The warmth coursing through me like a wave when we touch is almost more than I can take.

"Thanks for doing this for us. It means a lot." I stare down at our hands to avoid her eyes. My voice is suddenly full of more gravel than air. If I look up at her now, I *will* jump over this bar.

She doesn't pull her hand back right away, and we stay silently touching for what afterward seems like only a millisecond. She's staring at our hands too, and all the air in the room vanishes, and we're in a vacuum. Neither of us says anything or moves for a long while. Eventually, Sarah straightens and slides her hand away from mine, and my fingers instantly feel cold at the loss of touching her. *But that was progress, right?* A step in the right direction, anyway.

"This Friday night is open for you guys if you want." She clears her throat and runs a slender finger down the schedule on different dates. "We wouldn't have much time for advertising, though. How much of a crowd do you guys want for these? Do you want to advertise, or are these secret, and you'll take the regulars? Is your new material ready for prime time?" She looks genuinely interested but might be acting professionally. Like I should be doing, instead of fixating on her god-damned hands.

"You know what? You just rapid fire asked a shit ton of questions. I have no idea about the advertising," I say honestly, trying to switch my mind back into the game and absorb her questions. "I didn't know I needed that kind of information for this meeting. I am not prepared." *Ain't that the truth?*

She nods at my phone, "Well, that thing's not broken, right?"

"Nope."

"Then maybe," she smiles at me with a sarcastic glint in her eyes that is a total turn on, "you could use it to reach out to the rest of your band, or your manager, and find out that information, so we can get you on the schedule." Each word is overly annunciated and emphasized for effect.

I slap my forehead in playful disbelief, falling back quickly into our old pseudo-comedy improv that we used to do. "Oh my god, is that what this electronic thing is for? You're a genius! What would I do without you?"

We laugh, but then we both catch ourselves having fun together, and it dies out awkwardly. I grab my phone and start texting the questions to the rest of the guys.

"Indeed," she whispers to herself as she turns away, but I catch it. "Indeed."

We wrap up the meeting with us arranging to play next weekend instead, and with limited social media mentions of a "Special Guest" and not the band name to keep the crowd manageable. Amazingly, we keep everything friendly and professional without either of us breaking out in more tears. I even succeed in not jumping the bar and accosting her like the animal I apparently have become. Seeing her again has definitely awakened something within me. Emotions I buried deep long ago when they hurt too much surface and are bubbling up. I'm not sure what to do with all of it. I was right. Spending time with Sarah is going to be dangerous for me. I'm at risk of losing myself all over again.

Once our business is settled and customers start to trickle in, I leave, so she can carry on with her job. Even though we're getting along again like a damn house on fire, things are quickly starting to reach that very awkward, are-we-going-to-talk-about-anything-important phase, and I can tell neither of us wants to go there. As I'm walking out, I notice a flyer on the bulletin board full of ads and announcements, inviting musicians to regular open mic nights hosted by none other than Miss Sarah Lawrence herself. I commit the posted days and times to memory. That could be interesting. *Indeed.*

Rewrite The Stars

RYAN

Back at my mother's house, I find her cooking up a storm in the kitchen. The table in the small eat-in kitchen is full of plates piled with food enough for an army. There's no way in hell the two of us can eat all of it.

"Ma, what are you doing?" I ask, waving at the large spread. "Are you throwing a party? Who is this all for?"

"For you, silly," she says, stirring something on the stove I'm sure will be delicious. "I didn't know if your friends were coming back with you, so I made a little extra, just in case." My mother is famous for her 'just in case' food. I'm surprised I was never overweight with the number of calories she made me eat daily. I couldn't leave the house when I was younger without an extra sandwich at the ready.

I sigh and pull out my phone. "I guess I'll see what the guys are up to." I send them a quick text, inviting them over for dinner. The reply is instant and in the affirmative. I figured they wouldn't pass up a homemade meal. Especially since I did nothing but complain about missing my mom's cooking the whole time on the road. "Matt and Jude will be here shortly to help." I take a seat at the table and grab a taquito from a plate piled high with them, but before biting into it, I say, "Ma, take a seat for a minute. I need to talk to you about something."

She eyes me warily but then turns off the stove and joins me. She folds her hands together tightly and stares at them. She knows what's coming. "What is it?" Her words are clipped and sharp, already defensive.

"Why didn't you tell me?" I don't raise my voice, even though the thought of her purposely keeping that from me pisses me off to no end. She brought me up better than that. "Why didn't you tell me about Mrs. Lawrence?"

She doesn't answer right away, weighing her words carefully. "I didn't want to distract you."

"Distract me?" I'm incredulous. I can't believe that's her reasoning.

"Yes. Distract you," she nods. "You were busy in LA making something of yourself. Becoming the success I knew you would be. I didn't want anything to get in the way of that."

I drag both my hands down my face with a long groan. My mother. Thinking she's the wizard behind the curtain for my entire life. While in some ways she was and still is - in this, she got it all wrong. I count slowly to ten in my head before speaking again. *One Mississippi... Two Mississippi...* "That was not your place, Ma. You should have told me. I had a right to know."

"Why?" she asks, throwing her hands up in frustration. "What could you do anyway? What would you do? Run back here and throw your career away? For what? There was nothing for you to do, Ryan."

"That wasn't your decision to make for me," I shout, and we both still as my words reverberate around the kitchen. I lower my voice, trying to reign my emotions in. "You still should tell me these things."

She lowers her head, but refuses to admit her guilt. "I went to the funeral and paid respect for both of us. Nobody saw me, but I was there. I know you would've wanted to go, so I went for you. She was a mother, so she would understand why I did what I did. How we protect our children." She makes a quick sign of the cross and puts a fist over her heart.

"I'm not a child..."

"You're *my* child," she hisses, jumping up from her chair. "You will *always* be my child until I can no longer breathe. You being a grown man doesn't change this."

"I could have been there for -"

"For Sarah?" she goes back to cooking and nods her head. "That girl is an angel. I felt inside that she would understand. She would get it. She basically did the same thing for you." She puts a hand over her mouth to stop herself from saying anything more.

"What?" I lunge out of my seat. "What are you talking about? What did she do?"

My mother avoids looking at me, staring at the food as

she stirs, her lips pressed into a hard line. She's said something she didn't mean to, but she can't take it back. Not now.

"Tell me what Sarah did."

"Can't you figure it out now, Einstein?" She reaches up and lightly taps the side of my head. "When her mom got sick with the cancer, she didn't tell you, and she pushed you away. She forced you to follow your dreams and not give them up for her like the dumb love-sick puppy you were. I noticed the way you two looked at each other. It was only a matter of time before you both realized it. She did the right thing for you. The honorable thing. And I'll be forever grateful to her for doing that for you."

All the pieces finally clicked into place in my brain, and I feel like the biggest dupe on the planet. *Oh my God. It all makes sense now.* How she had changed so suddenly and so brutally. She wasn't herself at all, but I had no choice but to take her words for what they were at the time. I had to believe her. *What else could I do, call her a liar?* As much as I was sure something didn't feel right about anything she had said to me, I had to leave it alone. I had to leave Chandler without her. Sliding back into my seat at the table, I bury my head in my hands, pulling at my hair. *I'm such a fucking idiot. Wait - Does this mean that she had feelings for me back then? Could she still? Do I dare even hope now?* This only raises even more questions.

My mom gently rubs my back, "Sometimes sacrifice is a better secret than a story. And when you love someone, sometimes you sacrifice for them to succeed. It's just a part of love and life."

I lift my head and look up at her, trying to absorb her

wisdom. I know she's right. I don't agree with either of their methods, but they did what they thought they had to do. Because I do know about sacrifice and love. I *would* have stayed if I had known. I would have given up LA. I would have given up everything for Sarah, and they both knew it. While part of me feels played like a fiddle, another part of me is nothing but grateful for these two selfless women. They did what was best for me regardless of what it did to them. I can never repay that kind of sacrifice. *Ever.*

"Thank you," I whisper.

"Oof. Idiota," she smiles and smacks me upside the head again, then leans down and wraps me into a warm hug.

There's No Way

SARAH

The next couple of days are thankfully Ryan-free, so I can finally concentrate on essential things -- like my crazy finances. Going over everything with Jenny, who, while a total scatterbrain is astoundingly also a mathematical genius, it appears we'll be able to survive my two-month hiatus from the studio unscathed. It will take some of her magic with a few investments, but I'm relieved to be in the clear. That's a massive weight off of my shoulders, and I finally feel like I can breathe again since being laid off.

Jenny's helping me prepare the stage for tonight's open mic night and run the quick sound check to ensure everything is ready. Hosting so many of these, the routine for getting ready is down pat. However, I'm not sure how many performers will show up tonight, with it being late summer. We're in between the nearby art college semesters, so it might either be packed to the rafters or completely dead. We'll need to wait and see what the evening holds. My guitar is always ready to go if I need to fill empty spots. Sometimes I'll accompany other musicians if they ask me to as well.

I enjoy performing almost as much as I love writing the songs I play. The love of music initially brought Ryan and me together in the first place. We both collected rare vinyl records and often saw each other at the local record store, Harmony Lane, which was right by the big box store I worked at during college. The owner, Rusty, would set aside albums he thought each of us would like. It got to the point where our tastes in music were so similar, we'd end up arguing over who got what record. Eventually, we figured out sharing was our best course of action, and we became fast friends from then on, practically joined at the hip. It led to us writing music together. Ryan would even perform with me for composition reviews for my professors if I needed him to. He's an incredible guitarist with a fantastic singing voice. He's the complete package. A true star.

Seeing his prodigious talent wasted here in Chandler forced me to push him away when my mom got sick. If I had told him the real reason why I couldn't go with him to LA, he would never have left. He would've insisted on staying and helping, and I couldn't let him do that. I couldn't watch him throw away the opportunity to follow his dreams. His big break. Those don't come by very often, so you grab them while you can, and this chance happened to knock at the right time for him and the wrong time for me. Besides, the label didn't want me, they wanted him. He insisted he could convince them we were a package deal, and he would fight them for me to go with him. I *had* to hurt him to get him to go. And to stay away. I couldn't risk still speaking with him while everything happened. I had to tell the big lie up front, to avoid all the little lies later.

And the big lie was huge. Telling him a musical career was his dream and not mine. That he was forcing his plans onto me and didn't really know me at all. I said it hurt me that he thought I would want to give up my own life to chase him across the country. I called him names like 'rock star' which I knew he hated, and that I didn't want anything to do with him ever again. But the truth is I would've chased him. I would have followed him around the world if I could. I would have gone anywhere. It crushed me to watch him go, but I know in my heart it was the right thing to do, no matter how much it hurt myself.

The one thing that has allowed me to live with those lies all these years is that he believed me. He truly believed I thought so little of him and his dreams. He was easily convinced I was a completely different person who could be mean, uncaring, and brutal towards him. If he thought so little of me, he didn't know me. Understanding that is the only thing that got me through my mom's ordeal and the years afterward. It makes everything else bearable.

Jenny takes off to spend the evening with her fiancée, and as the start time for open mic night comes and goes, only a few regulars arrive. It looks like it's going to be a pretty quiet night, so maybe I'll be able to try out my new material. I only recently began writing again and am extremely out of practice. The crowds here are kind and encouraging, so I'm not too worried about playing new songs. Being the only bartender and the MC these nights can be challenging, but I've become skilled at juggling both. Mark only likes to bartend on nights and events that will tip well and says the starving artists that come to play are cheapskates. He's not wrong, it is a low tip night, but the experience of seeing some true artists at work is totally worth it for me. I wait for a few more stragglers to sign up and then head to the stage to begin the night's festivities.

Killing me Softly

RYAN

Jude and I find a seat at a corner booth in the shadows at the Stout Hideout. I had to come. I had to bring someone with me because I'm a fucking chicken, and Jude was looking for something to do. I gave him the briefest rundown of my history with Sarah without getting too much into it. Just the basics: we were friends; I wanted to be more than friends but never had the nerve to tell her; I asked her to go to LA with me to pursue music; and she freaked and never wanted to see me again; and that it was all a lie of some kind to get me to go to LA without her. He also heard about our strange interactions the last few days. Just the bare bones. Nothing about real emotions. Jude's not really the guy you talk to about *feelings*.

Sarah's behind the bar when we arrive, so I enlist Jude to buy our drinks and take a seat. He shakes his head but yanks his baseball cap a little lower and fetches us a couple of beers without incident.

"I don't see what the problem is." He slides my beer across the table to me. "She's perfectly normal. Not a single whiff of bat-shit crazy."

"I never said she was crazy."

"Well, you made her sound like she's cuckoo for cocoa puffs," he shrugs. "She's drop-dead gorgeous, though, so I totally understand that angle."

"Don't even think about it, dude," I warn. Thinking of anyone else hitting on Sarah makes my stomach clench. Especially Jude, who is a total player, with a 'girlfriend' in every town we've been to.

"Hey man, this is your movie. I'm just a supporting actor. Don't sweat it."

I can't help but study Sarah's every move. Every patron or fellow musician interaction is handled with grace and a genuine smile. She's really in her element when she's around people, and she shines like the god damn lighthouse down the lake during a storm. She introduces each act as though they are the headliners of an arena show. With every minute that passes as I secretly examine her, I find myself falling head over heels for her again. I can't stop it now. Every move reminds me of how she used to move. Every smile reminds me of how she used to smile. Despite everything that happened between us, she's still *my* Sarah deep down. Even if she doesn't know it.

Sarah examines the sign-up sheet and scans the crowd before heading back to the stage.

"Hey guys," Sarah says smoothly into the mic. "It looks

like we've finished our first round of musicians, so I'm going to steal the stage for a few minutes, and then we'll start again from the top if you don't mind?"

The crowd cheers her on enthusiastically, and I join in, careful not to be too rowdy with my encouragement for anyone to notice us. I lean over to Jude with a proud nod in Sarah's direction. "Buckle up, buddy." He smirks at me acting as though he's hard to impress -- and he is. On top of being a philosopher, he's also a music snob. He crosses his arms over his chest and sits back, waiting to be wowed. I surreptitiously pull out my phone and am ready to record. This memory will be immortalized of seeing her perform one last time if nothing else.

She sits on a stool with her guitar and adjusts the microphone. "This is a song I call 'I'll Never,' I wrote about a year ago. I hope you like it."

I can't help but hold my breath until she starts, and the sound of her singing voice allows me to breathe for what seems like the first time in years.

I'll never be all that you need
I'm incomplete; cut at the knees
You deserve more...

I'll never see the tunnel's light
My eyes are shut; no need for sight
You deserve more...

I've tried to be something I'm not
To give you more than what I've got
Or will ever.

I'll never be the choice to make
I'll only be the worst mistake
You deserve more...

I'll never have a love to share
I'm resigned to life not being fair
You deserved more...

I've tried to be something I'm not
To give you more than what I've got
Or will ever.

When she finishes, the entire bar erupts into raucous applause. Even Jude stands and whistles. I keep my seat to stay unseen, but I'd be front row tossing roses on stage if I could. Watching her on stage, singing from her heart as she always does, flips yet another switch inside me. My emotions are thrown back in time three years. I'm in love with Sarah all over. There's no mistaking this feeling. It's now a physical need to be in her presence, like oxygen to breathe. I honestly believe if I leave this bar now, I might suffocate.

I stare as Sarah introduces the next act and makes her way through the tables back to the bar. She blushes as she graciously thanks everyone who compliments her. And everyone is, of course, complimenting her. She was amazing.

"Duuuuuude," Jude smacks my arm. "You said she was good, but you didn't say she was *gooooood*. What the hell? And she didn't want to start a music career? That's literally the definition of insanity. I take back my previous non-crazy assessment."

"I know," I say as I shake my head in agreement, even though I know now that wasn't the reason she stayed here. "You know the line in the business about stars needing to have the *it* factor. Well, she's got *it* in spades. She always has."

"Damn skippy," he agrees. "Didn't you say she works at the recording studio or something? Maybe we could ask her to help with the new album. Think she'd be down for that?"

I shift uncomfortably in my seat, remembering our encounter outside the studio and how upset she was about her job disappearing for the two months we will record. I never did find out what her job was we were blocking her from. *I am a selfish asshat, aren't I?* "I'm not sure," I shrug. "We're not exactly the best of buddies anymore, remember? And what about Reese?" I'm not sure where Sarah and I stand with each other. It got pretty intense the other day, but we kept it professional. Reese is the producer the label hired to work with us on our last album, and this one as well. We have a bit of a history, and things could become complicated quickly.

"Well, jump on that man," Jude frowns, his brow deeply furrows as if he'll throw a tantrum if he doesn't get his way. "We. Need. Her. You know this. Our new songs are shite, and we don't have much time. Reese can't be here for at least another two weeks anyway. We need to get ahead of it. And whatever you and Reese got going on…"

"You know there's nothing there."

"Well, whatever it is or isn't needs to be set aside."

A mixture of dread and excitement courses through me at the thought of asking Sarah to work with us in the studio. Jude is right. Our latest writing sessions produced only mediocrity at best. We could use a fresh set of eyes and ears to help us out. And I know for a fact that when Sarah and I write together, we're like freaking lightning in a bottle. Well, it used to be. *Would we still have that magic now?* Reese should be a non-issue. We're both adults. We can deal with our past like adults.

"All I can do is ask," I say.

"No," Jude plants a fist on the table. "You crawl on your knees and beg the woman for help. Shit, I'll go and grab Matt, and all three of us can grovel at her feet."

That makes me laugh out loud. "I don't think we'll need to go that far. First and foremost, we'll need to talk to Vanessa to make sure we can pay Sarah for any work she does. Put that down as a demand from me. I doubt the label will want to pay for two producers."

"Done." Jude pulls his phone out of his pocket, sends a quick text, then drums his fingers rapidly, waiting for a reply.

"Did you seriously just text Vanessa to ask her?" I'm incredulous. Sometimes the balls on Jude are just too big.

"Yup."

"Are you crazy? She'll have your skull for a soup bowl."

"Yup."

We both stare anxiously at his phone, lying dormant and quiet for an eternity. When it finally lights up with a notification, we both grab for it eagerly. Jude gets to it first, reads the response, and smiles.

"10-4 good buddy, we are a go. I repeat we are a go." He smiles wickedly at me, showing me the reply. "Apparently, we're label darlings, who can have whatever we want now. Who knew?"

"You are so fucking weird," I laugh, lifting my cap briefly to run my hand through my hair.

"Yup." He gets up from his seat. "I will go and grab you a few more beers so you can work up your little boy nerves to talk to a girl, and then I'm heading back to the hotel to hit the hot tub."

"Eww," I wrinkle my nose at the thought of a hotel hot tub.

"Don't," he points an angry finger at me, his jaw muscles tight and teeth clenched. "Don't you dare kill my hot tub dreams."

I throw my hands up, laughing. "I wouldn't ever do that. I swear."

"Damn right, you wouldn't," he jabs his finger again, and I swipe at it. He pays the tab and brings me my last few beers before leaving. "Get it done, son."

I wave him off, watch him leave, take a long draw off my beer, and settle in to strategize my approach to Sarah on this. It's one thing to ask for us to play here, and an entirely different animal to ask her to work with us. I don't know how she's going to react. It hasn't been smooth sailing between us since I got back. Not only that but can I work with her again? I already know that I'm in dangerous waters with my feelings for her, and working closely with her could make things one hundred times worse. I'm not sure I can separate myself from the equation anymore. Regardless of the work situation, I don't think I can stay away from Sarah for much longer. I don't know if I possess that kind of strength.

I stay in the shadows at my table for the rest of the night. Sarah still hasn't noticed that I'm here, and luckily nobody else either, so I'm able to observe her all night without interruption. As the evening comes to a close, I start racking my brain for how to approach Sarah with all this. *Should I play it cool like it doesn't matter to me? Nah, aloof has never been my style. How about playing up the Jude angle, that it was his idea? Nope. That would go to his head, and I don't want Sarah to care anything for him. Man, I'm a selfish bastard. How about just telling her the truth about how you feel? A novel concept, but history has shown that to be a dumb move that gets your heart shattered. Well then, I guess I'm fucked.*

13

the words

SARAH

Another successful mic night is in the books, and I think everything went well. The response to my new songs was encouragingly positive, so they might be ready to record for my EP. If I can ever get back in the studio, that is. I'm cleaning up the patio area and emptying the ashtray when I sense the presence of someone behind me on the steps out to the beach. This is a safe neighborhood, but these days you never know. At almost two-thirty in the morning, there shouldn't be anyone else here but me.

"Sarah..."

That voice again. Ryan's voice: strong but gentle and one I would recognize anywhere. My spine tingles in that way you know someone's eyes are on you as I halt mid-movement and freeze in place. I think my imagination is playing tricks on me. I am tired enough for that to be the case. Turning around, I find Ryan leaning against the railing with his arms crossed. His baseball cap is low, and he's keeping his face in shadow from the string lights overhead. My breath catches as I take him in, pulling in the scent of the roses still attached to the lights from Jenny's party, making me a little lightheaded.

"Ryan, what are you doing here?" I ask, confused as to why he's here so late.

"You're fucking amazing, you know that?" His words are slightly mashed together. He's been drinking.

"Are you drunk?" He never used to drink to the point of slurring his words. I guess he drinks now. Not unheard of in the music business. *And what is he talking about?*

"No, but did you know that you're fucking amazing?" he repeats, pushing off the railing and stepping cautiously toward me. "Because you are. You're a fucking amazing person."

I can't help but blush at the compliments, particularly since they're coming from Ryan. Lorelai always tells me someone tipsy usually speaks their heart. Being a bartender, this proves true more often than I care to admit. This could be interesting if I allow it. "Oh yeah?" I give in, "what makes me so amazing?" *Am I really getting into a conversation like this with Ryan? Should I?*

"Not just amazing. *Fucking* amazing." He repeats, almost to me now, and I can finally see his gorgeous face. His eyes are bright and mischievous. He's apparently damned cute when he's tipsy. I can't remember ever seeing him like this. He reaches over and drapes his arms gingerly on my shoulders, like he does this all the time, and gazes into my eyes intently. The contact makes me shudder. "Those songs you played tonight... Jesus Christ, Sarah. Those songs are fucking amazing. But -- I have a secret. Wait. No. Nix that. I know *your* secret." His smile is sly, confident, and full of pride, and I have no idea what he's talking about, but suspicions are running rampant in my head.

"Oh?" I smile up at him, trying to match his confidence. His mood is infectious, and the heat of him being so close makes me a little crazy. A little reckless. "What is this secret to my amazing-ness?" I scrunch my face at the made-up word. I don't know what's happening here, and I can't help but go with the flow. Ryan Fucking Crawford has his arms around my neck, and I'm in heaven.

"Fucking amazing-ness," he corrects, pointing a finger at my nose. He's adorable.

"Right. We've established that part."

"I know that you're a liar," he flashes a smile lighting up his face from within. "And you lied to me. *To me.*" He hits himself in the chest with the flat of his hand as if mortally wounded. But his tone changes swiftly, growing softer, huskier. "Thank you for lying to me, Sarah."

I stare at him in disbelief, trying to read his face to check if he's serious about this. If he does know I lied to him. If he does know how I felt about him back then. He's not making this up. He appears to know everything. "Who told..." I can't finish the question. I'm so dumbfounded. *Who could've known?*

"My mother." His voice is flat. He's not happy about it.

"How...how did she know?" I barely get the words out. I'm so confused. His mother who hates me so much she didn't even tell Ryan when my mother died. *What does she have to do with this?*

"She's a smart cookie." He sighs heavily and locks his fingers around the back of my neck like we do this every day. I'm surprised by it, but it feels too good to call him on it. I still can't tell what's happening, but I like it. "She saw what you did for me and called you an angel, and she's not wrong..." he starts to lean in for a kiss, but I push back lightly on his chest to stop him.

"Ryan, you're drunk." Regret drips from my words. I can't believe I'm turning down a kiss from him. Something I dreamed of for years. But he's been drinking, and I can't tell if he'll be able to remember any of this tomorrow. I don't want to be something he regrets in the morning. Just another conquest to him.

"Actually, I'm not." He focuses his eyes intensely on mine, ensuring he has my attention. "A little tipsy? Absolutely. But not drunk. I swear. Matt played the role of awesome wingman, and brought me coffee and Taco Bell in the parking lot a while ago, so that's starting to kick in." He frowns. "I'm going to regret that, aren't I?"

"Oh yeah," I giggle. "But-"

"But nothing." He turns solemn, moving his hands down my arms and grabbing my waist, pulling me against him. His body is so solid and strong, and it's driving me crazy being this close to him. I can't concentrate on what he's saying. "I know what I'm saying, and I know what you did for me. And I know *why* you did it, and I'll be forever grateful to you for it." His jaw tightens, and his eyes grow hard with determination as he continues, "But I'm not holding back anymore, Sarah. I thought all this time apart would make me feel differently about you, but it didn't. My feelings are exactly the same, if not stronger, now I that know what you did for me. But I didn't tell you back then because I was a chicken shit insecure asshole who was unsure of everything, especially you. But being back here only confirms it. You're it, Sarah. You've always been it for me. End of the story. Coda. El fin. And I have a feeling you felt the same way about me back then. I need to know that I wasn't crazy to believe we could have had something three years ago."

I can't help but blush, and I can't hide it from him either. "You're not crazy."

"And what about now?" He runs a finger along my jaw line, and under my chin, tilting my face up to him, and the sensation echoes through me. "Do you still have feelings for me now? My feelings never stopped."

"How I feel doesn't matter…"

"Since when do your feelings not matter, Sarah? You can't keep doing this." He puts a hand to his head, and yanks at his hair in frustration. "You deserve to be happy. I deserve to be happy. *Everyone* fucking deserves to be happy. Why not be happy together?"

"But Ryan," I say into his chest, still dizzy from his proximity, and now from us finally expressing our true feelings. "How can this possibly work?" And I mean it. I can't imagine a path forward that ends well for either of us. We lead completely different lives now, and combining the two seems like an insurmountable obstacle. I've literally only had seconds to absorb his feelings for me, and I already see it ending horribly. That can't be a good sign.

"I don't know, but we'll find a way. Where there's a will, there's a way. We almost had something great back then, and I truly think we can create something fantastic now."

I want to believe him so badly. I want to let my heart have what it wants with no restrictions and no limits. No more sacrifices. To be able to love him freely is an impossible dream, even now. I'm so swept up in everything, I can only look up at him and nod. He just said the words my heart has longed to hear since I met him six years ago. The words my heart has wanted to say to him for the longest time. The words I've had to bury just as long. Hearing them now, after everything I've been through, feels like a gate opening wide that I've been locked behind. Chains being released.

We stand there, gazing into each other's eyes in silence, for I don't know how long, but it's not long enough. His eyes are always so intense, like they're looking right through me and straight to my soul. *Could these magnificent eyes really be looking at me with feelings that are more than friendship? Could that really be happening?*

He smacks the top of his head, suddenly remembering something, and puts me at arm's length. "Oh yeah, what are you doing tomorrow?"

I'm thrown off balance by the quick subject change, and need to take a second to regain my bearings. "Um, nothing? You hijacked my place of employment, remember?" I can't help but scowl at him, reiterating my displeasure at that little factoid. Despite whatever is happening between us, I'm determined to keep reminding him of that.

"Well, what if I told you that we, Indigo King, would like to invite you to work with us, and help write and produce our new album?" His enthusiasm is infectious, and I can't help but mirror the grin spreading on his face.

"Really? That can't be a real thing. You don't just ask someone to help you write and produce an album out of the blue like that." Because you don't. *How can that even be possible?*

"Really, really. Jude was here with me tonight, and we recorded you and sent the video to Matt, who also agrees with us. And our manager, Vanessa. We'll even give you real cash money for your time and effort. C'mon. You know us writing together is magic…" The way he says that twists something inside me in such a sexy way, I squirm.

"Well, what if I told you I would love to?" And I would. Ryan is right, when the two of us work on a song together, something magical does happen.

"Then you would make me the happiest musician in the world because now I know our album is going to kick ass."

"Is this going to be a problem?" I point at each of us, indicating us as a couple. This new thing I always wanted to be a thing but didn't think I could have thing -- thing. Such an odd sensation, so foreign to my usual self. The circuits in my brain are frying, and I can almost smell the smoke. My entire life could have just changed in a matter of the last few minutes. This is total insanity, but I'm caught up in his enthusiasm.

"It doesn't need to be. I can keep work separate from us."

He chuckles to himself, intertwining his fingers with mine, "Us. I like the sound of that."

"Me too," I smile at him, a wave of warmth washing over me at the sound of it.

He pulls my hand to his mouth and kisses my palm, never breaking eye contact. "Good."

A thrill pulses through me as I gaze back into his eyes. I haven't had a drop to drink tonight, but I might be drunker than Ryan. *Is this happening? Is this my life?* A few days ago, I was ugly crying in my car thinking he was a selfish asshole. *How did we get to this so fast? Or were we always here?* If I look long and hard at it and examined our relationship, I'd have to admit we were always "us." Maybe some things are just inevitable.

Complicated

RYAN

The next day, I'm still stunned by the previous night's events and how well things went with Sarah. I couldn't have imagined it any better. Well, a few things come to mind that would have made it even more incredible, but I can't think about those things in the middle of a band meeting. Most critical bits are clear, but some details are fuzzy from the alcohol. I know Sarah drove me home, but I couldn't say how I got to bed. I can only hope I didn't do anything majorly embarrassing or out of line. That would be my luck - finally get the girl of my dreams, and drunkenly make an ass of myself in front of her on the first night. This means the odds of Sarah showing up today to work with us might not be very high after all.

The entire studio is ours today, and as we wait in a conference room for Sarah to arrive, I show Matt and Jude the rest of the videos I surreptitiously took of her performances the previous night with my phone. She played two additional songs Jude missed, and they are both impressed with her talent, as I'd known they would be. It almost makes me giddy others can see what I always knew. I'm halfway through showing them the videos Sarah and I made of songs we wrote together before I left, when she comes in, guitar in hand, and a nervous smile painted on her face. She can hear what I'm playing for them, and her cheeks flush the cutest pink. She's adorable, but there are slight shadows under her eyes, as if she had a stormy night of sleep. I wonder if she's okay.

I stop the video and practically jump out of my chair. "Guys, this is Sarah. Sarah, this is the rest of the band, Jude and Matt." All of it comes out in such a relieved rush, that I hope everyone understands what I'm saying. The guys are surprisingly polite in their greetings, apparently on their best behavior.

"I caught your first song last night." Jude indicates for Sarah to pull up a chair to join us, which she does. "I saw your talent right away, and I told Ryan we needed to enlist your help if you were available. He was against it at first, but I convinced him in the end." He glances sideways at me with a smirk, overplaying his cards, and egging me on to argue with him, which I won't.

"Cool, thanks." Sarah nods at him, meaning, that scenario doesn't surprise her in the least, but I still don't take Jude's bait. We all stare at each other awkwardly until Sarah takes control and breaks the silence. "So, how do you want to do this? Are we working with what you have? Or writing new songs?"

Everyone turns expectantly to me like I'm going to be directing everything. I hate that. "How about you listen to what we've recorded so far, and you can let us know if you think any of the songs are worth salvaging, and go from there?" Someone does need to take charge, even though the decisions are always made as a group, but damn the curse of the lead singer. Some long-standing ipso facto assumption we're born to automatically be some kind of leader. It's a fucking myth. I sure as hell don't feel like one. If anything, Jude is the pushy one.

"Sure, that would be great." Sarah gets up and heads straight for the control room without checking if we're following. Jude and Matt stare at me from across the table, their faces unreadable.

"Aren't you guys coming?" I ask from the doorway, confused as to why they're not getting up.

They give each other a weird look, and Jude complains, "It'll take like an hour to listen to all those songs."

"And?"

Matt chimes in. "We've heard it all, man. We were there when we wrote the songs."

"Yeah, dude. No offense, but I don't want to witness that kind of carnage," Jude shakes his head.

"They're not *that* bad," I say.

"If she's any good, which we all know she is, she's going to be brutal, and my weak ass self-esteem can't take any kind of rejection today," Matt grabs at his heart briefly in mock pain. "We'll be back after lunch."

I roll my eyes. This is how it's going to be today. There is no getting either of them to work if they are determined to play hooky. "Fine. Get out of here then. We'll catch you later."

Once they go, I realize my situation. I'll be alone with Sarah in the control room. The thought both excites me and scares the shit out of me. Then it dawns on me Jude and Matt most likely left on purpose for this very thing to happen. I don't know whether to punch them both or high-five them. *Professional. You're a fucking professional.*

In the control room, Sarah's already at the digital workstation, trying to locate the files of our recordings. "I can't find your stuff," she says without turning around. I walk up next to her, and in the low light of the monitors, her eyes shine brightly, reflecting the screens. She looks so comfortable here, but I guess she would be, seeing how she works here. It's nice to see her so relaxed with this.

"Ryan?" She's snapping her fingers in front of my face. *How long have I just been staring at her? I must have spaced out. Jesus.*

"Yo," I laugh, blinking a few times, trying to gather my shit together, and my voice comes out shaky. "Present and accounted for." I snatch up the external hard drive with our music files and hand it to her. "For your listening pleasure." She's cautious not to let our fingers touch as she takes it from me, and something pings in my chest. *Is she regretting our connection last night? Or is she just being professional like we discussed? Like I should be right now.* However, we haven't addressed what happened between us, which is making this awkward.

She plugs the drive in, pulls up the first song, and our

music starts pumping through the room's speakers. I sit on the couch across from the workstation and watch her as she listens, her eyes closed, taking everything in. Every once in a while, she pauses the music to take notes, and it drives me crazy wanting to know what she's writing in that damned notebook, but I don't interrupt. Her face gives nothing away. She's completely stoic. All business. I can't gain any sort of reading if she likes any of it. In some songs, she takes a million notes; other's only a couple.

We arrive at the final song, and I cringe inwardly as the music starts. It's an acoustic song I wrote about her the day I got back, after seeing her at the gas station. I forgot it would be on the external drive. I also had no clue at the time I recorded it she'd be listening to the damned thing in front of me a week later. *Fuck my life right now.* I throw my head back on the couch and drape an arm over my face. This is going to suck. The song is called 'Almost,' and is about how we were so close to being together way back when, and how broken my heart was we ended the way we did. The song is a 'what if?' scenario, imagining what we could have experienced together if she didn't push me away. I don't have a clue how she's reacting to it with my face hidden. When the song ends, quiet settles in the room, and I peek out from under my arm to check out what's happening. Sarah is leaning over her notebook, and I can't see her face. *Fuuuuuck.* She hated the song, and is ripping it to shreds in that fucking book of hers. *The Notebook of Death.*

"That bad, huh?" I groan.

She doesn't respond, and she's trying to hide her face from me as she wipes tears from her eyes. *Shit, I made her fucking cry again. Trying for a new high score? Way to go, shithead.* I don't know what to do. Half of me wants to play this cool and be professional, whatever the fuck that means in this situation. And the other half wants to go and pull her into a hug and apologize for whatever I did this time to make her cry.

She's able to compose herself, so I don't need to decide, thank god. "Sorry. I'm just tired, and I guess the last song hit me wrong."

"Don't apologize. Seriously." She has zero to apologize for. I gaze down at the silver ring on my right index finger and spin it anxiously. I'm not sure if we're in a place in our new relationship where I can dig deeper into feelings yet, so I don't. This is all uncharted territory, and I need to be cautious. I don't want to scare her away again. "So, other than the last one smacking you upside the feels, what do you think overall?"

She laughs, and seeing her smile again makes my entire day. It lights up her entire face. "Well..." she raises an eyebrow, "we should wait for Jude and Matt to come back, so we don't have to go through my notes twice."

At that moment, my stomach decides to growl loud enough for anyone in the surrounding zip codes to hear. "Well, shit. Can we grab some lunch while we wait? I'm either extremely hungry, or an alien is about to burst out of my chest."

"Yeah, we better not risk it. Let's head across the street." She stands and extends her hand to me to help me off the couch.

I grab it, and when I'm next to her, our eyes meet, and I can tell we're both holding our breath. Both waiting for the other to do something. I brush her hair back off her shoulders, exposing her long neck I now can't pull my gaze away from. *I bet her neck is delicious. And everything else...*

Before I can find out what anything tastes like, she reaches up on tiptoe and places a light kiss on my cheek. I get the message. That is as much as we're doing here, and that's fair. I squeeze the hand I'm holding and bring it to my lips, kissing her knuckles. I waited this long for any kind of relationship with her. I can pace myself. I think.

15

Please, Please, Please, Let Me Get What I Want

SARAH

We go to the Greasy Spoon Diner across the street from Lakeshore. Carla, the waitress who is here most days I work at the studio, greets me with a broad smile and a raised eyebrow. I'm sure she's dying to know who the extremely handsome guy I'm with is. But I'm wrong. She doesn't need to wonder; she already knows.

"Aren't you the lead singer of Indigo King?" She addresses Ryan as she takes us to a booth and hands us menus. She gives me a quick wink of approval.

"Yup, I'm Ryan." He holds a hand out to shake hers. "Nice to meet you." He's smiling, but I can't tell if the expression is practiced for the public or genuine. He's not an egomaniac, at least. The fame hasn't gotten to his head yet.

"Likewise. Well damn, are you recording at Lakeshore?" Shaking his hand in return. "My daughter Lara will freak when I tell her I met you. She's followed you since that first song of yours, 'Killing Time,' came out a few years ago. She loves you." Glancing at me, "Sorry honey, if I didn't say something, Lara would kill me."

"No worries," I chuckle.

"Please tell Lara thank you from all of us for her support. It does mean a lot." I can tell he means every word. He appears really grateful for his fans. It says a lot about his character that part of him hasn't changed over the years. He still cares about people the way he used to.

"I'll be back in a bit to take your orders." Carla winks at Ryan this time and goes to greet the new customers just coming in.

The Greasy Spoon Diner is true to its name with its checkerboard floor, bright red booths, chrome stools, and a sit-down counter with an old-fashioned pie-of-the-day display case in the corner. The outside of the building resembles a retro silver train car that is becoming a little worse for wear. The diner's been a staple in Chandler for as long as I can remember. Being the only place in town open 24 hours, the Greasy Spoon becomes the 'cool' place to go when the bars close. And, the greasy food is as tasty as you'd expect things that are bad for you to be — delicious.

I watch Ryan as he glances around the diner, taking in the surroundings. "Man, I haven't been here in... forever," his voice waxing nostalgic. "Carla's new, though, right? What happened to...what was her name...?" He squeezes his eyes shut, trying to remember the former waitress that worked here.

"Mary," I answer, shifting my eyes down quickly at the menu and pretending to read intently, though I know the whole thing by heart. "She passed away around the same time...." My voice drifts to nothing, unable to speak the words, 'as my mother.' It's not that I should be entirely over my mother's death or anything, but the feelings are fresh as I experience the pain again with Ryan. I'm reliving every heartache all over. Ryan's warm hand covers mine and envelops my fingers, and he rubs my knuckles lightly with his thumb.

"That's right, Mary. She was a character. Man, she swore like a sailor. Even the tough biker guys that came in here would blush," he chuckles.

He's trying to distract me, and I love him even more if somehow possible. But while he takes my mind off of my mother, he puts it onto memories of us being here together before. It seems like a lifetime ago now. So much happened the last few years, so this is all kind of brand new. A fresh start for both of us. And I think in that respect, this could be promising.

We order and eat our lunch with a few awkward moments popping up between us, which isn't all bad. We were always decent at small talk or comfortable silences. It would be strange if there were no awkwardness between us. The fact there is some tentativeness lets me know what is happening is authentic, and neither of us is pretending. That eases my nerves somewhat. Not completely, but enough.

The butterflies flying around my stomach make eating anything a challenge, and I eventually push my plate to the table's edge. Ryan doesn't have the same problem, and he's not lying about being hungry. He devours an enormous burger and both of our fries. He even orders a slice of the pie-of-the-day for us to share, but I can only muster a few bites.

When we finish, he holds his palm up on the table and motions his fingers for me to take his hand, so I do. The butterflies flutter more frantically when our skin meets.

"So..." He gazes at our intertwined hands on the table. He's got a small smile, but his brow is furrowed, worrying about something.

"So?"

"Are we going to talk about what happened last night? Or...this?" He lifts our joined hands from the table. "Or are we just going to pretend the last three years didn't happen?" His eyes meet mine, and I sense something in his that didn't use to be there. Something close to fear, but definitely hurt. Back when I pushed him away, he never showed any pain. I suspected I'd hurt him, but anger and resignation were all I saw in him. He had believed every word I said and taken my harsh words so readily; I just assumed he expected me to say those things, or they didn't bother him. To be honest, I had a hard time looking him in the eye back then, so I could've missed a lot.

"Do you want to dive into everything here at the diner?" I ask, glancing around at the lunch crowd. "Or in the middle of a workday?"

His response surprises me. "Actually, yes I do." The

intensity is back, and the gold flecks in his eyes seem to shimmer in the diner lights. "Now that I'm clear headed, I want to make sure we're on the same page about us. I want us to have clear communication."

"Okay…Clarity is great."

"And no more lying." His tone says he won't argue that point. I don't blame him.

I nod. "No lies between us."

"Good. Because I want you to know that you were probably right for what you did back then. I would have stayed. I would have given everything up for you. I was in love with you, but I was too chicken shit to say anything because I didn't know how you felt about me." He catches my eye, but then quickly away, almost embarrassed. "I was just about to tell you too. I had asked you to come with me, and was going to say it was because of…how I felt. But you shot that right down." He half laughs, rubbing his thumb over mine nervously. "I couldn't say it after that. I knew there was no point."

My chest constricts hearing this. I had suspected he cared for me like I did him, but I was never sure. It was my only comfort all this time to believe that he didn't. Because if he did feel the same, surely he would have said something. I see now that's not true. If he had said to me what I said to him, I wouldn't have been able to say anything about how I really felt either. I don't know whether to feel pride that I did the right thing, or more guilt at how I had to do it. Once again, my heart and head are at war with each other.

"I am sorry for how I handled things back then." I force

93

my shoulders back. I need to take ownership for my actions. "But I'm not sorry that I did it."

His eyes widen briefly, but he nods. "Okay, I guess that's fair."

"Ryan, look at where you are now. You have a successful music career. Your band is recording their second album...."

"Still sorry about that."

"I'm not." I laugh, squeezing his fingers. "And you even admitted that you would have stayed if I had told you the truth. So, despite my screwy way of handling it, I really did have good intentions."

"Alright. Enough about the past." He sits up and clears his throat. "What about now? Where do we stand today?"

"I'm not sure," I say. And I'm not. I don't know what the right thing to do now is. This is a lot to deal with in a short period of time. "A lot has happened the last three years. We're different people than we were back then."

"It's true that a lot has happened. For both of us. But I don't believe our essences ever change, do you? Does who you really are as a person change that much over time?" He's being so sincere. So honest and open. I love that he's being so vulnerable with me. It gives me real hope for our future.

"Maybe not?" I shrug. "I don't know. We'll have to play it by ear."

He grins, and his smile lights up the whole diner. "I see what you did there."

I smile back at him, but then get more serious. "So, can I assume you don't have a girlfriend?" He's probably had lots of girlfriends, but I want to be sure I'm not just taking a number.

"You would be correct in that assumption." He answers so quickly that I have no doubt he's telling the truth. "And what about you? Are you currently... unattached?" The hope in his eyes is so heartwarming, I melt a little inside.

"I am. So, how do we do this?" I can't help but smile to myself, because I can't believe I'm sitting in the Greasy Spoon with Ryan Crawford talking about the future of our relationship. It's surreal.

"Well, we should probably, oh I don't know, date or something?" He's being so charming I feel like swooning right here in front of Carla's lunch crowd.

"Oh, really? A date, huh?" I'm blushing like crazy, and I can neither stop nor hide it. "I can see that being a thing we could maybe do."

"Then, how about dinner tonight?"

"Geez, you move fast."

"I have a few years to make up for." His eyes dance with mirth as they meet mine.

I slide out of the booth to head back to the studio. "Me too. Where do you want to go for dinner?" Ryan throws some cash on the table and waves goodbye to Carla as we leave.

"How about my place?"

I stop in my tracks, unable to move my feet any further after hearing that suggestion. "Your mom's house? I don't know...." I'm not too fond of the idea of going over there and having to face his mother. I still haven't processed everything she's done. I'm not sure how I feel about her or how she feels about me. *Ryan did say she called me an angel, but what would she say about us being together now?*

"I'll make sure she's on her best behavior." He notices my trepidation. Stopping, he pulls me into him, resting his forehead on mine and catching my eyes with his. "I promise. It will be fine."

"Fine." I echo and sigh heavily, his warm eyes and gorgeous smile convincing me again. I used to be able to resist those things, and my free will is now melting away to nothing as I fall under his charms.

He wraps me into a firm hug. "It'll be fantastic. You'll see."

# # #

When we return to the studio, we find Matt and Jude are waiting for us on the couch in the control room, so I take a seat at the workstation and grab my notebook. They're about to witness precisely what their record label's money can buy when it comes to my musical expertise.

Once everyone looks settled, I start in. "So, you've got fifteen songs to work with, which is an admirable start, but we can eliminate a couple right off the bat."

"Oh no, she's killing our darlings!" Jude clutches at his hair in mock panic. "The humanity!"

I laugh but go on. "Track four needs to go. It copies the same chord progressions and beat as 'Killing Time,' and you don't want to rehash anything from your first album. You need to be original and fresh." They glance at each other and nod agreement, so I move track four from the current folder into one I labeled 'Dead Songs.' I notice Ryan's look is a little perplexed, but I continue. "Tracks nine and fourteen kind of drag everything else down and don't fit the overall tone of the others, so we should consider letting those go as well."

"Which ones are those again?" Matt asks. "I knew what you were referring to with the other one, but I don't know the songs by track number."

I check the folder on the computer, "Track nine is called 'Make Sure,' and track fourteen is 'Fall Back?'"

"Oh wow, I thought 'Fall Back' was fucking killer." Jude sits forward, ready to argue.

"We can totally keep that one if you guys want," I say and put my notebook down. "I guess I should ask you all first if there are thoughts on what songs should go before we get into my notes?"

They all look at each other again and shrug. Not helpful at all. This might be more difficult than I initially thought. Ryan, at least, doesn't have a confusing fog in his eyes anymore.

"That's kind of why you're here," Matt says, glancing at his bandmates. "We suck at making decisions like this."

"Okay, we'll work through it. Let's be democratic and have a show of hands then. Who wants to keep 'Fall Back' in the lineup?" I look at the three of them expectantly.

Jude is the only one to raise his hand, glaring at the other two. "I'll remember this when it comes to something you guys like."

"Sorry, dude," Ryan says.

"Well, wait," I say, not wanting to cause a rift between them. "Jude, what exactly do you like about this particular song? The lyrics? The bass line? The beat or tone? Maybe if I know what sticks with you in that song, we can incorporate it into another one."

He thinks for about a second, and he blushes slightly and turns his head away from the other two. "The bass line." I almost don't hear what he says; he's so quiet. He must be embarrassed to show the part he likes is *his* part, but I agree.

"I love that part too, especially in the bridge." I check my notebook, knowing I reference the change somewhere. After turning a few pages, I find what I wrote. "Actually, I made a note the bass line in that would work well in track ten, which is...." I check the folder for the song name, ''Take It With You.' Here, I'll play a little of what I'm thinking." I isolate the bass line of the bridge section of 'Fall Back' and overlay it onto the 'Take It With You' track I think will work better, and play the part for them.

Jude and Matt are jamming out to the music, and Ryan has that confused fog around him again. I'm not sure what he's unsure about, but I'm glad the other two appreciate the change. "I take it you like it better now?" I ask though I can tell they do. They're too distracted to answer me, but I meet Ryan's eyes and share a quick moment of success. Proving all the work I put in at the studio over the years is paying off now. Producing has never been my goal, but I took several college courses while getting my music degree, and I had to learn a lot while recording my own songs. I think I've gotten pretty good at the job if I do say so.

They're all grinning at me like goofballs when I stop the song. Their silence and smiles are a bit unnerving the longer they go on. "What?" I ask. "Seriously, what? You're creeping me out."

"We like," Matt nods at the others. "We like, right?" They nod along with him, and a knot I didn't know was there unfurls in my chest. I didn't have a lot of time to build up too much, but my anxiety about this not working out is erased right in that moment. This could be a great two months after all. *But then what?*

16

You Shouldn't Kiss Me Like This

RYAN

When I get home from the studio, my mother's reaction to the news that Sarah is coming for dinner is not what I expected. She doesn't say a single word, and nods her head with no expression on her face. I thought for sure I would be blasted with at least a scrutinizing look from her, but she gives absolutely nothing away. I suppose it's better than what I thought would happen, but it scares me a little for some reason. My mother is a hothead and opinionated, and sometimes I never know what will fly out of her mouth. This could either go really well or be a complete nightmare.

"Ma," I say to her back while she's at the stove, already preparing dinner. "Please be nice." I'm trying not to sound too demanding, but I want to make sure I express that this is important to me.

She doesn't respond, but glances back over her shoulder and nods again. It is so not like her to say nothing. This raises my anxiety for the dinner to go smoothly even higher. I sigh inwardly and head upstairs to take a quick shower before Sarah arrives.

I'm like a fucking high schooler getting ready for my first damned date the way my hands shake as I prepare. Fumbling with the buttons of my shirt, it takes three times longer to dress than it should. I'm in no way a fashionista and am not wearing anything fancy, only jeans and a button-down shirt, but they're my 'better' jeans and 'better' shirt. Things others said looked good on me, so I'm taking their word. I glance at myself in the mirror, run a hand through my messy hair to tame it a little to no avail, say, "Fuck it," and head downstairs to wait for Sarah.

This isn't the first time Sarah's been to our house for dinner. Far from it. But this is the first time since everything happened. Before I left for LA, it was rare for us not to spend at least part of each day together. So, I think my nerves are primarily due to how weird this is becoming. It never used to be, so it shouldn't be strange to invite her over. But things have changed way too much for each of us for that to happen. We need to start over with everything. I didn't even truly consider the dynamic of my mother when I invited Sarah over. I'd said it would be fine, but I don't know that to be true. This could completely blow up in my face. *What have I gotten myself into?*

The house smells fantastic with the promise of an exquisite meal, making my mouth water. I avoid going into the kitchen to let my mother do her thing since she doesn't like being crowded while cooking. And, apparently she's not speaking to me right now. As I pace around the rest of the house, I notice our small dining room, which we never use, is cleared and set with a tablecloth and the good plates and glasses. There are even a couple of candles, though not yet lit. My heart tightens a little, knowing my mom is going to all this trouble for Sarah. At least, I hope it's for Sarah. *Jesus.*

I go over to the small liquor cabinet in the corner, pour myself a whiskey shot, and then make it a double for good measure. The amber liquid burns like a bitch on the way down, but if I'm going to get my dumb nerves under control, I need some liquid courage. I repeat the process one more time, just to make sure. Tonight is too important for me to clam up and be passive. I did that before, and lost three years.

I finally give in and go to the kitchen to check what my mother's up to. I sneak up behind her and give her a big hug, lifting her off the floor and kissing the top of her head. She screeches with laughter and bats at my arms to let her go.

"Put me down, Ryan! Put me down!"

I do as she demands but still am swatted again with a wooden spoon. "Ow! What was that for?"

"I'm sure I have reasons."

The doorbell rings, and I almost trip over myself in my rush to answer the door. My mother shakes her head at me with a smile as I open it. Sarah is simply radiant. She's wearing a deep red sundress that flatters everything about her. The setting sun behind her illuminates the aura around her and makes my heart skip a beat. She pushes the bottle she's holding into my chest, and I grab on to it before I can drop it.

"I figured your mom would be cooking something amazing and Mexican, so I brought some Sauvignon Blanc to pair with." Her words come out in a rushed run-on sentence leaving her breathless. She's almost as nervous as I am, her hands now fidgeting without something to hold. "I hope the wine is okay...."

"Yeah! Yeah, great. Thanks." My god, she's gorgeous. I can't help but stare. Our eyes lock, and something passes between us. I'm not sure what; a want, a need, something primal making my skin ache to touch hers. "You look...."

"Let the poor girl in, Ryan," my mother calls from the kitchen. "We're not having a picnic outdoors. Where are your manners?"

That breaks the spell we're under, and I step back to invite her in. My hand brushes the small of her back as I lead her to the dining room, and that tiny touch makes my fingers tingle. I'm acting like a fucking teenager who's never been with a girl or on a fucking date. I need to reign myself in.

Sarah waves at the table silently and raises a curious eyebrow at me in a '*Wow, aren't we fancy?*' expression. I shrug and point my thumb over my shoulder towards the kitchen, indicating this is all my mother's doing. Her eyebrows go up in surprise, and she mouths the word '*Wow.*' I nod and mouth back, '*I know.*' I love Sarah knows this isn't how we usually do things around here, and her coming for dinner is being treated as a special occasion by my mom. While she may be surprised, I'm kind of not. My discussion with my mother the other day proved how highly she thinks of Sarah, and she's not one to say things like that out loud. She shows her affection with her actions -- and *always* with food. But still only 'kind of' surprised, because you just never know with my mother.

There is the typical pre-meal flurry of activity as candles are lit, wine is poured, food is brought to the table and dished out, compliments to the chef are given, and that chef says a quick grace. Then silence falls over everyone as the delicious food gets devoured. My mother is surprisingly the first to break it.

"So, when does your Benji leave for school?"

Sarah's a little surprised at the question but composes herself. "He leaves next week, actually." She shifts her eyes down to her plate and pushes the food around.

"And he'll be a business major? Very practical of him."

"Yes. He received a couple of scholarships to the Fisher Business school he could defer to this year. He wants to go into analytics." Sarah again appears shocked at my mother knowing any of this. She glances at me to see if I somehow told my mother these things, but I didn't even know any of this, and all I can do is give her a bewildered shrug. Leave it to my mother to be in the know of the town goings-on.

"Are you saying I'm not practical?" I chuckle, trying to deflect from the interrogation of Sarah and refilling my wine glass.

"I don't need to say it. We all know it," my mother dead-pans. Then she does something I have never seen her do before. She leans over and squeezes Sarah's hand, looks her in the eye, and says, "Tell Benji I wish him only the best at school. I know he's had a hard time, so let him know that it does get better." My mother is not an effusive person with anyone but family, so for her to reach out to Sarah like this is remarkable. All the times Sarah's been here before, she's never been this affectionate. I think this is her way of thanking Sarah for her actions three years ago, and concern for everything she's been through. As much as I hate that she approves of her actions, I can tell her gesture and words mean a lot to Sarah.

"Thank you. I will tell him." She smiles, and some sort of understanding passes between them I can only partially comprehend.

"You two take your wine and go out back," my mother orders, standing and grabbing dirty dishes. "Out of my sight."

"But Mrs. Crawford-" Sarah starts to try to help clear the table, but my mother swats at her hands to stop her. Sarah yanks her hands out of the way before getting pummeled as I did earlier.

"But nothing. You are a guest. Go enjoy the warm evening while we still have them." She's flailing her arms and shooing us out the back door to the patio, hurling Spanish at us like a weapon. I barely have time to grab my wine glass without spilling a drop on the way out.

"Wow. So *that* happened." Sarah chuckles. She sits on the love seat glider, which has seen better days, and starts swaying back and forth. The rusty springs squeal loudly in protest into the quiet night.

I sit beside her and wrap an arm over her shoulders, the liquid courage doing its job nicely. I'm a little light-headed and can't tell if this is from the alcohol or emotion. The rising moon is full and bright, and the bluish hue it casts on Sarah's tanned skin seems iridescent. I brush the back of my hand along the arm closest to me, the one with the dragonfly tattoo. Up close, the detail in the wings is exquisite and so delicate.

"This is beautiful," I say. "Like you."

"Oh, thanks." Her cheeks are turning that glorious pink again.

"I love when your face turns pink like that," I say, my voice coming out low.

She brings her hand up to her face, touching the warm skin, suddenly shy she lowers her lashes. Her hair starts to fall across her face, but I stop it and tuck it behind her ear. My fingers tingle again as my skin meets hers. I'm still in some disbelief that we're here like this right now. That we've talked like adults about what happened, and how we feel. I never would have thought coming home would mean getting to be with Sarah like this.

"Are you having a good time?" I ask. I want to make sure this is going as well for her as it's going for me. We've spent so much time together over the years, that this feels rushed, but at the same time like it took forever for us to get here. It's hard to gauge where we are together.

She gives me a look that's part smolder, part burn. "I am."

Her nearness makes every muscle in my body tighten with need, and I have to take a long swig of my wine to distract myself, finishing the entire glass in one gulp. I lean over and set it down on the ground in front of the glider, breaking my connection with her for only a second. But it's a second too long. The craving inside of me is overpowering now. I shift my body towards her and place my hand along her cheek, caressing her silky soft skin, and gaze deeply into her eyes. I need to find out if she's feeling the same way about me right now. If she wants me as badly as I want and need her. I think she does.

"Ryan..." is all she gets out before my lips brush hers in the lightest of kisses, tentative and sweet. Electricity shoots from my lips to my core when our mouths touch. I've kissed girls before, plenty of them. But that simple kiss has jumped to the top of the list of all-time best kisses. Maybe because this has been such a long time coming, the kiss felt better than anything else I ever experienced. It's the first kiss I've only dreamed of until now.

I pull away briefly to check her reaction and then lean in to press my mouth to hers again, hesitantly at first, but then more assertive and more confident, until the two of us become a tangle of mouths, hands, and hungry sighs. My skin catches fire anywhere her hands or mouth touches my body, and I might internally combust right here in the backyard. The sensation of her lips on me is better than anything I ever allowed myself to imagine. We're engulfed in pure magic, and I don't want to break the spell, but she pulls away from me. She holds an arm extended between us to prevent me from getting closer.

"Did I do something wrong?" I ask, gasping for breath and trying to regain my bearings. My head is still swirling with recent memories of her touch, and I'm bewildered. It sure felt like she was reciprocating my feelings a second ago.

She stands quickly with her back to me, hugging herself in the slight chill of the evening. "No, you didn't do anything wrong. I don't know what we're doing. As much as I want this to work -- and I *do* want this to work, I don't see how this ever can. Our lives are so different now. And you're only here for a matter of weeks. This is just crazy...." She turns then, and heads toward the back door.

"Sarah, don't run away," I pull her arm around my waist and grab her face in my hands. Her beautiful eyes bore into mine, trying to read my scattered thoughts. "Not again," I whisper as I graze her bottom lip with my thumbs. I dust her forehead with a feather-light kiss and wrap her into my arms tightly. "Never again. I won't let you. You have no idea how long I have wanted this. How long I waited for this."

We stand like that for a long time, swaying in the moonlight. Both of us humming songs to one another as we slow dance. Not saying anything, just holding each other. Suddenly, a wave of gravity hits me, and I take a step back, which makes me giggle for some reason. I glance up at Sarah, confused, realizing I'm sitting on the ground with no memory of how I got here. *Am I fucking drunk? What the hell?* I try to think back to the alcohol I had this evening and remember the double whiskey shots. Both of them. And the wine. All the fucking wine. They don't go together, now that I think about it. *But I was kissing Sarah... Did I just fuck this up?* "Shit. I ruined the night, didn't I?"

"You didn't ruin anything. Apparently, you're a light-weight who can't handle their wine." She helps pull me up, and I drape an arm over her shoulders so she can lead me inside, "Let's get you to bed. Wait-"

"I like where your mind is at," I grin.

"I meant *your* bed, goofball."

"Well, we will be a tight fit, but I think we can manage. Keep in mind I still have a twin bed...." I laugh, and it comes out with a snort, "...in my mom's house. How old am I again?"

She's laughing with me and is so god-damned cute. "I don't know, twelve?"

"Eww, Do you kiss all twelve-year-olds like that, Miss Lawrence?"

She punches my arm, "You're so gross."

"But I'm funny."

"Yes. You are funny." She rolls her eyes at me.

"And handsome."

She shakes her head as she leads me into the house. "Yes. And handsome."

That's the last thing I remember of our first date...

Say You
Won't Let Go

SARAH

I spend the next week juggling the job at the recording studio, my job at the Stout Hideout, getting Benji ready to leave for college, and finding time to spend with Ryan. Every minute of every day is packed to overflowing. Time to myself is nearly non-existent. I almost have no time to spend with Jenny, and we're falling behind on our gossip. She's been begging me via text for details on Ryan and my relationship for days. Everything is still so new; I don't want to jinx anything and say everything is perfect. I know something will happen to screw things up as soon as I do. But things *are* kind of perfect with us. It's almost as Ryan suggested, and the last three years never happened. Like we've been together the whole time. There's no pretending, though. It feels completely natural to be with him now.

Saturday morning for Benji and Joe to head off for Columbus arrives, and I can't believe my little brother is actually leaving home to go to college. After his major depressive episode when mom died, I didn't think this day would ever come, and I'm so proud of him I want to burst. He's put in the work and deserves every bit of progress he's making. I don't need to handle him with kid gloves any more. I'll always be overprotective of him; this isn't something new for us. Even when we were younger, I felt the need to treat him with extra care and extra love. But now, my baby brother is all grown up and leaving the nest. Now I know what parents go through, I guess.

"I'm sorry not sorry, but I'll be leaving you with a mountain of dirty dishes," Joe announces to the kitchen, flipping a pancake expertly without looking. The enormous food piles on the island make up for any work I'll need to do when they leave. Joe is one of the best cooks ever, and the spread he's laid out for their send-off could feed the entire neighborhood. I texted Ryan to come over and bring his bandmates to help eat everything. Otherwise, there will be more leftovers than I can deal with, even with Gunner's help.

"Don't worry," I mutter, in between bites of a mouthwatering waffle, "I'll make Ryan's band clean up."

"I like the way you delegate." He points the spatula at me. "Way to be a badass boss lady."

Benji, who's been relatively withdrawn all morning, laughs, "You can say that again. You saw how she made me clean my room yesterday."

"Hey, you're going to be gone until Thanksgiving. I don't

want your mess in my face every day I pass your room until then," I say defensively.

"Just shut my door. We shut the door to the other room we don't want to deal with." His tone goes flat, and the smile on his face fades away so fast, it's like it was never there. He's talking about our mother's bedroom door that I still keep shut. I know I should empty the room and give her stuff away, but it's *her* room. I find it easier to put things out of sight and mind. I'm not ready yet. I'll get there. Just not yet.

"That's different, and you know it." My fork hits my plate with a clank as I drop it. I turn on my counter stool to face Benji head-on.

Joe turns back to the stove swiftly, suddenly very interested in the particular pancake in the frying pan, not wanting to be caught in the middle of this. I don't blame him. Benji and I don't usually create a lot of drama between us, but no relationship is flawless. Family drama is always messy.

"It might be different, but that doesn't mean it isn't still true." He stares at his plate. His face is unreadable, and I'm not sure what he's trying to do here. *Is he trying to start an argument with me before he leaves? Does he think that will make it easier to say goodbye? Or, does he think I should clear out that room?*

"What's your point, Benji?"

"I'm not trying to make a point. I'm just saying that is how things are dealt with in this house."

"Well, why didn't you say something if you wanted things handled differently?" His words are a punch to my chest. I was not aware that how I dealt with everything bothered him.

"What was I supposed to say? Hey Sarah, you're not handling mom's death right? There is no right or wrong way to grieve. There is comfortable and uncomfortable for everyone else. Mom died two years ago. And how you're *not* dealing with it is getting uncomfortable."

The doorbell rings, making Gunner bark his head off, and the super intense energy in the room amps up to eleven. Ryan and the rest of the band must be here.

"I got it." Joe quietly holds up a hand to us. "Keep going. This is good for you both. I'll snag you a couple more minutes." He turns off the stove and heads towards the front door.

"Why didn't you tell me any of this, Benji?" I ask, hurt that he thinks he can't talk to me. I thought we were able to be there for each other, no matter what. To know that this has been building up in him and making him uncomfortable hurts my heart. "You know you can tell me anything."

He nods but still doesn't meet my eyes. "I know. Some things are harder than others to talk about."

"Oh, Benji," I stand up and pull him into a hug, holding on to him tightly. "When I say you can talk to me about anything, I mean *anything*." I pull back to meet his gaze to emphasize my point. I need him to know this. "I am your big sister. I will always *be* your big sister. I can handle it if you've got something to say to me. Specifically, if I'm fucking up." I hug him again, squeezing him harder. "I love you. And I'm gonna miss the crap out of you."

"Okay, okay," he pretends to choke but laughs. "I'm gonna miss you too."

"I'll clear that *other* room by the time you come back for

Thanksgiving. Deal?" I hold out my hand for him to shake, and he grabs it.

"Deal."

Joe can't hold back the tide that is Indigo King any longer, and they all pile into the kitchen, anxious for their complimentary gourmet breakfast. Straggling behind them, Joe mouths the word 'sorry' and gives a helpless shrug.

Ryan gives Benji a quick fist bump and me a light peck on the cheek. Everyone stops for a second and stares at us, taking in Ryan's swift kiss, and then goes about what they were doing without a single word about it. I can feel myself blushing furiously and sit back down in my seat to finish my own breakfast while they grab theirs. We've been able to keep our relationship professional while working at the studio, so Jude and Matt don't know we're together. I almost feel guilty for keeping it from everyone, but to be honest, I kind of liked having that one secret with Ryan. We've only had stolen kisses and some extremely steamy moments here and there, but they've been fantastic. The cat's out of the bag, but nobody batted an eyelash. Maybe we weren't such a secret after all.

Ryan is still next to me and is playing with a lock of my hair, lost in thought. His touch sends instant shivers down my spine, and into places with no business feeling so good in front of so many people, especially my little brother, and I force myself not to physically react. The desire to squirm in pleasure is almost overwhelming.

I finally can't take it anymore and turn to him, "Aren't you going to have something to eat? Joe's really outdone himself this morning."

"Yeah, I'm waiting for an opening," he jokes, snapping out of it and chuckling. "I don't want to lose any fingers to these two trying to grab a pancake."

"Well, you'd better hurry up because we don't plan on leaving any leftovers," Jude says.

"FYI," Joe pipes in, "The kitchen is officially closed, so what is out now is all there is. May the odds be ever in your favor."

As the guys dig into their food, I put my empty plate into the sink to deal with later, and head out to the garage to check on my old SUV that is now Benji's. When our mom got sick, I gave it to him since it was so difficult for her to maneuver in and out of. It was easier for us to use her car when I took her to doctor's appointments. Turns out, the SUV is an excellent vehicle for moving to college. The back of it is packed to the brim with both Benji and Joe's things since almost nothing fits in the Prius. We packed it last night in what was the closest thing to live Tetris I'll ever witness. It will be amazing if they can duplicate it on move-out day.

I'm double-checking some old boxes from a shelf on the back wall to ensure we didn't miss anything, when a familiar arm snakes around my waist. My skin tingles as Ryan's hand glides under the hem of my shirt, his palm brushes my stomach, and his fingers barely graze the bottom of my bra. I put the box away and lean back into him, my hand instinctively reaching around and grabbing the back of his neck. He kisses my ear, tickling it with his tongue and warm breath. This is how our previous steamy moments have all started. When we're together, we can barely keep our hands off each other. It looks like today is no different.

"My god, you're beautiful," he whispers, and then kisses a trail down my neck. Every kiss and touch is an electrical storm, sparking sensations that drive straight to my core. He's hard against my back, and his hands slide up to grab my breasts. The throbbing between my legs grows more intense as he shifts his fingers under my bra and caresses my nipples that stiffen at his touch. My body's longing to have him inside me makes a breathy groan escape my lips.

Ryan reciprocates with his own spontaneous moan, and starts to turn me to face him. The intensity of our touches increases every time we're together, and each day we approach the point of no return. We hear voices coming our way from inside the house, and we intuitively jump apart from each other. We're trying to act naturally, but I know we're failing miserably by how Jude and Matt study us both as they pass through the garage. The heat in my cheeks is probably a dead give away too.

"There you are. We're heading back to the hotel," Matt says, deciding like an adult to avoid discussing what they walked into. "Joe said something about us doing the dishes, so we took care of that for you. Thanks for the invite."

"Cool..." is all I can manage. *Shit. How long have we been out here?*

"Yeah, we'll let you two go back to..." he swirls his hand around suggestively, "whatever it was you were doing." He gives Ryan a quick wink and heads down the driveway to their car.

I lean back against the shelving and let out a long breath. Had we not heard them coming and jumped away from each other, that would have been more embarrassing than it already was. And things were pretty uncomfortable to begin with. I glance over to Ryan, breathing heavily himself, and gazing at me with a hunger I've not seen in him before. His eyes are dark with desire, and he rakes a hand through his hair, his forearm flexing. *Damn, this man is hot. I can't believe he's mine.*

"That was close." His voice is husky and rough, and full of heat.

"It was."

He steps over to me, hooks his thumbs through the belt loops of my jean shorts, and pulls me to him. He's still hard, and my breath catches as he drives me carefully back into the shelf I was leaning against. Between the tiny amount of sleep I got last night and my hunger for him, my brain is buzzing. But it turns into a lovely kind of lost sensation. Intoxicating even.

His hands slide up to cup my face, and he presses his lips to mine in a kiss that holds the most yearning I ever felt from someone. That kiss alone lets me know how much he wants me. And not only the physical me. A kiss that conveys so much more than carnal need. So much more. As he slowly pulls away from me, my legs shake a little. I have never been so thoroughly kissed in my life. The thought makes me wonder what else he can be so thorough with, and I blush at my own thinking.

"Are you alright?" He's got a gleam in his eye like he

knows what I was thinking, but I don't care. I want him to know that I want him the same way.

"Are you?" I smile back.

"Fuck no, I'm not alright." He rests his forehead against mine, eyes closed, and grinds his hips against me slightly, letting me know exactly what's wrong with him. My body responds on its own, and I wrap my arms around his neck to pull him into a kiss. It grows deeper until we hear Benji and Joe nearby and pull ourselves apart again. "*Fuck me,*" Ryan mutters, making me giggle at him.

"Not today, apparently."

"Very funny," he grimaces at me. *Poor guy, can't catch a break today. But then, neither can I.*

Benji and Joe appear in the doorway, holding hands and looking too charming for words. I still can't believe they're leaving. My mind completely switches modes, and my eyes start to brim with tears as I look at the two of them. I'm going to miss them so much.

"Oh, here we go." Joe hands me a cloth handkerchief. "Waterworks time. Here. Use this, go on. Cry it out of your system. I thought you cried yourself out last night."

The tears overflow and start to fall as I ignore the handkerchief I'm holding, and pull Joe into a hug, crying on his shoulder. "I'm gonna miss you, Joe," I cry.

He pats the back of my head awkwardly, "There, there. Benji? Do something with your sister?" As much as Joe is an emotional guy, he doesn't deal with other people's emotions very well.

Benji steps into Joe's place in my hug, and I start bawling

all over on his shoulder. "I'm gonna miss you so much," I hiccup. "You better call me every day."

"I'm only going to be like two and a half hours away. Not that far."

"Shut up. Promise to call me. Or text at least." I pull back, dab at my eyes with the cloth, and ungracefully blow my nose.

"I promise, I will keep in touch."

I glare at him and sniffle. "Is that the best you can do?" I know I'm being a clingy asshole, but I don't care. This is super hard for me. I should be allowed to be an overbearing sister in situations like this.

"I don't want to promise what I can't deliver." Pride takes him over. "My therapist would be proud of me for that one."

"Make sure you keep in touch with her too." I can't help but laugh because he's right; his therapist would love that. And my mind instantly goes to the dark place he was at not too long ago. It scares me more to think that I won't be able to keep an eye on his moods or his medications. I need to trust that he'll be able to handle it. Maybe his promise is a sign that I can have that trust now.

Ryan steps up behind me and puts a hand on my shoulder. Such a small but comforting gesture, but I can't help putting a hand over his in thanks.

Benji gives Ryan a strange look and holds his hand out, "Take care of my sister."

"I'll do my best." Ryan's tone is stoic. He takes his hand and shakes it. Benji raises an eyebrow as if his response isn't good enough. "I don't want to promise what I can't deliver. I can only do my best." He echoes Benji's words back to him, but there isn't any sarcasm. Ryan means what he says. He's being sincere. That's good enough for Benji, and he nods his appreciation for the honesty.

"C'mon, people." Joe claps his hands like he's directing a bunch of actors. "We need to get this road on the show. Benji, check your Waze for the right destination address. Did you pack your charger?"

Benji rolls his eyes and hugs me again before heading to his car. I know I don't have anything to worry about with Joe on Benji's side. Even though I will. And Benji's come a long way from how low he was. I'm cautiously optimistic that this will go smoothly. I discussed this step with Benji's therapist. She thinks it may be time for him to be more independent and agrees that college is an excellent move. I can only trust her advice. And trust that his and Joe's relationship is strong enough to withstand any storm.

Ryan and I hold hands and watch as both of their cars disappear down the road and out of sight. We're at the end of the driveway, and he pulls me into a hug, wrapping his arms around me. A hollow sensation blooms in my chest once they're gone. My breath hitches a little, but I hold back the tears.

"What do you need from me?" he asks, his voice soft and full of concern.

I melt inside at the question and almost let loose the tears I held in. No one has ever asked me that before, and I'm unsure how to respond. "I don't know," I say, honestly. Because I *don't* know what I need. I haven't been on my own before. I hadn't thought this far ahead. The last few weeks were such a whirlwind, with Ryan coming back into my life, and then *really into my life*, and the producing/writing job with Indigo King, and Benji leaving, things have been insane.

"Let's go sit out back for a bit and figure it out." He pulls me back through the garage and leads me out to the spot on the large driftwood branch. This has now become 'our spot' since we started seeing each other. Gunner follows along, chasing his ghosts. The day is still a bit warm, but the area is shaded. I lean against Ryan, putting my head on his shoulder, and nestling comfortably in his arms. We fit so perfectly together all the time, no matter where we are. I love it.

"I'm almost afraid to go into the house," I say after a while, watching the lake waves crash into the beach rocks. Living along the lake doesn't mean you have a smooth sandy beach. It means you have a lot of treacherous stones to try to prevent premature land erosion. The rocks make for better wave crashing, though. It matches my mood. "I never lived alone before."

Ryan is quiet, but then asks, "Do you want me to stay with you for a while? Until you're more comfortable? Or, I could stay a few nights a week?"

I look up at him and examine his radiant face to see if he's being cheeky with his suggestion, but he's sincere. "Are you being serious? Or trying to sneak into my bed?"

The wind that always surrounds the lake's edge is whipping his dark hair around, but I can see the different trains of thought run through his head at my question. His lip twitches like he wants to smirk but keeps his face serious. "Can't it be both? Are the choices mutually exclusive?"

Considering his question before answering, I make a decision. "I think I want to try living alone for a while."

"Of course."

"No offense to you. I just never have. And I think I want to try it out."

"No offense taken. I understand." A smile creeps up his lips. "But I can still stay over sometimes, right?"

I push into him, laughing, "we'll see about that."

He squeezes me and kisses the top of my head. "We've got our whole lives ahead of us. We go at your pace. Always. Know that. I'm simply a bundle of testosterone trying to get into your pants. But only *your* pants, so we're clear."

18

Kissing A Fool

SARAH

The next night is the first of the Indigo King test shows, and the flurry of activity between the studio and the bar is frantic and kinetic. Mark is working with me tonight with the expected extra crowd coming to see the 'Special Guest.' Lorelai is here for the occasion as well. We've seen on social media that rumors got out who the band is, correct rumors. And rumors that may or may not have started with Jenny and me.

About an hour to go before we open the doors for the show, the band finishes their sound check. We don't keep a complex setup at the Stout Hideout, so they're getting straight spotlights and a simple audio mixer. Luckily, Indigo King isn't used to anything fancy yet.

"How's it sound at the bar?" Ryan's voice booms from the stage.

Lorelai and I give him two thumbs up, glance at each other, and break out in laughter. The whole day was hectic but satisfying. We spent the afternoon fine-tuning the playlist several times, and knowing that the songs they're going to play tonight are songs I had a key part in writing and shaping is still unbelievable. These will be my first official songwriting credits on an actual album, and I'm proud of our work. I'm excited for people to hear their songs. And I'm especially happy for Ryan, who worked so hard and deserves to bask in the glow of their praise.

The guys leave the stage and come over, and Ryan leans across the bar to give me a kiss. I catch Mark giving us a sideways glare but ignore him. I had told Ryan about our banter, and I think he kissed me to rub it in his face that we don't need to banter; we are the real thing. I don't mind, though. Any chance to kiss Ryan, I'll take.

"So, what's your poison?" Mark asks. He looks over at Lorelai, "I assume the band's drinks are free?" He doesn't seem happy about it.

"But of course." She gives the band a haughty wink. "We treat our bands well here at the Stout Hideout."

"In that case," Ryan rubs his hands together greedily, a thirsty grin on his face, "Glenfiddich for me then."

"Well," Lorelai qualifies, slapping on a panicked grin, "we love our Special Guests, but only as much as the lower shelves allow. You understand, of course. But I do approve of your taste in whiskey, love."

"I was only kidding," Ryan gives her a wink. "I wouldn't

want to take advantage of our host. I'll take a Jack and Coke, but please make it a double."

"I'll take that one." I grab a glass and start his drink for him. Mark takes the rest of the band's orders, and soon enough, time for us to open the doors arrives. My nerves are probably more on edge than the band in anticipation. I don't know why I'm worried; I know they'll do great. I'm just more invested than ever in someone's music than I ever have been.

I have the honor of introducing the band, and when the time comes, I make my way to the stage around the large crowd through the back green room area. On my way, I wave at Carla from the Greasy Spoon, and who I assume is her daughter, Lara, in the audience. We did let Carla in on the secret earlier in the week so that she would be here, and bring her daughter with her. Lara is ecstatic with anticipation, and it makes me smile.

"You guys ready?" I ask the band before I step on the stage. They're beginning to look almost as nervous as I am.

"Yup," they all say in unison.

"What are you guys nervous for? You're awesome. I know this because I helped you write your songs. So, it *must* be incredible." I'm hoping my pep talk has some effect.

"We're good," Jude nods. "We're good."

I give Ryan a smile and a quick kiss and head out to front stage. The crowd cheers but then quiets when they realize it's just me, which strikes me as funny but understandable. I'm not who they're here to see.

"Ladies and gentlemen." I play up the circus barker role I've taken on. "The Stout Hideout is happy to present you with a real treat tonight." There's a smattering of shouts and applause. I can distinctly make out a small scream from Lara, which makes me smile. "We have some superstars, some real rock stars with us tonight." I glance side stage and wink at Ryan cheekily. "One of whom is one of Chandler's own." This makes the crowd cheer louder. "They're here to try out some new material on you in secret," I put a finger up to my mouth to indicate the mystery. "No recording, please. And you need to be kind, but you need to be honest, okay?" The volume in the room turns up even more. "So, without further ado, I give you the one and only Indigo King!"

The crowd erupts into loud cheers and applause as Ryan, Matt, and Jude head out on the stage and proceed to command it with their presence and talent. This is my first time seeing Ryan at work live with a full band and crowd. There are videos on the internet of their performances, but seeing it in person is impressive. He displays such charisma with the audience and wins them over almost instantly. And the band works so well together; each new song goes smoothly and without a hitch. Ryan talks between them, explaining the writing process and thinking behind each one. They play a few songs that would be familiar to fans at the end, and after close to two and a half hours, everyone is won over and eating out of their hands.

Jenny and Luke arrive about halfway through the show since they had a dinner commitment with Luke's bosses that they couldn't wiggle out of. I fill their drinks for them, and they disappear into the crowd. I feel bad for not talking to them, but my attention is pretty focused on Ryan and the band.

Once the concert ends, Mark and I work for about another

hour and a half, serving the throng of happy patrons who I can tell think they've witnessed something remarkable. It makes me glad to know that I had a tiny part in it. Jenny says a quick goodbye before she and Luke leave, knowing that I can't chat when work is crazy like this. I'm dying to head to the back to be with Ryan, and let him know how well it went on this side of the stage; to share in the celebration of the new music we created. Once the crowd reaches a manageable level, I leave Mark to head back to the band to check in on them.

When I get to the backstage area, I'm intercepted by Lorelai, who seems scared to death as soon as she notices me. "Is everything alright up front, love? Are you sure Mark can handle the big crowd by himself?"

I stop and study her more closely, concerned for how she's acting. She's unsettled to the point of panic. It's so strange and unlike her. I haven't ever seen her like this. "Are you okay, Lorelai? Are you upset?"

"Oh, I'm fine honey, really." She grabs my arm and tries to turn me back to the bar. "I worry about Mark. He's not the brightest bartender...."

I start pulling my arm away gently, and my eyes catch the half-open doorway leading to the green room area, and my blood runs cold when I see what she's been trying to keep me from.

"Dear, let's head back to the bar; I thought I saw Jenny...." Lorelai tries again as my world falls apart before my eyes. Ryan is in the middle of passionately kissing a tall blonde woman I never laid eyes on before in my life. And I would notice her in the crowd, I'm sure. She's stunningly beautiful.

And she's obviously *very* familiar with Ryan. *What the fuck am I seeing? Who the hell is this?*

I'm half tempted to storm in and demand answers, but I'm too stunned to do that. I'm too shocked to move. Lorelai has to physically pull me away from the doorway. But, before I'm turned away, I swear that Ryan sees me, but I can't be sure. "What the..."

"Really, love. I think it'd be best if we go back...." I let myself be directed back to the bar area, but I'm not seeing anything anymore. I'm not feeling anything. I'm entirely numb.

I turn to Lorelai. "I need to go home."

"Go fetch your purse. I'll drive you. I'll let Mark know." Her eyes are hard on mine, communicating her shared emotion and committing herself to take care of me in my moment of need. I'm so grateful to her because I know that I could never drive myself in my state. The initial shock at what I just saw is starting to wear off, and I can begin to sense the pain that is about to double me over, and keep me up all night as it stabs at my heart.

I rush to the back of the bar and grab my bag, ignoring Mark's questions about what's wrong and going on. I leave any responses to him for Lorelai, and run outside to her car before completely breaking down. I have to clutch at my stomach to keep from literally screaming out loud or throwing up. Maybe both. The betrayal hitting me is like being run over by a bus. I'm totally blindsided, and such a god-damned fool. I thought Ryan wanted clarity. Open communication. He's wanted to be with me since he met me, blah blah blah. I was so wrong. *How could I have been so wrong about him?*

Didn't I know him at all? After all this time? I guess I didn't. And I let myself fall for him all over again. Like a stupid idiot. People do change after all.

Lorelai comes out of the bar, half running and waving her keys. "Let's get the ever-loving heck out of here." When she gets to me, she pulls me into one of her hugs, but it doesn't have the same effect it usually does. "You're going to be fine. No matter what. I swear. I've got your back." She pats my head. I'm still numb and confused about what happened; I can't digest it all. Let alone take any kind of comfort for it.

"I'm okay." I'm trying to convince her of something I don't believe, but I can tell how flat my voice is. "I'm okay. I just want to go home. I need to be home."

"I can do that, honey. I can do that." We don't have a long drive to my house from the bar, but it feels like months. When she pulls into my driveway, we stare straight ahead at the bright headlights harshly shining on my garage door, unsure of what to say. "Do you want me to call Jenny for you? Or Benji?"

"No. I'll talk to Jenny tomorrow, I'm sure." My voice is monotone. I have no emotions left. "Thank you for the ride." I turn to her, my thoughts scattered. "Tonight went well, though, right?"

She turns her head to me, confused. "Excuse me, honey?"

"The songs. Everyone liked the songs?"

"Sure, love," she says, her tone softening. "The songs were brilliant. You should be proud."

I nod. Not proud. Not anything.

"Thanks again for the ride." I step out of the car and head into my now extremely empty house.

19

Careless Whispers

RYAN

After the show, we're all surprised as our original record label producer, Reese, comes into the green room area. We weren't expecting her for a few days yet. I'd put off bringing her up to Sarah because I didn't know how. My relationship with Reese is complicated, to put it lightly. We both used each other to release tension in the past, nothing more. There were no expectations between us for any kind of emotional commitment because that would never happen. And we both knew those were the rules. At least, I thought we did. When she shows up at our show tonight, I'm caught by complete surprise. Not only at her early arrival but also at her reaction to seeing me. She basically jumps me as soon as she sees me. And being the asshole male I am, my body responds like a total fuckwad. Throw in the few double Jack and Cokes I drank, and fuck me. *Seriously. Fuck me.*

I swear I saw Sarah out of the corner of my eye in the middle of a compromising position between myself and Reese, but I hope to god I'm wrong. It isn't until I pull myself away from her that the expression on Matt and Jude's faces tells me I might not be wrong. *Was that Sarah? Fuck!* I try to push away from Reese to go after Sarah, but she holds me back.

"Where do you think you're going? We're celebrating here." She grabs a random drink from the table and hands it to me. "The new songs are amazing you guys! Cheers! I can't wait to jump in the studio with you to mix them. The label is going to love what we can do with these." She holds up another drink to cheers with mine, and I can't do anything else but go along with her. With Reese here, basically our label is here. We're held by the collar. The other guys join in, clinking their glasses and beers with ours in congratulations, but the cheerful mood is now forced, and they're both giving me dirty looks.

I down the drink in one swallow, willing the burn in my throat to sober me up to keep track of what's happened and what's going on now. My mind isn't playing along enough to realize that is the complete opposite of how alcohol works. I'm still completely confused. Part of me is elated at the show we just put on with new music Sarah helped us perfect, and another part of me is distraught at the thought she witnessed me kissing Reese. The adrenaline pumping through me is doing both good and harm. *Did she see us? Or did I imagine that? She'll never understand...*

A few minutes later, the male bartender I can't stand, Mark, comes to the back area, and he's got a genuinely shitty attitude. "Are you guys done?" His tone is agitated.

Reese turns on him, her bob hairdo cutting her features sharply, "No. We're not." Her voice is in her old, take-no-prisoners mode, and I almost feel bad for the guy she directs it at. "We could use another bottle of..." she holds up the now empty bottle of Jack Daniels, "...this. And the appropriate mixer to go with. If you please."

Even though she said please, her tone is so condescending, I can't let it pass. Not here. Not where Sarah works. "If you could, we'd appreciate it," I call to Mark's back since he's already turned away without a word, knowing my trying to be nice is now a moot point. I turn to Reese. "Why do you always have to do that?"

"Do what?"

"You know what." I glance at the others for agreement. They avoid my eyes and leave me on my own on this. "You didn't need to be that way with him."

She waves me off. "Whatever. You guys were fantastic, by the way. They should be thankful you played here."

"They are thankful." Matt stands up from the couch and leaves the room, and Jude glares at me hard, like the change in everyone's mood is my fault.

What the fuck did I do? I did fuck things up, didn't I? I need to fix this. Now.

"I need to go." I push past Reese out to the bar area. She tries to grab me, but I shrug her off. "Not now, Reese." I don't care if the label fires me, I need to explain to Sarah what happened. I need to talk to Sarah.

"But, Ryan..."

"Let him go, Reese," I hear Jude behind me as I stumble away.

I pull my phone out of my back pocket and try to order an Uber to Sarah's house, but I can't open my phone. It doesn't recognize my face for some reason. Maybe I'm too fucking drunk. "Fuck!"

"What's up, man?" A total stranger hears me and comes over to help.

"I can't open my fucking phone, and I need to get to Sarah." I'm slurring my words, and I cringe but push through. I need to get to Sarah's house. If this stranger can help me, so be it. I'll do anything.

"Sarah, that works here?"

"Yeah! Do you know her? Where she lives?"

"I know her, but not where she lives. Here, let's work on getting your phone opened." He holds it up, and I have to pull back as he pushes my phone into my face, too close for it to recognize me. I think he's as drunk as I am. *Shit. I am drunk now. Again. Not cute.*

"Dude. That was not helpful." I grab my useless phone back, more disappointed with myself than him.

At this point, angry bartender guy passes me again, holding the bottle of Jack Daniels he's delivering backstage.

"Hey, I know you're grumpy for some reason, but can you help me get to Sarah's house? I don't think I can drive. *Should* drive. And I need to talk at her. *To* her."

He gives me the most venomous glare I've ever gotten, but I take it because I think somehow I deserve it? I'm not sure why anymore, and the ground is looking really comfortable right now. "Go wait at the bar," he growls. "I'll take you. But you'll need some coffee first."

I garble my thanks to the stranger next to me who tried to help me but failed, and make my way to the bar where I park my drunk ass on a bar stool, put my head down, and wait as directed. Mark comes back what I think is a few minutes later, but could be an hour, and clears everyone else out. He's amazingly charming about it and doesn't upset anyone in the process, which is a sign of a great bartender, and I make a mental note to compliment him.

"Drink this," a voice booms, and I lift my head to find a cup of steaming coffee being held in front of my face. Mark is scowling behind the mug, and I grab it before he can dump the scalding liquid on me, disfiguring me forever like I'm sure he wants to. I don't think I blame him.

"Thanks," I mutter, grabbing the coffee and taking a tentative initial sip, then a full-blown gulp. I really need to sober up. I don't remember how I got so drunk in the first place. *What the fuck is going on with me lately?*

We sit in silence for a while as I attempt to pull my shit together as quickly as possible. I drink the hot coffee as fast as I can without burning the shit out of myself.

"Are you sure you want to go to Sarah's like this?" Mark waves a disapproving arm, indicating my mess of a person.

"I am."

"And what if she doesn't want to see you?"

I think about that for a minute. *What if she doesn't want to talk to me? What will I do? What can I do?* "I won't take no for an answer," I say and instantly regret it. That is totally not what I mean to say.

Mark stares at me. Doesn't raise an eyebrow. Just waits for me to dig out of the hole I just made for myself.

"What I mean is, I'm determined. I'm persistent. Once I explain everything, she'll understand how happened. *What* happened. I know she will." *I hope she will.*

"Look, I don't even know what you did, but from everyone else's reactions, it can't be hunky dory. How can you be so sure?"

"Because I know Sarah. And she knows me."

"Are you sure about that one, pal? The Sarah I know wouldn't tolerate bullshit from anyone. Especially a guy."

I examine him more closely. *How well does he know Sarah?* I never asked her about past boyfriends. *Did she use to date Mark?* She'd told me they didn't, but they have an odd relationship, for sure. I narrow my eyes at him, "I'm sure."

We lock stares for a minute; alpha to alpha in some sort of mental contest I don't quite know the rules of, but think I'm winning because he pushes off the bar and says, "Right. Let's go then." I guess I win.

A little while later, I'm not clear on the space-time continuum at this point; we're in Sarah's driveway. Mark steps out of the car, leaving it running, and rings the doorbell. I follow only slightly behind, trying to pull myself together. I notice Mark has a bank deposit bag in his hands, which throws me a second, but then I realize they're probably the night's receipts. Gunner goes crazy in the house at us intruders, and then Sarah opens the door. She must see Mark with the night's deposit bag and think it's safe to come out. As soon as she notices me, she stops cold.

"He held a gun to my head." Mark's voice is flat as he hands her the bag. "Because nothing says flattery like a gun to the head. I had no choice but to bring him here for fear of my safety."

We both look at him, confused. Who knew Mark was a reader?

"Hey, I get that reference." I point at him. "I think that's from a book I read once. I think. I'm not sure. I'm pretty dumb right now." But apparently I'm sober enough to recognize random urban fantasy quotes.

"My work here is done." Mark gives Sarah a look I don't quite understand but makes me immediately jealous for some reason, and he gets into his car and drives away, leaving us both to watch him go.

"Well, that was just weird."

Sarah isn't as amused as I am and tightly clutches the deposit bag to her torso. She's in an oversized t-shirt and pajama shorts, and I can't help but take in her tanned bare legs. I want to reach out and touch them. *I'm in the middle of a fucking crisis, and my drunk-ass mind is in the damned gutter.* "What are you doing here, Ryan?"

I move towards her, but she steps back with each of my steps forward. "I think I need to explain...."

"You think?" She thrusts a hand on her hip. *Damn those hips.* "Well, forget it. There is nothing to explain, Ryan. It was pretty fucking clear what I saw. Good night." She heads into the house and closes the door.

"Wait!" I rush and hold the door open before she can shut it on my face, surprised I can still be so agile in my current state. "Can't we talk?"

"Nothing for us to talk about. Go home, Ryan. We're done." She's so calm it scares me. It seems easy for her to throw everything away without letting me explain anything.

The finality of her words slaps me in the face. I know I deserve them, but they still hurt. "Sarah, I'm so sorry. Please talk to me." I need to explain to her Reese means absolutely nothing to me. I got caught up in the god-damned moment, but my mind isn't working as fast as I need it to.

She drags my hand off the door and steps back into the house. "Don't call me. Don't text. Don't show up here again. I'll see you at work Monday. To *work*, not discuss this bull-shit." Her bloodshot eyes are dry and dead. She's cried enough for me tonight, and I can't blame her. She slams the door in my face. Gunner doesn't even protest.

I deserve all the hate she's giving me. I know I do. And it kills me I can't fix this. One second of a bad reaction has just ruined my entire life. And there isn't a god-damned thing I can do about it. I don't need to worry about getting sober anymore. I'm entirely aware of the consequences I'm facing. I have fucked up beyond repair the one good thing I ever wanted, or thought I ever had for a brief moment in my life. I'm straight back to the '*Almost*' in my song about us, and it hurts more than I can even fathom any pain. My chest feels like it's caving in.

I want to bang the door down and beg for her forgiveness, but I have no choice but to let her be. She wants nothing to do with me, and I can't blame her. *I* want nothing to do with me. I reluctantly pull out my phone, and now there's no problem getting an Uber home. *Of course.*

20

Too Good At Goodbyes

SARAH

I'm awakened by a loud pounding on the front door the next day. Gunner, who is snuggled up against me in bed, lifts his head at the noise with his typical "boof" for when he's not sure what woke him up, but he doesn't go into a full bark mode yet. Maybe I was dreaming, and my jolting up woke him too. I fall back on the pillow, the memories of last night's events crashing down on me and pressing on my chest. The weight of the pain crushes me all over again, but I'm at least able to fend off tears. I don't think a single tear is left in me. I cried them all last night.

The doorbell rings several times, and the pounding returns. This time Gunner is on full alert and jumps from the bed to attack this side of the front door. I glare at the clock on the nightstand and see the time is almost one o'clock in the afternoon. Considering I didn't fall asleep until the sun was rising, I'm not too surprised at the time. I glance at my phone lying next to the clock, and remember I shut it off entirely after receiving approximately twenty incoherent texts and voicemails from Ryan. I couldn't take anymore and had to shut the thing off.

I pull the comforter over my head to block out Gunner's incessant barking. Maybe if I ignore whoever it is, they'll go away and leave me alone. It's probably Ryan again, and I have nothing to say to him. And I don't want to deal with him today. I will need to build up a thicker skin by Monday somehow if I'm still going to work with them on their album. Facing him when the pain is so fresh will only pour salt on my wounds and not allow me to process the finality of everything.

The next time the pounding on the door starts again, a voice calls my name and doesn't sound like Ryan, thank god. It sounds like Jenny's. I throw the comforter off and drag myself out of bed, grabbing a hoodie off the back of a chair on the way to the foyer. I give Gunner a quick pat for his reliable protection, and double-check the peephole in the door to ensure I'm not fooled into seeing Ryan as Mark did to me last night. *The asshole.* I don't see anyone but Jenny and open the door for her.

Before I can get a word out, she barrels into me, throwing her arms around my neck and nearly choking me with the force of her hug. The outpouring of emotion in my direction almost makes me break and start crying, but I hold myself together. On the inside, I want to shatter into a million pieces, but I'm an expert at covering my true feelings. I have years of practice now.

"Jenny... Jenny." I peel her off me. "You heard about last night?"

"Well, yeah, I heard." She shuts the front door and squats to pet Gunner. "I can't believe we left before any of that. I would kick his ass for you." She thinks about that for a second. "Honestly, I'm still game to do that. Do you want me to? I started taking a kickboxing class to get in shape for my wedding dress. I could mess him up for you."

That makes me smile, which now appears to be so foreign on my face. "No. But I'll keep you in mind for future reference."

"I'm serious," she stands up and makes some strange kicking moves to demonstrate, which forces a chuckle out of me. "Let me at him. I'll show him what happens when you fuck with my best friend."

"I appreciate the sentiment, but I swear I'm fine."

"I have been trying to call you all morning but kept getting your voicemail."

"Yeah, my phone is off. Ryan was relentless last night, and I didn't want to deal with him. Having to work with him again on Monday will be bad enough."

Jenny gets a strange expression on her face I can't read. "No offense, but you look like shit, girl. Do you want to day drink with me? We've not done that in forever. It just so happens there's wine in the car. I'll be right back." And before I can respond, she's gone and back in a flash with a box of wine in hand.

"Holy shit, Jenny." My eyes are wide. "I didn't even eat breakfast yet."

"We can make fruit smoothies with this!" She's getting even more excited. "It'll be totally healthy. You'll see." She fills the blender with frozen berries from my freezer and the white wine, and winds up with something oddly resembling a strawberry daiquiri. She pours the concoction into two margarita glasses with plenty left and hands me one.

I'm intrigued and take a sip. The coldness burns a little as I swallow, but it is surprisingly tasty. "Okay, I'm sold. This is the new breakfast of champions."

"Right?" She takes her glass, grabs the pitcher, and heads to the back sliding door. "Let's take in some sun before the snow starts flying."

"You know the temperature is colder here on the lake, right? September sunshine is deceiving." I glance down at my pajama shorts and bare legs and feet. No way I'm sitting outside like this. Particularly while drinking a frozen cocktail.

Jenny gets outside, places everything on the patio table, and turns right around. "Can I borrow a hoodie? It's a little chillier out here than I thought. You should probably change into something warmer too."

I roll my eyes and smile to myself. Same old Jenny. "Hang on." I throw some jeans and shoes on and grab another hoodie for Jenny.

An hour or so later, after we've had a couple of drinks, Jenny's been given full details of the previous night's turmoil, when she suddenly springs more drama on me.

"So, about you having to work with Ryan on Monday."

She examines her fingernails. "You don't need to worry about that."

"What do you mean?"

"My dad said the blonde you saw Ryan with is their original producer, Reese something-or-other. I don't care. And according to the label, she's here to take over as producer for the final mix of the album."

"Since when?" It feels like my gut's been kicked by one of Jenny's kickboxing moves. First, Ryan kisses this Reese person, and now I find out I'm no longer needed because of her. This also explains Jenny's strange look earlier when I mentioned going back to work Monday.

Jenny shrugs, "I don't know. I guess the plan was always to work with her; she's just been delayed? Didn't they tell you?"

"Nope. Not a word."

"Well, that's shitty. You sure you don't want me to kick his ass?"

"Tempting. Not gonna lie," I smirk. The frozen wine is starting to achieve its desired effect as anger rises instead of hurt. "To be honest, this will give me more time to work on my own songs. I'm pretty close to having a full album." I almost sound believable to my own ears.

"That's amazing!" She claps her hands energetically together. "When can I listen to it?"

"That remains to be seen." I'm unsure how to answer. The situation has shifted so fast I'm not sure what I'm doing. "I didn't plan anything official yet."

"You should do YouTube again like you used to do. That's how Ryan got signed, right?"

I internally shrink at the sound of his name, and the invisible knife in my back twists. "Yeah. That's how he got discovered by his label before he put the band together."

Awkward quiet settles in over us, and Jenny glances at her phone. "Damn, I need to start getting ready to meet Luke for dinner." She hesitates and studies me. "Do you want to come with us? Nothing fancy."

"No, I'm okay. Thanks." I appreciate the offer, but being the third wheel on a date night is not my idea of a fabulous evening. And knowing Jenny and Luke, they'll be all over each other the whole time. Usually, I wouldn't mind since they've been together forever, and I'm used to it. But my emotions are too raw to deal with that. "You guys enjoy yourselves."

Jenny helps bring everything back into the house before grabbing her bag. "You call me if you need *anything*, okay?"

"I will. I promise."

She gives me another hug. "You can keep the rest of the wine. Use it wisely." She winks knowingly, pets Gunner goodbye, and leaves.

I eye the pitcher on the counter, which appears to hold *just* enough for one more serving. I hesitate for only a second, remembering how drunk Ryan was last night. *Fuck it, if he can be irresponsible, so can I for one day.* I take Jenny's advice and pour the final dregs of the frozen concoction into my glass. The doorbell rings and Gunner proceeds to bark his head off once again. Jenny must've forgotten something. I scan the counters for anything she left behind as I head to the door, but don't see anything.

"What did you forget -" I stop mid-sentence because

Jenny isn't at the door. Jude stands on the doorstep. "Jude? What are you doing here?" I briefly survey behind him for any sign that this is a rouse to trick me into talking to Ryan. I'm still worried someone will try to pull something like that. My distrust of everyone now is slightly unnerving.

"Sorry, were you expecting someone else?" He's a bit sheepish. His hands are shoved in the pockets of his jeans, and the way he's standing, he looks younger for some reason. I can't quite put my finger on what it is.

"No, my friend just left, and I thought maybe you were her coming back for something."

"Oh."

We stand there looking at each other for a minute. I don't have the faintest idea what he could be doing here, but I finally remember my manners, "Come on in. Can I fetch you something to drink?"

He passes me and takes a seat at the kitchen counter. He's eyeing the empty blender pitcher and my full glass of frozen wine. "No thanks. I'm good."

I grab my glass and sip, unsure if I want to know why he's here. Is it his job to tell me I'm fired from working with them? His poker face could give mine a run for its money; he's so unreadable. "If you're here to tell me I'm fired, I already know. Thanks anyway."

"What? Since when?" He's genuinely surprised. *How could he not know?*

"Since the label sent your *'obviously preferred'* producer back to you." The words are sharp enough to cut my tongue as I speak them.

Jude shakes his head, confused. "I don't understand. We've been expecting Reese. We knew she would be late, but didn't expect her until next week."

"How long have you known?" I can't believe nobody told me any of this. Especially Ryan. *What else is he keeping from me?* The betrayal by him just keeps hammering away.

"We always knew." He's still perplexed. "Didn't anyone tell you about any of this? I assumed you knew."

I bark a laugh and take a long drink. "Apparently, I'm not worthy enough to know *many* things. Thanks for coming by Jude." I start walking toward the door, but he's not following me. "I really don't want to be rude, but you can go now. As you may or may not be able to tell, I'm not really up for company."

"Hold up. Let's get some things straight here. I didn't come here to talk to you about the album production because you're still working with us as far as we're all concerned."

"Yeah, I don't think so." I stop him before he can continue. "That's not happening. And I don't feel bad since you already have a replacement. So, if you don't mind...." I motion to the door. He still doesn't move. *What the actual fuck?*

"Sarah..."

"I'm sorry, Jude, but with the current circumstances being what they are, I don't have it in me to continue working with you guys. Please don't take this the wrong way. This has nothing to do with you or Matt. I'm satisfied with where all the songs are, so I don't see a problem stepping away for the final mixes."

"Well, I have a problem with it." He has a disgusted expression on his face.

"Excuse me?" I can't believe he's mad at me about this. I did nothing wrong here.

"I don't have a problem with you. That came out wrong." He runs his hands down his face in frustration. "I'm fucking pissed at this whole situation. I could kick Ryan's ass right now."

"Well, my friend Jenny's forming a line for that particular honor, so call her for your ticket."

He smirks at me. "Got any more of those fru-fru drinks?"

"I can make some," I suggest, because more alcohol sure sounds like a great idea.

I whip up another pitcher full of the boxed wine and frozen fruit, and hand Jude a glass. "Sorry, I'm fresh out of umbrellas to thoroughly embarrass you."

He takes a sample taste and smacks his lips. "Not bad. But don't you dare tell anybody I drank this. I might lose my man card."

"My lips are sealed. No worries. Your macho image remains intact. But come on, men should be able to drink what they want."

"Touché."

After a second, it dawns on me he acted surprised about me not working with them. "Jude, if you didn't come to tell me I'm fired, why did you come here?"

"Ah, yes, the other reason for kicking his ass." His features cloud over, remembering his original mission. "About Ryan and Reese..."

I stiffen, hearing their names together in a sentence. It does something to my nerves and sets my senses on edge.

"Jude, I don't want to hear about them. If Ryan sent you here to try to convince me...."

"He didn't. I swear. But that's just it, there is no 'them.' There never was."

"It sure as hell looked like there is. I'm not stupid, Jude. I know what I saw." I don't know how he expects me to ignore seeing them kissing last night with my own eyes. I'm not a fool. Or at least I won't be one anymore.

"But you don't. It's complicated."

"How? When he's got his tongue down someone else's throat, it's damned black and white. No gray area there." I'm starting to get indignant. There isn't any explaining this away. Not for me.

"I know things looked bad, but hear me out."

I scoff at him and cross my arms, ready to listen to this fairy tale. "This ought to be good."

"Have they slept together in the past? Yes. But do they have a relationship? Hell no. They never have and never will."

"Then what the fuck was last night?" Something inside me curdles at the thought of the two of them being so intimate with each other in ways that Ryan and I have only been close to.

"As I said, Reese showed up early. She knew nothing about you and Ryan."

"And this is supposed to make me feel better, how, exactly?"

"I'm not *trying* to make you feel better. I'm trying to explain what happened. We met Reese when we recorded our first album a couple of years ago, and she was going through a nasty breakup with her then-fiancé. Ryan seemed to be trying to get over somebody too, and they hooked up, but it wasn't an emotional thing between them. And it never got in the way of our working together because it isn't a thing."

"Did my being in a relationship with Ryan ever get in the way of *our* working together?"

"Of course not."

"So that doesn't mean a damned thing. And it doesn't negate the fact he was kissing her. *He was kissing her.* He was kissing her back whether she kissed him first or not."

Jude hangs his head, rests his face in his palms, and lets out a loud sigh. "I know it's not an excuse, but he'd had a little too much to drink, and as soon as he realized what was happening, he pushed her away and tried to go after you."

"Interesting. I wasn't that hard to catch. I didn't see him until hours later, when Mark dropped him off, drunk on my doorstep."

"He started after you, but...."

"But?"

"Reese stopped him...."

"Perfect. Just perfect." The picture is getting clearer, and it isn't making me feel any better. In fact, it's making me decidedly worse.

"Ryan's gotten himself in a tough spot. Reese works for the label. She's got power over us. Not that she would use that power against us, but I'm sure that weighs on Ryan too with how he deals with her. It could ruin things for all of us if it goes badly. He thinks he's responsible for everyone. He's always been that way."

Now that hits me like a ton of bricks. Could this Reese chick be power playing Ryan? "Well, she knows about me now, right? Is it going to screw things up for you?"

Jude shakes his head. "I don't think so. She's upset about what happened and wanted to come to talk to you herself and apologize. I didn't think that would go over too well with you, and decided to come myself instead."

"Well, thanks." I'm not sure what to think about any of this now. If anything, I'm even more confused. I don't know what to think, or who to believe. "I definitely do not want to see her or Ryan right now."

"And if I know Ryan, he's been calling and texting like crazy since last night to try to apologize and explain himself."

"Yeah, I had to shut my phone off."

Jude stands to leave. "Please think about what I said. If you have it in you, give him another chance. I know he's crazy about you, and he feels like absolute shit right now."

I nod. "I'll consider what you said. But, as for the band, I am set on not returning to the studio to work with you. And please don't take it personally. I just can't bring myself to do that. I wish you guys luck with it, though. I'm sure it will be fanfuckingtastic. I mean it."

"I understand and will let everyone know. No worries. And thanks for listening. And for the fru-fru drink. Remember our little secret." He conspiratorially puts a finger up to his mouth and smiles as he leaves.

Once he's gone, I head to my bedroom and turn my phone on. As soon as it powers up, I'm bombarded with a slew of alerts for both texts and voicemails. I skip most of them, text

Lorelai back that I'm alive and well, and the same for Mark. When I open the texts from Benji this morning, I get worried.

> BENJI: Hey sis, got a sec?
>
> BENJI: I need to talk to you. Can you pick up your phone?
>
> BENJI: I really need to talk to you. Please call me as soon as you get this. It's important.
>
> BENJI: SOS 911

My fingers press the call button so fast I don't even read the rest of my messages. I jump up and start pacing right away, my heart pounding in my throat. *Please be okay. Please be okay. Jesus.*

He finally picks up after three rings. "There you are, where were you?" he asks. "I have been trying to reach you all day." I can't tell his mood from his voice, but he's acting awfully calm for an emergency situation.

"Benji? What's wrong? What's happened? Are you okay? What's going on?" I can't seem to catch my breath, and any buzz I may have had from the frozen wine is gone as adrenaline floods my system.

"Whoa, chillax, sis," he laughs. "I'm all good. I've been trying to get hold of you to check on *you*. Since late last night, Ryan's been blowing up my phone saying he can't find you, and a bunch of other stuff I'm not sure I wanna talk about in mixed company."

"Chillax? Chillax, Benji?" I can't believe he's telling *me* to calm down. "You put 'SOS' and '911' in your text. That's only supposed to be for real emergencies."

"Well, it seemed like an emergency since we both couldn't reach you. I was worried."

I let out the breath I'm holding in a whoosh and sit on the edge of my bed to regain my bearings. I'm so relieved Benji is fine, but I'm also pissed Ryan thought to bring my brother into our drama after what he did to start it.

"I'm fine, Benji. My phone was off for a while."

"I kind of know what happened from Ryan. Are you going to be okay?"

I hesitate before answering. We don't like to talk about our love lives to each other. Not for any reason in particular; we've just always kept stuff private. "Yeah, it was bad. But I'll be fine. Don't worry about me."

"Well, for what it's worth, he sounds very sorry, and he's very aware he's an asshole. I agreed with him on the last part. It's only been a few weeks, and that 'best' he promised me isn't measuring up so far."

I'm reminded of the promises they each made the day Benji left for school to do their best. And yes, Ryan's certainly falling short. "Did he have anything of value to say? Or was he just groveling?"

"Mostly the groveling. I almost pity the guy."

"Yeah, well, don't. Are you having any issues? How's school going? How's Joe?"

"Way to change the subject," he laughs again, but there's a slight edge to it this time. "Everything is fine. Joe is Joe.

You know how he is. Living together is a bit of an adjustment, but nothing major so far. Just a few hiccups here and there. Nothing I can't handle."

"Good. I'll let you get back to your fun college life then. Enough of your sister's boring boyfriend drama."

"I'm glad you're okay. You let me know if that changes, alright?"

He sounds so grown up, I have to smile. Our caretaker roles reversing for a change. "Yes, sir. I'll let you know. Love you."

"Love you too."

21

Love Me Like You Do

RYAN

For the next two weeks, I send Sarah a daily morning text apologizing again, and letting her know I'm thinking about her and miss her like crazy. I also go to the Stout Hideout every evening to see her if she's working. I order one beer, tell her I would still love to talk to her if she ever wants to, and take a seat in a corner booth, nursing the beer until closing. Then I send her a goodnight text when I get home to tell her that my feelings for her are the same, and I'm a total asshole, but also the most patient man in the world. On open mic nights, I record her singing her songs and rewatch them, torturing myself for what could be a lost cause. Until one glorious hallelujah morning when I actually receive a reply to my text.

> RYAN: Good morning, beautiful. I hope your day is excellent. Just a reminder that I'm still thinking about you all day, every day.
>
> SARAH: Thanks

Thanks! She said Thanks! Sure, she sent only one fucking generic polite single-syllable word, but that is one more word than she's said to me in two weeks. Progress! I jump out of bed with my fist-pumping and barely miss the ceiling fan blades. That one word gives me hope, and I'll take all the hope I can muster. I'm only in Chandler for a few more weeks, and I need to make the most of them. I want to make the most of them with Sarah.

I'm not sure what to do here. *Do I text back again right away? Wait to visit her at the bar tonight? Head to her house and talk to her now?* I'm acting like a fucking teenager passing notes in school. But at least I got a 'thanks' today. It's something. I'll take it. I decide to not push my luck with a response right away.

Reese still does feel bad about what's happening and has offered several times to talk to Sarah for me, but I keep telling her no. Sarah would not respond well to Reese. She's not exactly the most subtle person in the world, and she can be abrasive. I'm sure any type of apology from her wouldn't come out right and make things worse. And if I know Sarah at all, I absolutely know that she already hates Reese, even though they've never met. Jude told me about his visit with Sarah and what they talked about. I appreciate him doing that for me, but I don't want anyone else to be involved in this. It wouldn't be right to bring in anyone else. And I already pulled her brother into it the night it happened like the idiot I am. Sarah and I need to work this out if we can. God, I pray that we can.

I go through the day on autopilot, repeatedly checking my phone for the time and for messages. As soon as we wrap for the day, I rush home to shower and grab some food before heading back out again to the bar. I have been able to avoid any conversation with my mother about how much I fucked things up so far, but I can't keep deflecting forever. I can't count how many times she's asked when Sarah's coming again for dinner. I say I don't know, and we're both swamped. I don't have the heart to tell her the truth yet. I'm disappointed enough in myself; I don't need to see it reflected back at me in her eyes too.

I arrive at the Hideout by eight o'clock, right on time for open mic night to start. I wasn't aware it was on for tonight since I haven't checked the board in days. I knew I would be here anyway. I get excited when I realize that there aren't too many musicians milling around, so I might be able to hear more of Sarah singing. That's when a crazy idea pops into my head.

After ordering my one beer for the night, I grab a napkin and steal the pen from the musician sign-up sheet.

> RYAN: Are you talking to me now? Check YES
> or Check NO

I fold the napkin and slide it to Sarah across the bar. She opens the paper and bites her lip to hold back a smile that's almost starting to form. My heart lurches with the hope that maybe we've passed the initial hurdle on our way to forgiveness. Dipped our toes in the communication pool once more. I wait at the bar in case she replies. She grabs another pen and turns to scribble on the napkin, then folds and slides it back to me, letting our fingers linger when they touch. I take the note from her, trying to read her reaction, but she's not giving anything else away. I open the napkin to find my response options crossed out and a new one in its place. She's added 'MAYBE' and circled it. This all gets my hopes up, and a thrill runs through me. I grin at her, but she's still not revealing any emotions. I reach out, steal her pen, and flip the napkin over to a blank side.

> RYAN: Can I see you after work? Greasy Spoon?
> Check YES or Check NO

When she opens it, she gives me an unreadable look, and I can't tell if I took things too far too soon or not. *Did I just misread that whole interaction?* She folds the napkin and puts it into the back pocket of her jeans before heading up to the stage to announce the first musician. As I savor watching her walk away, I have never wanted to be a bar napkin so badly in my life. She avoids me when she comes back to the bar, so either a 'no,' or she's still thinking things over. I tell myself to believe the latter to keep my hopes alive. I give a quick nod of understanding in her direction and head back to my usual booth to wait her out.

As the evening winds down and the crowd thins a bit, Sarah gets to the end of the musician list. "Thanks everyone, for coming out to our open mic night tonight. You've all been wonderful, as usual. Remember to check the board regularly as the dates change. And, our last musician tonight is…a newbie. R.C." She uses the clipboard to shield her eyes from the spotlight to scan into the crowd. "R.C.? Are you still here? Don't be shy. We don't bite." The audience titters a little.

I stand, adjust my cap, and weave my way to the stage. "I'm R.C.," I say, waving an arm at her sheepishly. There are a few whispers as I approach Sarah, but I can't make out what they're saying. I'm sure something about who I am, but maybe they're talking about me being the asshole that hurt Sarah. Who knows. When I reach her, she looks a little shell-shocked. Surprised that I signed up to perform. "Can I borrow your guitar?" I ask. She nods silently as she grabs the instrument from its case and hands it over. "Still not talking to me, huh?" She doesn't reply and leaves the stage in a hurry.

I sit on the stool, adjust the mic height, and check the guitar's tuning. I know it doesn't need it because Sarah played only a few minutes ago. I'm just stalling and working up my nerve. I don't usually get this nervous before performing, but tonight, I'm singing for Sarah, and Sarah alone. I take a deep breath and let it out slowly.

"I wrote this song about a month ago when I came back to Chandler about someone very special to me. Someone who, at the time, I didn't think cared for me at all. But I was wrong.

Turns out I am often wrong about a lot of things lately. Some of the song has changed a little since she heard it last. This song is for her. I call it, 'Almost.'"

Thought we were high enough, but fingertips just missed
Thought time would stand still for us, to catch up with it
Thought the show was at eight, but it was really at six
We almost had it

Through thick and through thin, but the thin disappeared
Through the mist and the vapor, the clouds never cleared
Leaving us in shadow, to hide with all our fears
But we almost made it

Almost
So close but yet so far
Almost
Wishing on the same stars
Almost
Tell me, which one of us lost the most?

We could have chased the sunsets, we could have raced our dreams
Instead, we held it all back, and ripped each other's seams
We could have held each other when the pain knocked down our doors
We really almost lost it all

Almost
So far but yet so close
Almost
Your wish, my dream, our hopes
Almost
Tell me, how to regain your trust

Now we have a fragile chance to turn it all around
To coax a raging fire from the embers that we found
Neither of us perfect, but our souls forever bound
Almost isn't good enough, anymore

Almost
Take my heart into your hands
Almost
Weave together our broken strands
Almost
Tell me, can we really, truly try?

When I initially end the song, I don't hear anything but the electric buzzing from the speakers behind me. My eyes were closed during the entire performance because I was afraid to see Sarah's reaction. I didn't know if she would stay to listen, and my heart couldn't take seeing her leave the room. I'm still afraid to open my eyes now, for fear that the whole bar has cleared, and I just sang my heart out to an empty room. One heartbeat passes, and then applause and cheers echo around the room. The crowd seems to have doubled since I stepped on stage. I know that's my imagination, but what an odd sensation.

With the spotlight glare still on me, I can't see to the bar, so I don't know yet if Sarah stuck around for the song. So, I thank the crowd, place the guitar carefully back into its case, and head to my corner booth. As I maneuver through the tables, I thank people for their kind words about the performance. I keep one eye on the bar, and Sarah's nowhere to be seen. Once I reach my table, I find a full beer resting on top of a napkin with writing on it. I slide the beer off quickly, and can hardly make it out since the ink is smeared from the condensation, but YES is circled. And not once, but several times. Grinning to myself like an idiot, I fold the napkin and put it into the inner pocket of my jacket. I take my seat, sip my beer, and wait for the damned bar to close.

Once everyone is gone and Sarah and I are the only ones left, I move to sit at the bar and watch her go through her closing routine. I offer to help, but she declines, so I'm mesmerized by the erotic ballet that is made up of Sarah's regular movements. The way she walks or pushes in a chair, or wipes down a table, or how she bites her lip, and moves a stray lock of hair behind her ear as she counts money from the register. This all accumulates into a dance of sensuality she doesn't even know she's performing for me. And the fact that she doesn't know how hot she is, with her hair piled up in a messy bun with random tendrils framing her makeup-less face, her sweatshirt constantly sliding off one beautiful shoulder, and the way her faded jeans accentuate her perfect ass, makes her even hotter. She hums 'Almost' to herself while she works, and it just yanks at my soul.

"I'll be right back." She heads into the office area. The overhead fixtures shut off one by one until the only light in the room comes from inside the glass shelves of alcohol across from me, casting a muted red glow. When Sarah reappears, my breath holds itself without any instruction from me. She simply takes my breath away. Noticing me staring at her, she clumsily grabs two shot glasses and a bottle of top-shelf tequila and pours us each a shot. She holds her glass up, and I echo her movements.

"To old friends." She steadily catches and holds my gaze. Her face shows no emotion, and I can't read her body language to know what she's trying to say at first.

My heart shrinks as her words sink in, and I swallow hard before nodding and meeting my glass to hers. "To old friends," I mutter, and drink the shot. Its burn in my throat now the only warmth in my body. Those three words stab me like icicles, leaving me cold and numb. This can't be how things end with us. I don't want to be 'just friends' with Sarah. Not now that I know how delicious her kisses are, and my hands know what it's like to touch her exquisite body. We can't go backward from that to some neutral platonic bullshit.

But what choices do I have here? She's making it difficult to visualize any other possibility for us. There's nothing else I can do. I tried everything and came up short yet again. I almost had everything, and I fucked it up. I grab the bottle and hastily pour each of us another shot, spilling a lot. Holding up my glass, I meet her eyes, and when I do, I have to force the words out of my mouth.

"To almost," I choke, and don't wait for her before shutting my eyes and downing the tequila. This time the liquid doesn't burn but slides down smoothly. I place my glass on the bar a little too loudly and see Sarah still holding a full shot. She's staring at me in confusion.

"Almost what?" she asks.

I can't believe she wants me to spell this all out. This is *her* choice, not mine. I don't understand how much clearer she can be. *Is she trying to punish me even more by making me say it out loud?* I wave my hand, indicating the two of us. "Almost... us. We were *this close*," I hold my thumb and forefinger close together, "to having everything I ever dreamed of, and I went and fucked everything up like the god-damned asshole that I am." The cracks I put in my own heart two weeks ago are starting to splinter, and I can feel sections breaking away. The parts that make up my love for Sarah, so, basically the entire thing is crumbling into pieces. "I'm sorry," I say, meeting her confused eyes with my own that are going blurry with unshed tears. "I can't just be your friend, Sarah. I can't go back to that."

I turn and head to the exit before those tears can start to fall. I don't need to add crying in front of Sarah to the list of my mortifications. I already made a big enough fool of myself over the last two weeks texting her and coming here every night.

"Ryan, where the hell are you going?" she yells from the bar.

I stop, but I don't turn around. I can't face her right now. I don't have that kind of strength left in me. "Home," I say, and continue towards the door. "Don't worry, I won't bother you anymore."

Her footsteps rush behind me as I approach the door. "Ryan, would you stop for a minute and look at me?"

I stop again, forcing myself to turn to look at her this time. I steel myself for the onslaught of pain it will cause, but I do it. I do not expect to find her smiling at me. *How fucking cruel can she be?*

"Would you stop being a fucking idiot and let me finish what I was going to say?"

"What are you talking about?" I ask, thoroughly confused.

She grabs my hand and leads me back to the bar. I don't protest and follow. This time we're both on the customer side of the bar and in deeper shadows as she pours two more shots. She hands one to me, and wipes a stray hair out of her eyes as she straightens her shoulders and faces me. *What is she trying to do here?*

"To old friends," she says again, but she holds up a finger to indicate more is coming, "who are destined to be much more."

I gape at her. *Did she just say what I think she said?* I study her, and she smiles cheekily at me before drinking her tequila. "Are you being serious?"

"Yes, you idiot." She playfully hits my arm. "I've been trying to forgive you here. You think you can sing a girl a song like that and-"

I don't even let her finish what she's saying. I down the tequila, and then my mouth crashes into hers, my fingers weaving into her hair as I guide her back against the bar. Our tongues slide together hungrily as we breathe each other in. Her hands glide under my shirt, and as soon as her fingers touch my skin, my body ignites, every inch of me burning for her; to touch her, taste her, be inside her, to worship her.

Encircling my hands around her waist, I lift her onto the bar, and my mouth traces the length of her elegant neck, down to her collarbone, and across her bare shoulder. She wraps her legs around my waist, and pulls me in to press my groin against her, and a small moan escapes from low in her throat, making me so much harder it hurts. But this is the best kind of pain I've ever felt. My entire body aches with hollow electricity with each touch. I missed the silkiness of her skin, the smell of her hair, her perfume.

"Sarah. I want you," I groan into her shoulder as I reach around and grab her ass, pulling her closer to me. Her hands are on my back, nails digging into my skin with a want I know is as desperate as my own. I cup my hands around her face, resting my forehead against hers, both of us breathing heavily. "I want you so much, but not here. Not like this."

She studies my face for a long minute. Trying to find something she's not vocalizing. She must find it, since her expression relaxes into a sly smile. "Then take me home," she whispers into my ear, then her teeth graze my neck, sending chills all along my skin. She doesn't have to tell me twice, and I reach under her and lift her off the bar, legs still wrapped around my waist. She yelps and locks her hands behind my neck as I make my way to the exit with her still attached to me.

22

Cold Sweat

SARAH

Ryan drives us to my house, and we barely make it inside with all our clothes still on; we can't keep our hands off each other. Once we're through the door, he grabs my wrists, and the next thing I know, I'm against the wall, arms above my head, and his mouth devours mine. He presses against me, but it's still not close enough. My skin yearns to be moving against his skin. He releases my hands, and I go straight for the bottom of his shirt, yanking on it.

"Off," I say, not caring if I sound demanding. His lips twitch with a smile as he reaches back and pulls his shirt over his head in one smooth movement, tossing it on the floor. I don't know why guys are so fucking hot when they do that, but seeing Ryan do it almost pushes me over the edge right then. I run my fingers across his chest, taking a second to admire the chiseled muscles and tattoos that were hidden under that shirt. I press my palm flat, and his heart is racing, probably as fast as mine is right now.

"Your turn." He gently pulls my sweatshirt off. I let my hair down in the car, and Ryan now runs his fingers through it, tugging on it, so my face tilts to meet his. He kisses my forehead, along my cheeks, and the tip of my nose, making his way down my jawline to my neck and shoulder. Each touch of his lips is powerful, sending shockwaves through me. He pulls away, and I immediately sense his absence from me, so I open my eyes.

"What's the matter?" I ask, concerned that he's changed his mind. I hope to God he's not changed his mind. This is way too good to stop now. I don't want to stop now.

He examines my face, caressing my cheek with the back of his hand, a curious expression in his eyes. He must find what he's looking for because he silently takes my hand and leads me upstairs to my bedroom. I think we've both taken time tonight to consider the magnitude of this step, and each other, and we're both in agreement. Once we get to my room, he maneuvers me to the end of the bed, his deft fingers removing the rest of my clothes with ease, leaving me in my bra and panties. But I'm not exposed at all. His breathing becomes ragged as he takes me in, making me feel more beautiful than I have ever felt. "You're perfect," he whispers.

He kicks off his shoes and slides out of his jeans, keeping his boxer briefs on. I can't help but see the extent of his desire on full display, and it's a *lot*. He's not a bulky muscular guy. He's more lithe and lean, but perfect. To me, anyway. He reaches around to unhook my bra, letting it drop on the floor, and cups the back of my head as he eases me back onto the bed, never breaking eye contact with me. The heat of his stare fans the flames already engulfing me. Once we're skin on skin, his arms caging me underneath him, I can't help gasp his name, "Ryan...." Every single nerve ending is alive and alert and yearning to be touched by him all at once. "I need you inside of me, *now*."

He sits up, kneels between my legs, and pulls my panties off slowly. He starts to run a line of kisses up my inner thigh, from my knee to my hip bone, teasing the area that wants it most. I squirm under him, my fingers running through his soft hair. Finally, his tongue is on my center, warm and wet, stroking with just the right amount of pressure to instantly send shudders of pleasure through me. My back automatically arches off the bed as I cry out, the waves of ecstasy pulsing through my entire body. When the frenzy subsides, he kisses my torso and takes my breast into his mouth, lightly sucking on the nipple, causing another round of pulsations to start building within me.

I reach down and pull on the waistband of his boxers. "Off," I command again. I have no idea when I became so demanding in bed, but I like this side of me, and Ryan seems to like it as well.

"Yes, ma'am." A sly smile plays on his gorgeous face. He slides off the end of the bed and out of his boxers. His naked body is glorious in the moonlight streaking through the window blinds, and the need to have him inside of me that instant becomes almost unbearable. He leans down and grabs his wallet out of his jeans on the floor, pulling out a foil packet.

He tosses the wallet behind him as he crawls up the bed to cover me with his body again. His length presses against me as he positions himself between my legs. He brushes each of my cheeks with feather-light kisses, then my forehead before looking me in the eyes. His are dark and serious. "Are you sure about this?" he asks. "I need to hear you say it, Sarah."

I give him a long look, considering him again, and all that's happened since he's been back in my life. The ups and downs. The misunderstandings and hurt. The laughs and the joys. The loud and the quiet. The closeness and the distance. It hasn't been perfect, but it has been *us*. "I've never wanted anything more, Ryan. I want all of you."

He takes my mouth with his, and I can sense his need, his hunger. And beyond that, I can feel his emotion, his desire for me. He leans on one elbow and opens the foil packet, and I take the condom from him. He raises a curious eyebrow, but I reach down and take him into my hand, stroking him firmly, and carefully roll it onto him. He closes his eyes, briefly lost, and lets out a long breath of air. "Jesus, Sarah. I almost came right then." His mouth twitches.

Running his fingers up my side, he grabs a breast, sucking on the nipple until it's taught, and my back arches again as he presses against me. This time he shifts his hips, teasing my center with his tip, moving in and out of me little by little, driving me insane, and running along the edge of my climax. This isn't enough; I need more. I need more of him. *Now.* His control is far beyond mine as I scrape and claw at his back, rocking against him, urging him to go deeper. He builds and builds with each stroke, the pressure about to release. When he thrusts into me completely, giving me all of himself, I'm pushed over the edge again. The spasm around him is exquisite and echoes through my veins, coursing throughout my body.

His mouth finds mine again, and our tongues dance as we trade gasps. His hand caresses my jawline then runs through my hair. He reaches behind my knee, pulling my leg over his shoulder, driving even deeper within me. I didn't think he could get any deeper, and the throbbing sensation starts to build again, so I'm taking him with me this time. I rub his nipple with my thumb and nip at his bottom lip, coaxing him to meet my oncoming orgasm.

"*Sarah...this is so good,*" he exhales into my ear as his thrusts speed up and deepen even further, becoming more frenetic and intense. My orgasm is so close, but I'm trying desperately to hold on to match him. The passion between us explodes, and his entire body stiffens as I arch into him and envelope him. Both of us collapse, panting, sweating, and entirely spent. We lay there, still joined together, my legs around him and his face buried in my neck. His rapid warm breath chills the dampness of my skin and it's simply delicious.

My entire body hums with pleasure as my fingers lazily trace random patterns on the smooth damp skin of his back. He props himself up on his elbows and gazes at me with wonder in his eyes.

"You are incredible." He brushes my nose playfully with his.

"You're not so bad yourself," I say, my smile growing as I soak in this euphoria.

He reluctantly pulls out of me and heads to the bathroom to dispose of the condom. The sudden chill as the air hits my flesh makes me grab the sheets and cover myself up. I slide over, making room for him on the bed as he returns and climbs in, pulling me against him with his strong arms. As I snuggle into him, this is all so perfect. So *right*. We fit together like we were made for each other. Being held by him like this feels like being home. I belong right here. I belong with him.

We fall asleep like this, with me wrapped in his arms, heartbeat to heartbeat. I can't help but think, *I've never been so happy or content in my life.*

23

Hazy

RYAN

I watch Sarah as she sleeps, her body warm against me. She shifts and grabs on to me every so often, pulling me closer to her, and I have died and gone to heaven. The gold and pink of the sunrise slant through the blinds and onto the bed, making her exposed skin glow. I haven't slept at all, and I don't feel tired one bit. I could lie here and hold her for the rest of my life if that were an option. Getting used to this would be so easy. Maybe *too* easy.

I occasionally hold my breath for fear of breaking whatever magical spell was cast on us for this to happen. For my dreams of Sarah forgiving me and this happening to come true. But I only have a couple of weeks left here at home. We leave to return to LA after our last test show on Halloween. *What is going to happen to us then?* We have such a short time left, and we've wasted the last few weeks not talking. My patience paid off, though, so maybe things will be fine. They *have* to be okay. I have fallen head over heels in love with Sarah. I'm not surprised by this; I knew I would if I saw her again and spent any amount of time with her. It was inevitable. I can only guess how she feels about me, and I'm not the greatest at reading her lately. It worries me how fragile this really is.

"Morning." Sarah pulls me close again and snaps me out of my daydreams. Seeing her smile at me sleepily as she wakes up makes me want her more.

"Good morning, beautiful," I press against her and show her just how much better the morning can be.

Her eyes close, and her smile broadens as she rocks her body into mine in response. We spend the rest of the morning languidly exploring and finding ways to please each other. All in all, not a horrible way to spend a morning.

The haze of the afterglow still surrounds us as we make our way to the kitchen to find sustenance. We're listening to the latest version of our new album as Sarah makes breakfast. My arms around her waist from behind, we sway together to the music as she sings along and cooks us eggs. We make a perfect domesticated tableau. It really is perfection. Just two tattooed musicians who had a wild night and peaceful morning of amazing sex making breakfast.

"So, what do you think of it?" I ask Sarah as we sit at the island to eat. I was initially nervous about playing it for her since she's not been involved in the project the last couple of weeks. But she insisted she wanted to hear it.

"I think the whole album is amazing," she says earnestly,

taking a bite of toast. "I hate to admit it, but some of the changes Reese made are pretty genius." She has to force Reese's name out.

"Well, you're the one that put us on the right path to begin with. We couldn't have done it without you." I never thought she'd admit something like that, so I grab her hand and squeeze it, trying to erase the doubt that I can see creeping up in her.

"Thanks for that."

"I mean it." I get up and clear our dishes. I turn to her, crossing my arms and studying her. What I want to ask her is the one question I'm most afraid to ask. The last time I did, it ended everything between us, and I don't want to go through that again. Never again. But I can't *not* ask her either. We're in it now, and it needs to go somewhere. I can't leave it here and go have a separate life from her, not after last night.

"What is it?" Her brow furrows with concern at my hesitation.

"If I ask you something, can you promise not to bite my head off?"

She laughs, "It depends on what you ask me."

"Seriously, promise me."

She stares at me, curious, but nods. "Of course. You can ask me anything, Ryan."

I still hesitate, afraid of making myself vulnerable like this again. Afraid that simple words in a question could ruin everything.

"Would you ever consider coming to live with me in LA?"

She doesn't react right away but stares at me, her face

unreadable. She's got such a damned good poker face. You'd think I could tell what she's thinking by now, but I seem to be getting worse at that instead of better.

"I might…." she starts, and my hopes jump way up. "But Ryan, I have responsibilities now that I didn't have before. The house….Benji…."

And my hopes crash down again. "Don't you want to pursue music? I thought you were working on your own album."

She squirms a little in her seat, making me more nervous and, to be honest, confused. "I do want to….eventually." She hesitates, staring down at her fidgeting hands. "I'm not ready, though. Nowhere near ready. I need to get back into the studio, and there's no way I could book free studio time in LA."

I nod my agreement at that. LA studio time is ridiculously expensive. Part of why we came here in the first place was the cost savings. "That's true, but how will this work when I leave in a couple of weeks?" I lean across the island, take her fidgeting hands into mine, and catch her eyes. Her beautiful, warm eyes. I need to express how serious I am about her. "I just got you back. I don't want to lose you again."

"Ryan…" she shifts her eyes down to our interlocked fingers, then leans over and kisses me. Then *really* kisses me. Then all discussion ceases in my brain, and we spend the rest of the day gloriously tangled in her bedsheets upstairs.

# # #

The following two weeks are a blur of trying to spend every second of every minute with Sarah that I can before our

Halloween show, and my imminent departure for LA the day after. I try to bring up her coming to LA, meeting me on the road, or how we'll keep in touch after I leave, and she either deflects or distracts me each time. Not that the distractions aren't perfectly wonderful, but it leaves me uneasy how much she's avoiding the topic altogether. She also avoids the studio while we complete the final mixing. She's yet to step into the same room as Reese, let alone meet her. Part of me is glad of that since it would be an extremely awkward situation for everyone, especially myself.

About two hours before the final show, everyone is getting into the costumes we rented for the night at the Stout Hideout. I'm going as Westley's Dread Pirate Roberts, and Sarah is Buttercup from the Princess Bride. We weren't going to dress up, but Jude and Matt talked us into it when we went with them to shop for costumes. Jude is dressed as Inigo Montoya, and Matt as Vizzini, and neither will stop quoting the movie. Every other word from Matt is, "Inconceivable!" and Jude is constantly saying, "You killed my father, prepare to die." Even more annoying, every time they see Sarah and me together, they call out, "Mawaaage."

Sarah is beautiful in her long light blue dress, blonde wig that looks remarkably real, and jeweled crown. She truly is a princess. Of course, I think that of her no matter what she wears. Since she's working the bar tonight along with Mark like our last show, she's wearing her Converse sneakers under the gown, which makes her cuter in my eyes.

We're hanging around the bar for a few pre-show drinks before the doors open, and Mark gives me a poisonous glare as he hands me my glass. I nod at him, letting him know the message is received, and that I won't be a drunken idiot by the night's end. I learned that lesson for sure.

We make our way backstage as the audience is let in, taking some photos for the band's Instagram account that Vanessa's been yelling at us long distance to do for weeks now. She'll be joining us in LA next week, now that her parent's situation has improved. She's been arranging our upcoming tour dates and press interviews, so we will be busy as soon as we're back. Everything is starting to ramp up now that we've finished the creative side of things. The first single from the new album is getting released in two weeks. It's exciting but leaves me a bit hollow knowing that Sarah won't be with me to share it.

"You ready?" Sarah asks, coming up behind me and sliding her arms around my waist.

"Mawaage," Jude and Matt say annoyingly in unison.

"Fuck off." I can't help but smile. I turn and frame my hands around her face and give her a deep kiss; her sweetness is intoxicating more than any drink. "I am now."

She pecks my cheek quickly, announces us to the crowd, and we take the stage. More people are here this time, and almost everyone is in costume. This is the most bizarre show we've ever done. Playing in front of literal clowns, rag dolls, and horror movie killers is not something I ever imagined doing, and it's more than surreal. I try my best not to look closely at anyone, and pretend to sing only for Sarah, somewhere beyond the spotlight.

We get to the night's last song, and I switch to my acoustic guitar. "Can we coerce Sarah Lawrence up here, please? Sarah Lawrence to the stage, please." Matt places a second stool next to me for her. The crowd's cheers escalate as she slowly makes her way up.

"I'm going to kill you," she whispers in my ear, and squeezes my bicep to the point of pain before taking a seat. A strained smile is stretched across her face.

I lean over to her and hand her the second microphone, our eyes locking. "Sing 'Almost' with me," I say. "I know you know it." Not a question, but a request. *Please say yes.*

Realization dawns on her, and the strained smile turns into a real one. "Oh. I thought you were just going to sing *at* me and embarrass me. I'd love to."

Singing the song, Sarah adds harmonies I never thought of, making the piece more special than it already is to me. I hope to god someone records this so I can view it again later. When we finish, the crowd goes crazy and chants Sarah's name until she blushes so much, she runs off the stage. I may or may not have been the person who started that chant. We thank everyone who came, and spend some time in the bar area signing autographs and taking photos. They'll make interesting memories for people, seeing as we're all in costume, but I'm happy to do it. Without fans, we'd be nothing, as my mother continues to remind me. She doesn't come to the shows, saying she'd be too nervous for me, but she keeps track of us on all our social media.

When the evening comes to an end, I go home with Sarah for my last night in Chandler. We've got seven months of touring the country and only a tiny break before taking off for Europe for another three months. It's going to be a grueling schedule. And after tonight, I'm dreading being away from Sarah for that long. Perfect for the Dread Pirate Roberts.

24

Let It Go

SARAH

The morning Ryan leaves for LA comes up so fast, I'm not prepared for the flood of different emotions crashing into me as we stand in my driveway, waiting for his ride to the airport. The day is cold and dreary, like my mood, and only a few leaves are left hanging on the trees. All the color from a few weeks ago now lays decaying on the ground. Autumn feels like she gave up and wants to step aside and let winter take over. I wish someone could take over for me today. This is going to be so hard. I barely slept last night since my thoughts kept churning, and decisions about the future kept getting weighed and made.

"So, which shows are you going to come to?" Ryan asks for the hundredth time, wrapping me in his arms to warm me up since I'm shivering. But not from the cold weather. "Detroit? Or Pittsburgh? Cleveland, for sure. Or we can go bat shit crazy and get hitched in Vegas." He wiggles his eyebrows at me.

"Ryan...." I'm trying to put him off again, and it's not working. Trying to put off this conversation altogether. I know I need to do this, though.

"Why can't you lie to me and say any city?" he laughs, throwing his head back. "Give me *some* hope, at least."

"Very funny." I'm not amused.

After that, we're quiet for a while, just standing and swaying, keeping each other warm as the drizzle falls. Neither of us moves to go back into the house. This rain fits the mood perfectly.

"I'm probably not going to see you until you're back here again." I'm unsure how to start this ending. Hopefully just a temporary ending, but one that needs to happen for us. This is the only smart choice with the huge amount of time we'll be apart in front of us. It doesn't make any sense to try to keep this going for almost a whole year. I almost fall apart as I think of being without him for so long. I can't imagine the ups and downs that a whole year of this would bring.

He leans back and meets my eyes, and I keep my gaze steady. Trying to express what I don't want to say aloud. "What are you saying, Sarah? I get the sense I'm missing something significant here. And I don't like where you're going with this."

"I just think you should keep your options open since you're going to be gone for so long. That's all."

"Options? I don't fucking want options, Sarah. I want you. Only you." Anxiety is taking him over. "Are you breaking up with me right as I'm about to leave? Are you doing this?" He pulls away from me and runs his hands through his hair. The pain in his eyes is killing me.

"Ryan, no." Suddenly, I want to take everything back. Maybe I'm wrong, and this could work somehow. The back and forth in my mind is tearing me apart. My brain is saying one thing, and my heart says another. "I don't want you to feel tied down to me. Like you owe me anything...."

"I do not feel tied down by you," he grabs my face in his hands and stares into my eyes, "at all. You are the only person that could ever make me happy. You saw how patient I can be. I can do that all fucking year if I have to. This is not fucking over."

"You say that now, but we don't know the future. You could meet someone next week, next month, or six months from now. I don't want to hold you back."

"I already met someone. Six years ago."

"Ryan, you know what I'm saying."

"How can you be so calm and say these things? Like what we have doesn't matter to you? Has this past month meant nothing to you?"

"Of course it has." He has to know how hard this is going to be. How impossible it will be.

His car service pulls up to the curb, and Ryan swears as he pulls me to him.

"I don't know what you're trying to do, Sarah, but I don't believe you mean anything you're saying. I refuse to believe after this past month, you seriously think this is a good idea." He leans back and makes sure I'm looking up at him. "I love *you*, Sarah. I fell in love with you the day we met at Harmony Lane, arguing over that Sex Pistols record Rusty had. You can't change that with a few words. Not anymore. I made the mistake of believing you last time. I don't believe you now."

The memory of that first argument makes me laugh, but his telling me he loves me right as he's about to leave doesn't seem fair either. My heart shuts my head up, melting me into him. Of course he's right. This relationship does matter to me. Sometimes more than I want to admit to myself. I should be tired of sacrificing myself, and allow something selfish to happen for a change. I should grow up already.

"I love you t-," I don't finish my sentence as his mouth is on mine, and I'm caught up in the moment's emotion, kissing him back with equal fervor. He doesn't fight fair when he kisses me like this. I can't believe I need to wait seven months for another one like it. I must be insane.

When we pull away from each other, Ryan whispers, "Promise me we'll keep talking about this. You need to escape your head, Sarah." He kisses me again, a light brush of the lips I think I'll miss more than the deeper one. "Promise me we'll try to make this work." The car at the end of the driveway honks impatiently, and Ryan turns to yell at the driver. "Fuck off! I'm saying goodbye to my woman here."

I want to laugh, but he's so serious. "I'll try," I grab his hand and head towards the street and the car so he doesn't miss his flight. The driver comes out, takes his bags and guitar case, and places them in the back.

Ryan turns to me, grabbing my waist, "Is that the best you can do?"

"I don't want to promise what I can't deliver," I smile, calling back to his conversation with my brother not so long ago.

He briefly hangs his head in defeat, then pulls me into another long kiss and a longer hug before getting in the car, not saying a word. I think we're both afraid of saying any more. I stand at the end of the driveway and watch the car until it disappears, something I have done a lot of lately; saying goodbye to people I love. A chill settles deep into my bones. I think I just watched my happiness drive away.

I promised to try, but I don't know whether or not to believe myself.

# # #

The next couple of weeks, Ryan and I try to talk every day or text if we're too busy. I'm back juggling my job at the Stout Hideout, and doing vocal and producing jobs at the studio. And now that I have studio access again, I make the most of it and work on my own songs. This makes staying in touch with Ryan hard at times. The last few days have been more hit or miss as the band takes the road for their tour. This will be even more difficult as he moves around the country into different time zones. I may be right after all about this not working out. I hope not. But I did promise to try.

By the end of the fourth week, I rarely hear from Ryan. We haven't talked on the phone directly in five days, and I only received one text. The last time we spoke, I could tell he was also drunk, as he was slurring his words while telling me how much he missed and loved me. I try to keep Lorelai's opinion on people who drunk dial in mind, but it's tough.

I run into Ryan's mother at the grocery store, and she seems happy to see me and not concerned about Ryan at all. We don't discuss how often we each speak to him, just how we'd heard the new song on the radio and how good it is. They released 'Take It With You' as their first single off the album, and the song is doing fantastic on the charts. The video is more impressive, and Ryan looks especially hot, but I don't say that to his mother. We make polite conversation and obligatory niceties about getting together soon. As soon as she walks away, I can tell we're not getting together. Something is very off with her, but I can't pinpoint it.

I try to distract myself from the lack of communication with Ryan by fulfilling my promise to Benji, and clearing out my mother's bedroom before they come home for Thanksgiving. Opening the door the first time was like stepping into a time machine. When she passed away, I cleaned the room but still set it up as though she would return at any moment. Her slippers are still under the side of the bed, waiting to be glided into upon waking up. But she's not here to ever wake up again. The thought breaks me, and I spend about an hour crying on the edge of her bed. The quietness of the room amplifies the loss of her.

Eventually, I shake everything off and get to work. I promised I would do this, propelling me to finish the task. Every piece of clothing, shoes, costume jewelry, and purses, are placed in bags and donated to the local charity. My mother wasn't one to collect knick-knacks, so there aren't a lot of those. The only things left are pictures in frames and several photo albums of Benji and me when we were younger. I set those aside to go through when Benji is back home. It takes me about three days to go through everything and turn it into an official guest bedroom. While it is technically the master bedroom, I can't bring myself to use it like one. It would be too weird. When I finish, I leave the door open.

# # #

The following week is Thanksgiving, and Benji and Joe come home for the long weekend before their semester finals and winter break. I missed them so much. The house is so empty with just me and Gunner here, even with Jenny's occasional visits; it can be nice to hear someone else's noise bouncing off the walls for a change. Both Benji and Joe turn misty-eyed when they find the guest bedroom door open, and my brother gives me a big hug.

"I knew you could do it." He's wiping at his eyes with his sleeve.

"Thanks for the push I needed," I tell him. And I mean what I say. I'm grateful he made me step out of my comfort zone. It was beyond time to deal with that.

Joe cooks us the most amazing Thanksgiving dinner, and I clean up the dishes before the oncoming turkey coma sets in. Benji comes to the sink to help me while Joe goes to lay down. He's earned the rest, for sure. The desserts alone were phenomenal and nap-worthy. Benji's been extra quiet since they got home. I don't notice any tension between him and Joe, but that doesn't necessarily mean anything.

"You okay?" I ask, handing him a freshly washed dish to dry. "You've been super quiet. Is school going okay?"

Benji frowns while either trying to figure out what to say, or how to say it. I give him time to answer, not wanting to rush him.

"I got a C- on one of my mid-terms," he says, his eyes cast down to the floor.

"And?"

"What do you mean, 'And?'" He throws the dishtowel on the island and starts pacing. "I can't have a C-, Sarah. We're talking failing. I can't fail a class. We can't afford for me to retake courses left and right-"

"Woah, dude." I step in front of him, grab his hands, make sure he's got physical contact, and meet his panicked eyes. "You're only a couple points from a C which *is* passing. You can make that up easily. Did you talk to your professor about it?" I'm surprised he's just now telling me since his mid-terms were weeks ago. *Has he been afraid to tell me all this time?*

"No." He breaks our eye contact, and I give his hands a supportive squeeze. "But I got a tutor, so that might help. I blank when it comes to tests, though. I can't help it."

"I used to do the same thing." And I did. I had major test anxiety in high school. Luckily, I was able to control it once I got into college. "There are some things you can do to reduce the anxiety. I can work with you on that if you want." I don't want to push myself and my advice on him.

"My therapist and I are talking about it, But thanks. I guess I'll let you know if I fail out of college."

"Yeah, a heads up would be perfect," I joke, but he's not laughing along with me. "Is there something else wrong?" I can tell there is, but I have a feeling I've gotten all I can get out of Benji for now.

"Nothing we can't handle." He forces a smile for me.

"Okay. You know I'm here if you want to talk." *Did he just say 'we?' Are he and Joe having problems?* Discussing problems with Benji can sometimes be like walking through a waterfall. You see the water, you know you'll be smacked in the face with it, but you step under it anyway and let yourself get drenched, then you step out of it and onto the other side. It can be that overwhelming and that quick. I guess the relationship waterfall he's standing in front of will need to wait until he's ready to walk through it.

"How about you? How are things with Ryan?"

"Things are great!" I try to sound sincere, though things are not great. Things are very far from great.

"She's lying." Joe enters the kitchen, pointing an accusing finger at me. "She's completely lying, I can tell."

"I thought you were taking a nap." I frown at him and try to change the subject.

"Well, I thought I was tired, but I'm not, so thinking is neither of our strong suits today. What's going on with that gorgeous rock star of yours?"

"Nothing."

"Well, there's your problem." He pours a glass of wine and hands it to me, even though I didn't ask for it. "If nothing is happening, you need to *make* things happen." He proceeds to pour wine for himself and Benji too. *Cool. I guess we're all drinking wine and discussing my love life now.*

"And how am I supposed to do that when I can't even

reach him on the phone?" I ask, my frustration starting to bubble up and over.

Joe thinks on it for a minute, tapping his chin with his finger. "You go to him."

"What? I can't just leave...."

"Sure you can. I'm sure Lorelai and Mark can cover for you, and Benji and I can stay here with Gunner for a couple of days. Right, Benji?" He nods in agreement. "We don't need to be back until Monday. This is perfect. Go and make a grand gesture for your hot man. Surprise him, and then rock his world."

I can't help but smile and get excited right along with Joe. *Could I up and fly across the country to visit him? Even for a couple of days?* Joe makes it sound so easy. Since I have his itinerary, I know where he is and where he'll be. Maybe I could surprise him and take us back to where we were. I did promise I would try. This would definitely count as trying.

"Fine. I'll do it." I'm unable to keep the excitement out of my voice. "If you're sure you're okay with staying here?"

"Go," Benji chuckles. "Do something for yourself for a change."

I give them a quick hug, much to Joe's annoyance, and rush upstairs to make all the arrangements. I can't believe I'm doing this. But I'm doing this. I have my own waterfall to walk through at the moment, and his name is Ryan.

1000 Times

RYAN

S pending Thanksgiving weekend in Las Vegas for two shows is not how I'd prefer to spend a holiday. It's not something you're ever used to when you're on the road. You're already missing everyone at home, and a holiday away makes that ten times worse. Trying to keep in touch with Sarah's been difficult, since I can't find a fucking private minute to myself to have an honest conversation with her. And finding personal time on a holiday is even more challenging. The timezone difference isn't helping matters either. I have been in a piss poor mood for days now, and I can't seem to shake it no matter what I do. Not being able to reach Sarah today is only magnifying the fact we're so far apart.

We texted briefly yesterday on Thanksgiving morning, but that was it. It took forever for her to respond to my text too. Each of her responses to me, both texts and calls are getting later and later every time, and shorter and shorter. I'm starting to wonder if she isn't right about this not working. If she's not willing to put in the effort to meet me halfway, I don't know what else to do. I know that I miss the ever-loving shit out of her, and I don't want to give up. But it's getting harder every day we're apart to keep a positive mindset.

Vanessa has us on the go so much more this tour than our last one; it's insane. This can be good insanity, though. It means we're doing well if people want a piece of us. That's the main problem, too - *everyone* wants a part of us. We're running out of parts to give away. Well, I am, at least. Matt and Jude get off a little easier than I do, which drives me crazy, but it is what it is.

By the end of any day, whether we play a show or not, which we most likely do, I'm so exhausted that I lack the energy to talk to anyone. Talking with Sarah when I can hardly think straight isn't fair to her. More often than not lately, I've had several drinks by the time I can call her, which never goes over well. I know I've made the mistake of drunk dialing her a few times, so I try not to contact her when I'm like that. Days I'm not like that are getting few and far between. But some days, I just need the extra motivation to keep going on this stupid long roller coaster of a tour. And we've only been at this a month. I doubt I can keep this pace up for much longer, the way I'm going, but it's the only way I can think of at the moment. Something's going to give. It's a matter of time before something does.

I find myself needing to numb the pain of being without Sarah more and more. I just got her back into my life, and in a way I could only dream about before. We had such a fantastic month before I had to leave on the tour, that being out here without her physically with me makes me ache with a loneliness I've never felt before. I can feel it carving me out each day, little by little, and soon there will be nothing left of me. The slight contact we have is not enough to fill me back up emotionally. I'm starting to be downright empty.

We go through the motions before our first Vegas show tonight at one of the smaller casinos, visiting the local radio stations and a signing at a record store. We made sure that our album came out on vinyl, so it's been cool to see those at signings along with band photos. We're headlining smaller venues at least the first half of the tour, and local bands open for us each show. So far, they've been decent, but the band opening for us tonight and tomorrow, Murderous Crows, is barely on this side of crazy. They're cool, but wow, I have a hard time keeping up. After a crazy dinner with them, we've got maybe an hour before our first show starts, and Jake, the lead singer, is pouring our third shot of the Mezcal his 'buddy' from Durango, Mexico, smuggles to Vegas especially for him. This stuff is strong enough to remove varnish from furniture, but I suck it down, still trying to fill that void in my chest. It still not working.

It doesn't fill anything, but it does warm me up for our show. The Vegas crowd is pretty cool, and the fans already know the words to our new songs, which is always lovely. Lucky thing, since later on in the show, there are a few songs that I forget the lyrics to, but I'm able to hold the mic out to the crowd and let them do the work for my drunk ass. It's a fucking lazy and dickhead way to perform, and Matt and Jude are none too pleased with me, but whatever. The crowd loves it. At least, I *think* they do. Definitely sounds like they do to my ears. By the end of the show, when we're performing our biggest song, 'Killing Time' for our encore, the crowd is more than happy to sing a weird live karaoke version of it without me.

As we leave the stage, and Matt is tossing his drum sticks into the crowd as he always does, I can hear people yelling for us to perform 'Almost,' and my heart craters. I refuse to play that song live. Well, at least without Sarah. That song is too personal for me to give to the fans in an intimate live performance by me. I can't stand to listen to it anymore as it is, since it makes me miss Sarah more.

Thinking of Sarah throws me into a downward emotional spiral. As usual, I try to call her one more time after the show and am now sent straight to voicemail. *She's not even taking my calls now? What the fuck?* Matt and Jude take off with Vanessa to I don't know where. Probably to be as far away from me as they can. I don't blame them. I wouldn't want to hang with me in this state either. This leaves me with Jake and his band to hang with the rest of the night. Since we play another show here in Vegas, we don't travel tomorrow, so tonight is a 'free' night. We don't get a lot of these.

One of the many magical things about Las Vegas is that the bars and clubs are open and serve twenty-four hours a day, seven days a week. I think we start the night at the bar in our hotel, then move on to at least three other bars. I can't remember. Turns out, Jake knows every single person in Vegas, which is helpful when seeking free drinks, and we've had a lot of those. We've circled back to the hotel, and the party moves to my room. And by party, I think there's at least ten of us now. I don't know. Math is hard. We kept accumulating people at each stop.

Matt and Jude are now being dicks about the noise, and some chick keeps trying to play 'Almost' on the wireless speaker that's blaring, and I keep changing the song to something else. She's starting to piss me off. I think there was a loud argument earlier. I may have been a part of that, but I don't think anybody got hurt or anything. I keep calling Sarah and keep going right to her voicemail. That's pissing me off too, and I tell her so. I tell her how mad she's making me. And how much I miss her. Someone takes my phone from me, so I'll stop. Definitely a good idea. That makes me *want* to play 'Almost,' and I do. Over and over, and over. I can almost feel her next to me, dancing with me and spinning when I close my eyes. We keep turning, and it's getting too fast and out of control. I need to lay down. I need to stop the spinning. Stop the song. Stop the spinning. Stop the world.

26

Never Again

SARAH

L anding in Las Vegas at 5AM makes me kick myself for the millionth time for not considering the difference in our time zones yet again. When I bought my ticket and left Ohio late last night, I guess I wasn't thinking straight. I thought it would be closer to 8AM, even though that's still super early. This time of the morning, it's hard to tell if it's early or late for the people milling about. It's a mixed bag of old couples trying their last round of luck on the slot machines lining the walkways, businesspeople racing to catch early flights, and bridal parties not sure if they're still drunk or already hungover.

Butterflies start to flutter in my stomach as I make my way to the parking deck to order a ride to the hotel. I didn't even pack a bag, just an oversized purse with a few necessities, so I could avoid having to deal with baggage claim. My return ticket is for tomorrow since Benji and Joe need to drive back to school. My phone's been off since I arrived at the airport last night and for the entire flight, so I'm surprised to discover so many messages from Ryan when I turn it on. I smile to myself, knowing what surprise is in store for him when I get to his hotel. I ignore the messages for now as I find the rideshare app and order a ride. Once my car arrives, I slide in and take a deep breath. I can't believe I'm here in Vegas.

It's still dark out on the ride to the hotel, but the strip is lit up in all its glory. I haven't been to Vegas before, and I'm amazed at how big the hotels are. When you see pictures of them or on TV, it looks like many smaller hotels right next to each other, but the strip is a lot bigger, and walking between hotels seems like it would take quite a while. No wonder there are so many cabs, limos, and ride-sharing cars on the road. I have a few minutes until I arrive at the hotel, so I read Ryan's texts from last night.

> RYAN: Hey beautiful. Getting ready to head to the venue. Thinking of you. Left you a voice-mail. Love you.

> RYAN: Hey there. Show bout to start. Tried to call. Miss you.

> RYAN: Are you mad at me. Did I do somehting

> RYAN: showz over tried called you

> RYAN: sarah damn it the hell ? Is going on

RYAN: last call for sarah. Last call. Fuck

RYAN: where are u? I need you talk to me

RYAN: sarahhhhhhhhhhh

Wow. That's a lot to take in for one night of texting, and from the looks of it, he was drinking again. Pretty heavily too. But it sounds like he was missing me, so he'll be even happier when I show up out of the blue. I'm getting anxious now on top of being excited. I didn't think I would be nervous to see him again, but it's been so long, and we have missed each other. This will be good for us to reconnect. Maybe he'll be able to believe that I do want to try to make us work as I promised.

After seeing the strip, I'm reminded of the comment Ryan made before leaving about us being crazy and getting hitched in Vegas. *Could that ever happen for us someday?* Someday.... I think I wrote a song about that a long time ago, but can't be sure. *Someday, married to Ryan.* It's something to definitely keep in mind.

The driver pulls up to the casino where the band is staying and lets me out. It's a little seedier than a strip hotel, closer to the downtown area, but overall doesn't look too bad. I make my way through the casino floor scattered with people up early or late, depending on your definition, playing the loud slot machines, and walk up to the reception desk where a petite blonde greets me.

"Welcome to Newton's Resort. Are you checking in?"

"No, I'm here to visit someone staying here." I chuckle to myself at anyone using the word 'resort' to describe this hotel. That's a little ambitious, I think.

"Oh, okay. Who is it you're here to see? I'll need to check if you're approved to give that information to you first."

"Westley Roberts." A happy memory of Ryan in his pirate costume crosses my mind and makes me smile. "My name is Sarah Lawrence? I should be on the approved list." At least, I hope I'm still on the approved list. I show her my I.D. Ryan had told me I'd be listed at every hotel and venue to have access to him. I pray that's still the case. I could always switch to Plan B and call him to have him come downstairs and surprise him here, but that wouldn't be near as fun. Or as sexy. I'm wearing his favorite bra and panties to greet him properly when we're alone. He's not the only one who has been missing the other. Thinking about being with him shortly makes my body hum. I can't wait.

"Oh good, you are approved. Mr. Roberts is in room 1712. You can follow the blue carpet to the elevators over there." She points the direction, and I thank her as I head that way. Now that I'm so close to him, I'm dying to get upstairs as soon as possible. I feel like it's Ryan's birthday, and I arranged a surprise party for him, and he's about to walk in the door. It's such a weird sensation, but it makes me giddy as the elevator climbs up to his floor. It rises at a snail's pace, and I bounce on the balls of my feet in anticipation.

Finally, the doors slowly creak open on the seventeenth floor, and I step out into the hallway, checking the signs for the direction of room 1712. As I walk the hall towards his room, it looks and smells like a frat party exploded. Bottles of different alcohols and beers, various remnants of food, and even some pieces of clothing are scattered on the carpet in-between room doors. A guy is lying on the floor in front of room 1710 and I can't tell if he's sleeping, drunk, or dead. He's about my age, but it's hard to say if the reek of alcohol is from him or the general surrounding area. I stop to check his breathing, and his chest rises and falls, so he's still alive, thank god. So, I was right, and Ryan was partying last night. I hope he's not too hungover to be happy to see me.

As I'm stepping over him, the sleeping guy's eyes pop open, scaring the shit out of me, and I jump back, covering my mouth to stifle a yelp.

"Hey," he says. At least, I *think* that's what he says.

"Hey," I say, moving away and continuing toward Ryan's room, not turning my back on him.

"You're pretty," he slurs, but instantly closes his eyes and snores.

"Thanks," I whisper. Not exactly sure why I'm being polite to a sleeping drunk stranger, but I am.

I find Ryan's room, and before I knock on the door, I listen for any more movement or voices from any surrounding rooms. It seems quiet, so everyone must be sleeping. Trying not to wake anyone up, I knock as softly as I can on the door. After no answer, I knock again, a little harder this time. I sense movement from inside the room and glance down to straighten myself out a little. I realize then that I didn't stop to check my appearance after landing. I've been stuck in an airplane for hours and look like shit. That's okay, though. I'm sure Ryan won't mind. Hopefully, I won't be in these clothes much longer anyway.

The door opens, and an attractive woman about my height with long brown hair stares at me blankly. She's wrapped in a bedsheet and nothing else. My mouth goes dry, and I can't breathe. All the blood running through my veins, and my heart freezes.

"What do you want?" She's squinting at me against the hallway lighting. I've obviously woken her up.

"Who are you?" I ask, not answering her question and not believing what is right in front of me. *Who the fuck is this chick? And what is she doing in Ryan's room?* I double check the room number, and this *is* the right room. *What the hell?*

She's indignant at my question, and the door opens more as she leans against it. "Who the fuck are *you*?" Her attitude is annoyed. Like she has any right to be upset with me.

My eyes travel from her further into the room, where I find Ryan laying face down on the bed in nothing but his boxer briefs. I know it's him from his tattoos, but I would know it was him without them. I know that body, and so does this bitch now.

"Nobody," I croak. "I'm nobody." I turn from her and head back to the elevators, stepping over the hallway drunk on the way. I don't even know if she says anything else or if the door shuts behind me. Once I make it to the lobby, I walk outside as if in a trance. I'm not crying. I'm not raging. I'm not thinking. I'm not feeling anything. I'm just walking. And I keep walking until the sun rises, and then I keep walking after that. It was surprisingly cold when I first came outside, but I didn't feel that either. The temperature is beginning to warm up now, and I'm starting to come around to myself.

I find a coffee shop and grab a coffee to keep me going. I start walking again, still reeling from what I saw, and it dawns on me to listen to Ryan's voicemails from last night. Maybe that will give me some clue or idea about what happened because I am so confused right now. Turns out they are enlightening.

> RYAN: "Hey, Beautiful. Just wanted to hear your voice before the show. Haven't heard it in a while. Hope you're good. Love you."

"Fuck you, Ryan Crawford," I say at the phone. Yup. I'm feeling something, and it's definitely anger that raises its ugly head first.

> RYAN: "Hey, it's me again. Not sure why all my calls are going straight to voicemail lately. Kind of freaking me out. Miss you. Call me. Love you.

"Freaking you out? I was on a fucking plane coming to see *you* dickhead. Fuck you, Ryan Crawford."

> RYAN: "Hey...still can't reach you. Fuck. Did I do something to upset you? Or are you mad about something? Call me back, please."

"Ha! Did you do something? Really? Fuck you. Just fuck you."

RYAN: "Sarah. Where are you? Why won't you talk to me anymore? Fuck.

"Where am I? Where am I? Fuck you."

RYAN: "Sarah. Sarah. Sarah. What are you doing? What are we doing? This is bullshit. Fuck. Fuck me.

"Bingo. Fuck you, Ryan."

RYAN: "Hey...fuck...why do I even...(unintelligible female voice) no, I know. I know. It's not cool. But it's...(wrestling sounds)."

"What the actual fuck? Fuck you."

RYAN: "... (faint music, unintelligible voices talking and laughing for about a minute)...."

"What drunk dialing fuckery is this? Fuck you, Ryan Crawford."

As I swear at my phone, a couple passing me by gives me a look but then chimes in, "Yeah, fuck you, Ryan!" It doesn't make me feel better, but it stops me enough to take stock of my surroundings. I've walked so much in the last several hours that I have no clue where I am. And I'm stuck here until my flight home tomorrow, with no place to stay. I've traveled to a not-so-great part of Vegas, and the buildings that aren't abandoned and boarded up, are covered with graffiti, and the parking lots are full of trash. Suddenly I don't feel safe being out here on my own, and my feet are killing me. I didn't have any problem taking a flight by myself, but I thought Ryan and I would be together the rest of the time once I got here. Now that I'm truly alone, I'm a little frightened.

I turn back to examine the casinos on the strip to pick one to go to and rent a room. The only thing that sticks out to me as familiar is the Eiffel Tower replica of the Paris Hotel. I head to a more populated area and order a rideshare car to drive me there. I didn't plan on springing for a hotel room on top of the airfare, but this entire trip is costing me a lot more than I thought it would in so many ways. To think, only a few hours ago, I was thinking about us being married.

I should have known this would happen. I really should have. Actually, I *did* know this would happen. This is why I didn't want to commit to a relationship before he left. It's why this hurts so much more now since I did commit. Too bad Ryan didn't.

Tell Her This

RYAN

I wake up to my phone buzzing somewhere across the room. When I lift my head to search for it, a tidal wave of nausea takes over, and I barely stumble in time to the bathroom to empty my stomach of everything I've ever eaten. *That's the last time I ever drink Mezcal.* I rinse my mouth out and head back into the room when I notice someone else in my bed. There's a woman whose back is to me, but her long brown hair makes my heart skip a beat.

"Sarah? Is that you?" I kneel on the bed and gently pull on her shoulder to turn her over. My heart expands at the thought of Sarah here with me in Vegas and in my bed to boot. I start to lean down to kiss her when her hair falls away from her face, and I can plainly tell this woman in my bed isn't Sarah. I don't know who the fuck this is. *What the fuck did I do last night?* I'm about to pull away when the strange woman reaches up and wraps her hands around my neck, locking me in place.

"Good morning," she moans, a just-waking-up languid smile on her lips. When she opens her eyes and meets mine, she yanks her hands away and pulls the sheets up to her chin. She shrieks, panic growing. "Who the hell are you?"

I jump just as quickly off the bed, raising my hands in defense. I glance around briefly, confirming this is, in fact, my hotel room. "Well, this is my room, and I don't know who you are, how you got here, or if...." I wave at her and the bed. I'd like to think I would remember if I had sex with someone last night, especially someone I don't know. But I was *so* fucked up; maybe that theory is right out the fucking window. Maybe I did have sex with this woman. The guilt at the prospect tears my insides to shreds.

"Give me a minute." The woman covers her eyes and pushes her head back into her pillow. I take the opportunity to throw the jeans I find in the corner on. My hands shake as I fumble with the button and zipper. "Where's Jake?" She sits up on her elbows and glances around.

"Jake?" I ask, the question throwing me off.

"Yeah, my boyfriend, Jake. His band opened for yours last night?"

"Oh, him. I don't know."

She examines me for a minute and chuckles. "Don't worry, we didn't fuck if that's what you're worried about."

The stone in my gut lifts at her words, but I'm still thoroughly confused. "Then what are you doing...here?" I again indicate her laying in my bed. That still doesn't make any sense.

She gets out of bed, pulling the sheet along with her, and I divert my eyes to avoid seeing anything I shouldn't. She starts picking up various pieces of clothing from the floor. "Well, Jake and I were about to have some fun in your bathroom since you passed out on your bed, but I think we were both too drunk. Jake insisted he was heading home, but I crawled into the closest bed to sleep it off. You were on top of the sheets, so I didn't think it mattered."

"Why was I just in my underwear? Who did that?" I'm still mortified I did something terrible.

"You did. When you were kicking everyone out. That's when Jake and I snuck into the bathroom. When we came out, you were face down on the bed in your skivvies."

I run my hands down my face in relief. The stubble on my chin reminds me that I'm sure I look as bad as I feel right now. I need food and coffee. Lots and lots of coffee.

As the woman, whose name I still don't know, heads into the bathroom, she says, "Oh, I think there was a chick here looking for you." She glances at the window, confused for a minute, and then at the clock on the nightstand. "Damn, I can't believe it's noon already."

My heart stutters. "A girl? When? Did she give her name?" *Please don't be Sarah. I can't believe I wish Sarah wasn't here, but if it was her...*

"Geez, so many questions."

"Well, it's fucking important," My voice rises with anxiety.

"It was super early and still dark out, I don't know. And she didn't say her name. Just said she was nobody and left. I tried to call after her, but she ignored me. She was *gorgeous*, but kind of a bitch if you ask me."

I clench my jaw and fists to restrain myself from punching the wall. "What did she look like?"

She shrugs, starting to close the bathroom door, "I don't know. Kind of like me actually, same height, same hair kinda." She pulls at the bottom of the bedsheet, dragging it into the bathroom with her, and shuts the door.

I fall onto the edge of the bed, my face in my hands, trying to catch my breath. It had to be Sarah. *Fuck! There's no way she's going to believe any of this. I'm fucked. I'm totally fucked.*

A knock sounds at the door, and I jump up to open it and find Jake on the other side. My heart sinks. I don't know why Sarah would come back after what she witnessed, but I had hoped.

"Hey man," He has a goofy smile as he comes in. "Last night was wild, am I right?"

"Yeah, that's a good word for it,"

"Is my girl still here? I tried to make it home last night but only got as far as one door down in the hallway." He laughs at himself, like being that wasted is entirely normal and funny. I don't find it funny. *I was as drunk as he was, and if I hadn't passed out on my own bed, would I have woken up in some random hotel hallway too? Or someone else's bed like Jake's girlfriend? What the fuck am I doing?*

He doesn't seem the slightest bit phased that he left his girlfriend to spend the night in another guy's bed. That's some severe dysfunction. "She's getting dressed in the bathroom."

"Oh, cool." He makes himself comfortable in one of the

room's chairs and cracks open a warm beer from the few left on the table. "Ready to buck up and do it all again tonight?" He chuckles as though this is all fucking normal for him.

"Actually, no," I say, searching for my phone that I can hear buzzing again. "I think I'll be avoiding Mezcal for a while, if not permanently."

"Yeah, the first time with that stuff can be pretty intense. You need to get used to it. Build up a tolerance." He flexes his biceps like that has anything to do with alcohol consumption.

I nod as I finally locate my phone under my duffle bag on the floor. There are a few messages from Matt and Jude telling me about breakfast plans and then lunch plans, which I've obviously missed. But then there are a few texts from Sarah's brother Benji that fill me with dread and panic.

> BENJI: Hey Ryan, did Sarah find you? I know it's early, but she hasn't texted that she arrived safely. Hopefully, this doesn't spoil her surprise for you.

> BENJI: Hey Ryan, starting to get a little worried here. We still haven't heard from Sarah. Please have her call, or at least text us. Thanks

> BENJI: Very worried now that we're not hearing from either of you. Please let us know all is okay soon, or we're flying out ourselves.

That's the last text, and I also notice a couple of voice-mails from him, but nothing from Sarah. I listen to the last message as I throw a shirt over my head and slide into my shoes before heading out, leaving Jake and his girlfriend behind in my room.

> BENJI: "Hey Ryan, it's Benji. I probably shouldn't be telling you this, but we located Sarah. She's still in Vegas ("at the Paris Hotel!" Joe yells from the background), (Benji - muffled: Joe! What the fuck?). Anyway, wanted to let you know we found her."

His tone lets me know he only made that call begrudgingly, most likely at Joe's insistence. *Thank you, Joe.* I was about to go from hotel to hotel to find her, which would be pointless, considering how many fucking hotels there are in this god-damned city. I never would have found her. Even now, knowing which hotel she's at, I have no idea what room she's in or if she'll ever leave it for me to see her.

I order a car and arrive at her hotel not long after. This isn't my first time at the Paris since we've played Vegas a few times, and we've already done the tourist thing. This time I don't bother taking in the beautiful architecture or decorations, concentrating instead on examining the people I pass by, desperate to find Sarah. I have no clue what I'll say to her if or when I do find her, but I need to find her first. I decide to check the food areas since it's around lunchtime. Hoping she's gotten hungry and ventured out for something to eat. Investigating each restaurant and food counter turns up nothing. I realize, knowing Sarah, she's not going to eat at all today, but I had to check for myself.

Making my way to the front desk, a group of teenage girls

surrounds me, fawning over me and begging for selfies and autographs. I oblige with forced enthusiasm and gratitude, but pull myself out of their suffocating circle with my most winning public smile, and walk up to the desk. The young woman behind the counter, who witnessed the entire interaction, smiles at me eagerly. She apparently recognizes who I am too. Maybe I can use my pseudo fame for good for once. I decide to turn on the charm to help this along and get to Sarah as soon as possible.

"How can I help you?" The receptionist clears her throat and smooths her extremely tight ponytail.

I turn the smile up another notch for her, and lean over the counter as if to share a secret with her. "I'm here to surprise my girlfriend," I put a finger to my lips, "shhh."

Her eyes drop to my lips and hover there a little too long before she answers. "A surprise?"

I play up the puppy dog eyes and nod, "It would really mean a lot to me, to *us*, if you could just give me her room number...." I hold my breath while she considers.

She glances around, "What's her name?"

One selfie with a hotel front desk clerk later, I have the room number and practically fly to her floor. Housekeeping is making its rounds, and it gives me an idea. I know deep down there is no way Sarah will open the door for me, so I convince, okay, bribe, one of the housekeepers to pretend to have extra towels for her while I stay just out of sight. Once the towels are exchanged, I slide in front of the housekeeper, thanking her, and into Sarah's doorway.

"Hear me out," I say, hands up in surrender. "What you think you saw isn't what you think happened."

She literally jumps away from me as if my being within a few feet of her physically repulses her. Throwing the towels at me, she whispers, "Get the fuck out of here, Ryan." Then her voice rises, "Get out!"

I take advantage of her backing away and step in, closing the door behind me. I lean against it, hands still raised. "Sarah, please. Please listen. I can explain everything. I swear." Her eyes are swollen from crying, and she looks so much smaller, like she's folding in on herself in front of me. It's shattering my heart to see her in so much pain. The pain *I* caused. I didn't know I was causing it, but ultimately it *is* my fault. I did this to her. She turns away from me before her brimming tears can fall, hugging herself tightly as she steps further into the room. I want to rush over and wrap her into my arms and make everything okay. I need to make this all okay. I can't stand this.

"Just go, Ryan. I don't want you here. I don't want to see you at all. I don't want anything to do with you."

Her words are daggers into my soul. "This is all a misunderstanding, Sarah. That woman-"

She whips around; her voice is now full of venom. "Misunderstanding? How could I possibly misunderstand a naked woman in your hotel room, wrapped in *your* bedsheet, and then you basically naked in the only bed in the room, Ryan? I'm not a fucking idiot. I know what I saw."

I shake my head desperately, trying to explain, "That was Jake's girlfriend. She-"

"Oh, so your fucking other people's girlfriends now?

That's low, even for you." She laughs, and the sound of it chills my spine, "I thought you only cheated on people with your former producers, but what the fuck do I know, right? Apparently, you'll screw anything and anyone."

That one hits hard, and I feel it all slipping away from me. Her eyes tell me all I need to know. She's given up on me. On us. Anything I say now, no matter how true, will fall on deaf ears. But I have to fucking try. We've come too far for a misunderstanding to come between us.

I try to calm my shaking voice; I'm so scared I'm losing her, "I love you, Sarah, please let me explain what happened. I'll call Jake, and he'll tell you the same thing...."

"I don't want to hear from your so-called friends who would lie for you. I don't want to hear any more from anyone, actually. Especially you. Go. Get out of my room, or I'll call security."

"Security? What the fuck Sarah? Can't we talk about this like adults?" I can't believe she's not giving me a chance to explain. If she'd give me a fucking chance...

"Adults? Adults don't wind up so fucking drunk they call their girlfriends to swear at them in voicemails with giggling females in the background. Adults don't end up in bed with random women, who are complete bitches to their girlfriends when they show up to surprise the person they were fucking stupid enough to fall in love with. Adults don't do that, Ryan." She starts advancing on me with her arms crossed over her chest, and stops about a foot away; her gaze is unwavering on mine. I want to reach out and hold her, but she's not done with me yet. "So, to answer your question, no. We can't be adults.

So, go. Get out of my room, and get out of my life. I never want to see you again, Ryan."

I deserve that. I put myself in this position, and I deserve all of it. I know I do, but that doesn't make this hurt any less. I take one last long look at her, trying to memorize everything about her because I know this look on her face will haunt me for the rest of my life. Remembering this moment is going to crush me day by day until I'm only an empty husk of a person. If I thought I felt empty before, it's nothing compared to the gaping void I'm falling through now.

My eyes are filling with tears, and I can't stop them. I don't *want* to stop them. "I do love you, Sarah," I somehow choke the words out, and her tears begin to fall again, matching mine. My hand automatically rises to try to wipe hers off her cheek, but she turns her head away from me. My arm drops down to my side, defeated. I've just lost her. I've fucking lost everything. "I'll leave, but I swear to you on my soul, nothing happened…" I hang my head and quietly leave, heading to the stairwell. I sit on the stairs and ball my eyes out like I haven't done since I was a little child. *Maybe, if I didn't act like a fucking child, I wouldn't be in this fucking mess.*

Wrong Direction

SARAH

When I get home from Vegas, I throw myself back into my work and my music, doing my best to do everything within my power to try to forget Ryan. It's impossible with everything in the town now reminding me of him. The studio where we worked together and shared stolen moments before anyone knew we were a couple, and the bar with too many memories to count, both good and bad, but mostly good. Especially the night he won me back with his little notes on the napkin, which turned into so much more for us. The night I gave my heart and more to him, that will be my downfall forever. I let myself get swept up in the romance of it all, but I wanted to believe him so badly. I wanted to believe I could trust him, that he loved me as much as I loved him. That my dream of us could come true.

And for a while, it felt like he did feel the same way for me.

I truly felt loved by him. He made me feel special whenever we were together. Like I was the sun he revolved around, and now when I dare to think of him, thinking about these things cuts more of my heartstrings. But even with the hurt he's caused me, I can't bring myself to hate him. I should, but I can't. By letting him convince me to commit to a relationship, I painted him into a corner he couldn't maintain. And I knew he couldn't. I basically set him up to fail miserably. It's hard to hate someone who you put into an impossible situation. I only have myself to blame for that. But even with that self-knowledge, I don't feel any better. In fact, I feel the lowest I've ever felt in my life. Even worse than I did when he left the first time years ago. Worse because I had a hint of what could have been if things were different this time. If I hadn't given in and let myself fall deeper in love with him than I was, maybe I could function like a normal person.

I'm barely functioning at all now, even though I'm working my ass off. I'm distracted, making mistakes, and missing simple things I shouldn't be missing. Everyone is more than patient with me, but I can tell I'm reaching a line I shouldn't cross. Both Marty and Lorelai have been lovely, but I don't want to let my personal life bleed into my professional one any more than it already has.

The only thing that has been going well is my songwriting. Heartbreak always makes for better songs, but writing about the real thing that happened to you makes performing it near impossible without breaking down. I can't bring myself to perform them on open mic nights. I haven't sung at a single one since Ryan's band played there last. I can't bring myself to be on the stage we both sang 'Almost' on for more than a few seconds to announce another musician. I know it's foolish, but I am a fool. I proved that much.

I spend most of my spare time in the studio, even though it's hard to be there, working on producing my songs. They're all written and recorded, and I'm actually done recording my very first album. I decided to release the album myself, with a videographer friend from college recording the videos for a couple of the songs to give me a head start. While I was self-conscious filming because I am no actor, she made me comfortable, and they came out amazing. The songs are genuinely complete and my friend has finished editing the first video, so I bit the bullet and set it all free into the world. Feedback has been fantastic so far, and I'm excited for potential sales.

Joe and Benji are home for winter break, and convinced Lorelai I need to have an album release party between Christmas and New Year's at the Stout Hideout, since I finally released the album. She seems more excited about the party than I am, and won't let me handle any details. Joe has taken over that task and given Lorelai a shopping list of what he'll need for food and decorations. While I'm happy to be hands-off on that project, being done with the album leaves me with a lot of free time. Even with two jobs, my free time feels too free, and I don't know what to do with myself when I'm not working. I check social media to see how the first single is doing but try not to do that too much because, well, internet people.

As for Ryan, he still tries calling and leaving messages,

but I delete them all without reading or listening to them. It was a flurry at first three weeks ago when the Vegas incident happened, but it has tapered off since I don't respond. There's still at least a couple each day. Jenny tells me to block his number and be done with him, but I can't bring myself to do that. *Yet.* A small part of me likes knowing he's still thinking about me. I don't know if it's an evil, vengeful side of me that likes it, hoping it tortures him, or the side of me that still longs to be with him, lies be damned. When I do receive a message from him, my stomach does a little flip, even though I don't read or listen to it. Just knowing he sent it is enough for me. Part of me still loves him, and probably always will.

I sit on the couch with Gunner, and gaze at the lit-up Christmas tree with no other house lights on, drinking a cup of hot cocoa. Fat flakes of snow are blowing around on the other side of the window, and a blazing fire is in the fireplace. My mom and I used to do this all the time, making me miss her fiercely. This was her favorite holiday, and she'd be so happy since it's beginning to look a lot like Christmas, as the song says, which is next week. We've been hit with about a foot of snow so far and expect more in the coming days. The only positive thing about the weather in Ohio is the high odds of having a white Christmas.

Benji and Joe decorated the house almost the second they got back from school, and it's like walking into Santa's workshop every time I come home. I half expect little elves to pop out of the closets with wooden toys they've put together. I wouldn't put it past Joe to design something fantastic like that. The two fought like cats and dogs while putting up the decorations, but then made up right away. It's almost endearing, but I worry things aren't as perfect as they want everyone to believe. I really wish Benji would talk to me about it. I'm not exactly the ideal person to go to for relationship advice, so I completely understand why he doesn't.

They went downtown to spend the day last-minute gift shopping, which is crazy. Not only because the crowds of shoppers will be insane, but the pile of gifts under the tree is way taller than it has any right to be for just the three of us grown adults. It's not like we're giving each other X-boxes or toys or anything. I'm sure they're primarily sweaters and scarves, so apparently, we're each getting new winter wardrobes. Even Gunner has a few packages with his name 'From, Santa.' And like he knows I'm thinking about him, he whines a little and puts his head on my lap.

"Yeah, yeah," I say, scratching behind his ear. "You've been a good boy this year. You'll get presents too. Don't worry." Turns out, we should have worried.

29

Not In That Way

RYAN

Watching Sarah's new video for the hundredth time makes my heart crack open even farther than it already is. As usual, she looks and sounds terrific, but I wouldn't expect any less of her. The song is called 'Listen,' and it's about how she should have listened to the waves of the lake that told her not to listen to her heart, which is now broken. The message isn't lost on me, obviously. I understand it's about me and how I broke her heart. The worst part is the video shows her sitting on "our" driftwood branch by the water, watching the sunset, and it kills me seeing her sit without me there with my arms around her, as they should be. Where they belong. The song is beautiful and heartfelt, and it's gained a lot of views and positive comments.

"Dude, you're going to skew her streaming analytics if

218

you keep watching that repeatedly like that," Jude shakes his head at me. I have my earbuds in but can still hear him.

"She should know people are watching hundreds of times. What's wrong with that?"

"People?" he smirks.

"What? I'm people."

"Barely."

"Not arguing that point," I turn back to my phone to play the video again.

My fingers are itching to text her or dial her number just one more time, but I think I'm hitting the wall on my perseverance. After three-plus weeks of trying without a single response, my ambition is flagging. But I can't find it in me to give up. Not yet. Not after finally getting everything I wanted. Being so close to having it all. I know for a fact that I did nothing wrong this time. I just need to get Sarah to realize that. And I could if she would ever let me speak to her and explain. It doesn't seem like I'm ever going to get that chance, though.

I'm about to send that text when my mother's face pops up on my phone, calling me. I haven't really talked to her these past few weeks. Just quick hellos and gotta-runs to avoid discussing Sarah and what happened. I'm disappointed enough in myself. I don't want to hear the disappointment in my mother's voice on top of that. But I suppose I've skirted this conversation as long as I possibly could. My mother has more dogged determination than I do sometimes. It's time for me to face it.

I sigh heavily and move back to the bunk area of the tour

bus and slide into mine before answering. No one else is back here, so I'll have a little privacy. "Hey Ma, how are you?"

There's a brief silence before, "Oh, is my son talking to me now?"

I chuckle, "Ma, I talked to you twice this week. Of course, I'm talking to you."

"No, you haven't *talked* to me in weeks. You're too-busy-Mr. Rockstar anymore to talk to his own mother."

I can tell she's smiling while she says this, so I'm not worried she's mad at me, but I cringe at the 'Mr. Rockstar' comment just the same. She knows that bugs the shit out of me, and only says it when she wants to annoy me. "Well, I'm sorry about that. I have some time now if you do. We're on the road to Phoenix."

"Well, be careful."

"I'm not driving the bus," I laugh.

"Pfft. You know what I mean," she says sternly. "Be careful in strange new places."

"I will. I promise." I'm dying to hear any gossip on the off chance it involves Sarah. "How are things at home? Is it snowing yet? What's the latest and greatest in the land of Chandler?"

"Yes, it's a real blizzard here. I almost didn't make it home from work; the roads are so bad. You're lucky you're in the sunshine right now. You should take your mother on tour during the winter."

I laugh at the mental picture of my mother on the tour bus with us. If anything, we would eat better than we have been lately, and probably have clean clothes more often.

"As for gossip, you are the hot topic, of course," she brags. "All the ladies in my book club talk about is my son, the famous musician, whose song is now in the top ten on the charts. The big la dee da."

That little fact is pretty amazing too. Our first single is precisely number ten, so barely "top ten," but it's still a massive accomplishment. I only wish we could celebrate with Sarah since she had so much to do with it. She deserves a lot of credit for her work on the arrangement of that song. It improved one hundred percent on the first day she worked with us, and then went even further.

"Why does that make you so quiet?" she asks, knowing instinctively, like only a mother can that something is wrong.

I need to take a few deep breaths before speaking, or else I'm going to lose it. I don't want to be crying to my mother like a fucking teenager. I've been an emotional wreck since Vegas, and I can't seem to pull my shit together. "I fucked up. I truly fucked everything up."

"With Sarah." She doesn't ask a question, just makes the statement. She doesn't have to ask. She knows.

"Yes. With Sarah. And I think this time it's beyond repair."

There's silence for a minute before she asks, "What did you do, Ryan?" There's no blame or accusation in her voice, not the disappointment I expected. Just expressing deep concern, which honestly feels worse. I want someone to yell and scream at me for what happened. Punch me or something physical, something tangible to make me feel the pain outside that I'm feeling inside.

I tell her the gory details of that night, and of all my

attempts to explain to Sarah what happened to no avail. I also begrudgingly include the sordid history and episode with Reese that started all the trust issues in the first place. I'm not proud of any of it, but I need to get it out.

"I'll be honest with you, son, if she were me, I'd be exactly the same way. I'd be done with you too."

This doesn't surprise me one bit. My mother doesn't put up with bullshit, just like Sarah. I mostly expected this response. "I know. I don't blame her. I just need to know how to fix this. *Can* I fix this?"

"The only thing that can help something like this is time," A sadness grows in her voice. "And that's not a guaranteed fix either. Just give her some more time. Maybe she'll come around."

"Should I even keep trying to talk to her? I feel like an idiot sending her all these texts she never reads and leaving her voicemails she never listens to. If I'm wasting my time, why should I keep doing it? Why keep trying?"

"Time spent telling someone you love them is never wasted, Ryan. Remember that," she says. "Even if they don't say it back, the universe hears you. And you'll be surprised how the universe responds sometimes. Keep doing what you're doing. You just need to be patient."

I sigh, frustrated with the entire situation, knowing she's right. "Patience is my middle name."

"No, it's not. It's James. I know, I gave it to you. Check your birth certificate," she deadpans. My mother, the comedian.

# # #

The show in Phoenix is a massive deal for us since big wigs from the record label will be there to see our show, and discuss a possible tour change up this summer to open for another band in bigger venues. It would be an excellent opportunity to get our faces and music in front of more people. Once our song hit the top fifty with a bullet, and radio stations started to really push us in their rotations, the song took off like wildfire. Vanessa is nearly beside herself with excitement at meeting with the label to discuss any details. Right now, it's just supposed to be a meet and greet, but she's optimistic it will turn into a bigger conversation.

Backstage before the show, I sit with my phone and my earbuds in, watching Sarah's video again and sipping a water bottle. I haven't touched a drop of alcohol since the Vegas incident, and to be honest, I don't miss it. Watching any of Sarah's videos calms my nerves enough to make me functional for our shows. I realized I didn't need the alcohol after all. I just needed Sarah. I also know I'm lucky to be able to just stop drinking as I have, since so many others in my position can't. I think about that each and every time I turn down a drink and get a, "Are you sure?" question, like there's a requirement to be drinking since I'm in a fucking rock band. I'm lucky I can just smile and say, "no thanks" and be done. Sure, I get weird looks when I pass on a drink, but if that makes me a nerd, I'm a fucking nerd. And I'm damned proud of it too.

The label execs arrive, and smiles and handshakes are passed around with introductions. I am so horrible at names, though; once I hear a name, it flies out of my head, never to be remembered again. That's no different now. I caught maybe one name out of the five thrown at me. I also recognize only one guy from when we first signed our deal, and the only reason I remember him is his slight British accent. He's an ex-pat from England who is determined to lose his poshness. "Ian, good to see you again."

"Good to see you too," he says. "It's an exciting time for you guys, eh? The new record is brilliant, by the way."

"Thanks. That's kind of you to say."

"What's that you're watching?" He notices my phone and curiously looks at the screen. "Isn't that Sarah...something... Lawrence?"

"Yeah! You know Sarah?"

"I know *of* her. That song is getting a lot of buzz on the streaming sites. She's on my list to watch the next couple of months. Hopefully, her next release is just as good. She has promise."

"Are you kidding? She helped us write this album."

Ian looks taken aback. "She did? I need to start paying attention to album credits better...How well do you know her?"

"I know her really well," I say, and the pang in my heart is so strong, I almost lose my cool in front of this label exec. *That's the second time today. What the fuck?* I clear my throat and press on. "I've got more video of her singing other songs live that aren't on her channel yet. If you like this one, you'll love those."

"Can you send them to me? I'd love to see them and see where we can go from there." He hands me a business card with his email address, and I nod and immediately put it into my wallet so I don't lose it. Sarah deserves a shot at getting her music out there as much as we did, if not more.

"So, you like the new album?" I ask, not wanting to forget the reason they're actually here.

"Absolutely. It's genius. We all think so, which is why we're here. Josh over there," he points to the short man at the end of their group who looks a bit like Danny DeVito, "is the manager for Incendiary Ink, and he wants to see you guys live before deciding on adding you to the bill for the summer."

We all look at Danny DeVito/Josh with nervous smiles and nods, unsure what to say to that.

"Well, after you watch the show, we're sure you'll see why Indigo King would be a perfect addition to your tour," Vanessa's smile is so wide I'm surprised her jaw doesn't creak. "The songs speak for themselves practically. And these guys know how to put on a show. You'll love it."

"Well then," Ian glances at his watch, claps his hands together, and ushers the rest out the door with Vanessa following. "We'll let you get to it. Have a good show."

"Thanks," the three of us say in unison as they leave the green room, then we look at each other and start silently high-fiving and fist-bumping. To open for Incendiary Ink would be too amazing for words. Their summer shed tours are infamous for selling out in minutes.

Vanessa comes back after a little while with a strange expression. "Did you all forget how to speak? 'Thanks?' That's all you can say to those guys? Really?" She crosses her arms across her chest to emphasize her displeasure.

We all stand there, gaping at her in silence. Apparently,

we're not men of many words today. She looks furious, though. *Why would she be so mad?* We were perfectly polite. I didn't even swear once.

"I'm just kidding." Her smile is back, and she throws her arms out wide for a group hug. "You guys were fantastic. Thanks for not swearing or embarrassing me."

"We would never dream of it," Jude winks at me and joins in the hug.

"Never," I echo with a broad smile of my own. But my mind is still on Sarah. I'm so excited that Ian seemed genuinely interested in her music. *I know she didn't want to go on tour with my band and me, but would that be different if she performed her own music? On her own tour? How much more would that complicate things between us?* Right. Like there's anything between us now to begin with.

Before we head out on stage, I take my mother's advice and send another text to Sarah.

> RYAN: Hey Sarah. Hope you're doing well. Just ran into a label exec who knew about you and your music. So, I bragged you up to him of course, because you are fucking amazing if you recall. Keep an eye out for something from my label. Maybe chase your own dream for a change? Love, Ryan.

We then put on the best fucking show of our tour so far, and jump right back on the bus to take over the next city and do it all over again.

30

The River

SARAH

Accident. Traumatic brain injury. Internal bleeding. Third-degree burns. Critical condition. Surgery. These are all words. They are words that I'm sure I've heard before at some point in my life. But as I listen to them now coming from the strange man on the phone, they don't make any sense to me at all. None of these words have anything to do with my little brother, so why does he keep saying they do? As he keeps talking, he tells me that I'm probably in shock, but that's just dumb. I'm not in shock. There's nothing for me to be in shock about. He also says that someone will be coming to my house to get me, but why would they do that? I don't want to go anywhere. Benji and Joe will be home any minute now, and I need to wait here for them. I put Gunner in his crate so he can wait too.

I glance down and see a broken mug on the kitchen floor

with sprays of hot chocolate on the nearby cupboard and wonder how that got there, but the thought skitters away and out of my head. I'm supposed to be doing something, but I can't remember what it is. I see that my phone is still on a call, and I hang it up. *Benji might be trying to call me. Or Joe. Maybe I should try calling them.* As I lift my phone, water drips onto the screen, and I raise a hand to my face. My cheeks are wet. I'm crying. *Why the hell am I crying?* A shiver runs through my whole body, and I'm suddenly ice cold all over. *I need a sweater.* I head towards the stairs to grab one from my room when the doorbell rings. *Maybe Benji forgot his key. It's absolutely going to be Benji. It's going to be Benji and Joe, and they're both going to be totally fine and tell me all about their shopping escapades. It's totally fine.*

When I open the door, the flashing red and blue lights of the police car blind me, and the stupor I'm in lifts briefly. The windshield wipers squeak as they slide back and forth on glass, pausing for a second in between. The surrounding snow seems to muffle every sound except the blood rushing loudly through my ears. That's not muffled at all. It's a roar.

The police officer on the doorstep takes off her uniform cap, and the falling snow sticks to her hair. I can't stop looking at it as the snowflakes turn red and blue with the lights. *This isn't happening. This cannot be happening.*

"Are you Sarah Lawrence?"

Her voice pulls me back again, and I start to shake uncontrollably. "Yes," I whisper, begging her with my eyes to be a figment of my overactive imagination. But she doesn't disappear. "I'm Sarah Lawrence."

The officer nods, "Are you related to Benjamin Lawrence, ma'am?"

She called me ma'am. *So formal.* My fists clench and my nails dig into my palms until it hurts. "He's my little brother. Well, he's a lot taller than me, but I still call him my little brother. Even though he hates it, but I can't help it. It's a habit, you know?" My voice is getting higher and higher in pitch with each word, and I can't seem to stop talking or catch my breath. "Where is he? Where's Benji?"

"Can we step inside the house, ma'am?" she asks, stepping forward.

"Nooo," I keen, unmoving. "Where is my baby brother?" The hair on the back of my neck is standing straight up, and the goosebumps on my arms aren't from the frigid night air. I keep asking her the same question, but I don't really want to know.

She nods at me, understanding that I'm not moving until I get an answer. That I *need* an answer now. "There's been an accident with one of the city's snowplow trucks and your brother's vehicle. He's been taken to Memorial hospital along with his passenger. We were called and asked to take you there as soon as possible since the storm is worsening. I'm sorry, but that's all I know." Her eyes are wide with dread and pity, and I don't know how to interpret that.

I stand still, staring at her blankly. All the words I heard in the last ten minutes tumble endlessly through my brain, but no words of my own are making their way to my throat. *Take me as soon as possible. What does that even mean? What does any of this mean?*

I can't handle it anymore. My breath turns shallow as my heart feels like it's slowing down and stopping. My ears build up pressure as if they're about to pop like I'm in an airplane again. *Maybe I'm still on my way to Las Vegas, and I'm just having a bad dream on the flight. The last few weeks haven't even happened.*

"Ma'am? You should grab a coat and some shoes. We need to go...."

All at once, the avalanche of emotions trapped inside my soul rips itself loose. Reality crashes into me with the force of a hundred hurricanes. My shaking turns into full-on shudders, and I grab my stomach, bend over, and let out the most gut-wrenching scream ever heard by human ears.

31

Home

RYAN

We played Tucson the next night and are now on our way to our gig in El Paso scheduled for tomorrow night. Incendiary Ink's manager was impressed enough by our show in Phoenix that we've been added to their summer tour as their opening band. We've been riding that high ever since Vanessa gave us the news. Even though this is a huge milestone, it's still bittersweet having to celebrate alone. I know I have Matt and Jude, and even my mother, but it's nowhere near the same thing. It still leaves me feeling a bit empty like something is missing. That missing piece is Sarah.

The drive to El Paso is long and lackluster, with nothing but desert scenery flying by, all brown earth and blue sky with occasional bits of green for flavor. None of my usual time wasters are working today for some reason. I tried playing my guitar, but nothing sounded right. Played some cards with Matt but got bored within minutes. Tried reading and watching a movie, but my attention span is like that of a gnat today. I feel like I'm jumping out of my skin, I'm so fucking restless, and I don't know why. I head to the back and try some push-ups and chin-ups to expend all this excess energy, but these aren't cutting it either. When my phone rings, I'm sitting on the floor between bunks, catching my breath after a set of sit-ups. It's my mother, at an odd time for her to call, but I don't mind. *Good. Maybe she can distract me for a while.*

"Hey there, Ma," I get up, sit on my bunk, and get comfortable for a time-wasting conversation.

"Hey Ryan, how are you?" There's something very off in her voice. I can't pinpoint exactly what it is, just something decidedly *wrong.*

"Mom? What's wrong?"

She doesn't answer right away, and I can hear her breathing on the other end of the line. She's choosing her words very carefully for some reason.

"Mom. Tell me what's wrong," I demand. A million thoughts of a million different horrible scenarios are racing through my imagination. So many things that could be wrong. And I'm a million miles away.

"It's...Benji Lawrence," Her voice is tentative, like there is so much more for her to say.

"What about him?" My chest is clenching so tightly I can barely breathe. *What the fuck happened to Benji?* My mind continues its race, veering off even more imaginary side roads. "Just spit it out. What happened with Benji? Is Sarah alright?"

"There was an accident the other night. Remember I told you how bad the weather was?"

"I remember. Go on."

"Benji's car got hit by a snowplow that ran a red light, right in the driver's side."

"Oh my god. Oh my god. Please tell me he's okay." I jump up and hit my head on the bunk above me, but I don't care. I run my hand through my hair and shake my hand out.

She hesitates again before going on. "I don't know for sure. I'm only hearing rumors and people talking. You know how it is here."

"Well, what are they saying?"

"His boyfriend is okay, I guess, just a broken leg and a few other small things, thank goodness. But Benji...they had to put him in a coma because of how bad his injuries are."

"How bad are they?" Suddenly I'm super aware of the road rolling by under the bus, and I'm lightheaded. I sit back down again before I fall down.

"I don't know. Pretty bad. They're still saying critical condition...He might not make it." I drop my head into my hand. Benji didn't deserve this. He's a good kid. Sure he had some trouble when his mom died, but who wouldn't? He wouldn't hurt a fly, even if he had to. This isn't fair. This isn't fucking fair.

"What about Sarah? Who's with her? Who's taking care of her?" She's got to be going out of her mind right now. Sarah and her brother are so close. I've never seen siblings that care about each other as much as they do. This has got to be killing her.

"Jenny's been there as much as she can," she says. "Luke's mom is in my book club, and she's the one I heard the news from. Lorelai goes to be with her too, bless her heart."

"Okay," I head toward the front of the bus. "I'll be there as soon as I can." Matt, Jude, and Vanessa all look at me, surprised. I hold a finger up to them to wait before barraging me with the questions I know they will throw at me.

"Ryan, what about your tour? I can go sit with her. I don't mind. I was thinking of doing that anyway...."

"Go if you want, but I'll be there as fast as I can get there."

"But we're in the middle of another snowstorm. Flights might not...."

"I don't care if I need to drive straight across the whole fucking country. I'm coming." Surely, she must know she can't talk me out of this. Nothing could stop me from going. *Nothing.*

"Fine. Just be careful and keep me posted on your travels."

"I will. And Mom, thanks for letting me know."

"Of course, Ryan. I knew it was the right thing to do this time."

We hang up, and I sit down heavily on the couch at the front of the bus, elbows on my knees and face in my hands. I need to get home, but how the fuck am I going to do that in the middle of a fucking tour? I impulsively said I'd go, but I realize now that I can't just up and leave. We have tickets sold. People depend on us. On *me.* I run my hands down my face. My heart is being ripped to shreds right now.

"Ryan, what's happened?" Vanessa asks softly, as she sits

across from me and lays a concerned hand on my knee. Matt and Jude turn to me from their card game.

"Sarah's brother, Benji, was in an accident, and he's in critical condition," I say, somehow able to keep it together. "He's in an induced coma due to his injuries. But he might not make it." I choke on the last sentence but still hold back the tears.

"Oh my gosh," Vanessa gasps, a hand going to her chest in shock. Matt and Jude have equal reactions.

"You've got to go, dude," Matt says, and Jude nods his agreement, looking a little pale at the news.

"Of course," Vanessa says. "Family first, remember?"

I look at each of them, astounded at their response. "But what about the tour? People depend on us...."

Vanessa gives my knee a light squeeze. "We only have a couple of shows between now and New Year. I kind of wanted to go home to check on my parents and spend the holiday with them anyway. It'll be fine."

"Yeah, don't sweat it, man," Jude says. "Go be with Sarah. And tell her we're all pulling for her brother. He seems like a real sweet kid."

"I'll try to find a flight home for you out of El Paso," Vanessa pulls out her laptop. "We should be there in about two hours? I think? Don't worry. I'll arrange everything."

I am so grateful for this group of people who are beyond understanding and unselfish. The knot that had formed in my chest with worry about the tour unfurls, but then wraps itself around the concern I feel for Benji and for Sarah. The thought of Sarah alone in a hospital waiting room or at Benji's bedside by herself shatters me. I want to be there for both of them. Whether she wants me there or not. To be there for them in any way I can, *if* I can. I want to be home. I *need* to be home.

"I found a flight for you that leaves tonight at nine o'clock, stops over in Vegas, but gets you to Cleveland around seven in the morning. It's not the greatest airline, but it seems like the best option, is that okay?"

"Yeah, I don't care. That's fine," I'm relieved that there's something to get me there. I wasn't kidding about driving if I need to. "Thanks, Vanessa."

We arrive at the hotel in El Paso where I was going to stay, but instead, I immediately order a car to take me to the airport to grab my flight to Vegas. We all say our goodbyes and half-hearted holiday wishes with a plan to reconvene the tour after New Year. I sincerely thank each of them for letting me do this. I know it's a sudden change to our immediate plans, and I'm nothing but grateful.

Once my car finally arrives, I begin my journey home and to Sarah's side. If she'll let me.

Only A Lifetime

SARAH

E very room I pass as I come and go has the same soft lights and beeps and hisses of machines escaping their open doors. The beeping of the machines keeping track of Benji's vital signs and keeping him alive doesn't register in my head anymore. They've become part of the background noise that permeates this hospital floor, along with the antiseptic smell. I'm only supposed to be in his room for fifteen minutes at a time, but the nurses usually let me stay as long as I want. When I do step out to go to the cafeteria or visit with someone who's come to see us, I sneak down to Joe's room to check on him. He doesn't have any family, so I try to prioritize visiting him. His families' death found him in the same grief support group Benji was in. That's where they fell in love.

He was fortunate to only suffer a broken right leg and

some second-degree burns on his left. He's also got some soft tissue damage in his neck from the impact and some cuts and bruises, but he'll fully recover in time. Benji wasn't so fortunate and took the full brunt of the snowplow. The police said he did have some luck on his side. Had he been in a regular vehicle and not an SUV, he wouldn't be here now. I like to think our mom had a hand in that bit of saving grace, seeing as how I traded cars so he'd have the SUV instead of me. The universe knew he needed it more than I did. Now the universe needs to bring him back to me completely.

I rap lightly on Joe's door before peeking my head in when I hear more than one voice inside, and find Joe laughing with a young woman with a platinum blonde pixie haircut that could pass as Tinkerbell with only the slightest effort.

"Hey," I don't want to interrupt their visit. "I can come back later...."

"No, no. Come on in," Joe says. "Sarah, this is my extremely talented artist friend, Olivia, who has volunteered to paint a replica of Van Gogh's 'Starry Night' on my hideous cast for me. Olivia, this is Benji's lovely, if fashion stunted sister, Sarah."

I give her a small wave as the magnitude of her project hits me. "Wow, that's ambitious of you. I can't wait to see it."

"Liv's the most amazing artist I know." Joe pats Olivia's hand. "I wouldn't trust my canvas of a cast to anyone else."

"Well then, it's an honor to meet you, Olivia," I head back to the door. "I don't want to intrude on your visit...."

"No, it's okay," Olivia stands and grabs her bag. "I need to get going anyway. The storm looks to be picking up again. It was lovely to meet you, Sarah. And Joe, I'll be by in the morning to take you home when you're released. Just text me." She leans over, and they air kiss like Joe always does, and gives me a quick wave as she leaves.

"Isn't she darling?" Joe asks, once Olivia is gone.

"She is." I sit on the edge of his bed, careful not to disturb his leg. "You're being released tomorrow?" I ask, not sure how I feel about that. I've liked having him in the same building to come to visit and talk to when sitting and staring at Benji becomes too much. If he's not here for me to do that with, I'm not sure what I'll do.

"That's what my hot doctor tells me." He forces a smile. We both have been doing that a lot lately. However, his eyes are especially poignant, bloodshot from crying mixing with his bruises from the accident. It becomes a severe contradiction that is hard to look at.

"Well, I'm glad you have Olivia to help you. Did you want to stay at our house? You're more than welcome to."

"I would, but I'm now allergic to stairs of any kind. And no offense, but you could build another dog with the hair that comes off of Gunner daily. No thank you very much."

That makes me chuckle. "No offense taken."

Joe's face grows serious and sad, and he stares down at his hands that are also cut up and bruised. "I won't be able to visit him, will I?"

"What?"

"Because I'm not immediate family. I won't be able to visit with him."

"Yes, you will. This is a twenty-first-century hospital.

Significant others are allowed to visit patients. Plus, I think I'm the one who approves visits."

Relief washes over him, and I can see the worry lift from his shoulders. "I'll do that first thing tomorrow before I leave then. Is there any change?"

"No, not really," I glance down at my own hands. "Though the doctor did say his brain swelling is going down, so we might be able to try to take him off the ventilator earlier than we thought. So some good news, I guess." I shrug a shoulder, knowing it's not the spectacular news we both want to hear so badly. But Benji's poor body has been through so much; any improvement is a miracle.

"He's a fighter," Joe says, and our eyes meet, both of us knowing his words are untrue, but wanting desperately to believe the lie. It's just something you say when someone faces what Benji is facing. I've never before wished with every fiber of my being that my brother was a real spitfire, a god-damned warrior, willing to fight for his life. A small part of me wonders what part of Benji is winning the battle within himself. I'm not a praying person, but I pray he finds the fighter inside.

"Only with you," I joke, trying to lighten the mood, but Joe's mouth doesn't even twitch towards a smile.

"Did I tell you we were fighting?" His voice is barely the ghost of a whisper. He glances up at me with so much guilt in his eyes that I almost fall apart. "We were arguing about a stupid candle we bought you for Christmas. By the way, we got you a stupid candle for Christmas, but it's probably shattered or burnt up and melted on Huron Road somewhere." He takes a deep breath before continuing. "Anyway, we were fighting about what scent we got versus what scent we should have gotten when the accident happened. It was so dumb." His eyes are now full, and the tears are overflowing down his cheeks. He grabs the top of his sheet to wipe at them.

"Joe, honey." I reach out for his arm, and he lets me rest my hand on his. "The police already determined you guys weren't at fault. It was the plow truck driver's fault for running that red light."

"I know, I know," he sniffles. "That's not what I'm talking about. I'm saying that my last conversation with Benji was an argument. My last memory of him will be of us fucking fighting, instead of kind and loving words I know we both felt, and I hate it. He deserved such a better memory than that. He just deserved better."

"Stop it. Just stop it." My tears are falling now too, and I'm surprised I even have any left anymore.

"But it's true...."

"No, I mean stop talking about Benji in the past tense. He is not dead. And he's not going to die either, so just stop it right now, Joe."

"I'm sorry, I didn't mean to -"

"And you'll have plenty of opportunities to tell him how much you love him, with as many kind words as you can come up with, and say them to his face." I have to get up. I need to leave the room. "I'm sorry. I'll talk to you later." I can hear Joe call after me as I open and close his door behind me, but I don't stop.

Our conversation got too close to feelings I don't want to face. I sounded tough and positive in there, but I don't know that I believe anything I just said. It's what you tell yourself, though. And what you tell others in situations like these. It's just what you do. Just words you say. They don't really have any meaning or truth, just like when Joe said Benji was a fighter. We both know that's not true, and he would just as soon give up on life if it was an option. Even though that knowledge claws at both of us, we want to believe so hard he'd fight, we try to convince ourselves of it.

I get a cup of burnt tasting coffee from the cafeteria and sit at one of the round tables to people watch for a while. I can't bring myself to go back to Benji's room yet. Sometimes I need to work myself up to it. Watching people come and go, it's easy to see that nobody likes being in a hospital; even the people who work here seem depressed. It's interesting to observe how worry and pain show themselves on different faces. Some have red-rimmed eyes, some are stoic and reserved, and some flash forced cheer as if willing themselves to be happy will erase their problems. I'm probably some weird combination of all three. Honestly, it seems to change from minute to minute.

As night falls outside and the snow continues to whip around in the parking lot lights, I realize we're nearing two days since the accident. Almost forty-eight hours have passed since Benji was thrown into this hell, since we all were. Tomorrow is Christmas Eve, and I can't think about celebrating in any way. I won't be able to celebrate anything until Benji comes back to us. And even then, the road in front of him to get back to one hundred percent will be so hard. But I hold on to that thought. I'll take a hard road instead of a dead end. I'll take an uphill battle over a hole in the ground. I'll take anything, so long as he isn't taken from me.

"Are you doing okay, honey?" A familiar voice breaks through my reverie, and I look up from my coffee to find Mrs. Crawford standing across the table from me. I didn't expect her here. She's one of the last people I expected to see.

"Mrs. Crawford." I nod, confused. "I'll be okay. What are you doing here?" Maybe she has a friend who has a hospital stay that she came to visit. Hopefully, they're in a better situation than we are.

"I came to see you." She pulls out the chair across from me and sits down, dropping her purse on the chair between us. "I promised my son I would check in on you." She eyes me, "Plus, I wanted to come. So, here I am. How is poor Benji? And how are *you* doing, niñita?" She reaches across the table and takes my hand into hers, and I fall apart.

I don't know why her simple act of holding my hand, or asking how I'm doing, or being reminded of Ryan, and all I've lost and might still lose, or everything all at once, but the last strand of strength I was holding on to snaps when she touches me. I cry so hard I almost can't breathe. Mrs. Crawford comes around the table and pulls me into a hug. She holds me until I cry myself out and don't have a tear left to drop. People around the cafeteria are trying to avoid looking in our direction, and seeing such raw emotion they're trying to deny themselves, but I don't care. I needed that so bad. I've cried, sure, but only bits here and there, never letting go and allowing myself to feel this deep pain. I haven't had someone I could let go like that with until she showed up.

She grabs a tissue out of her purse and hands it to me. "Here, clean yourself up now." She rubs my back as I attempt to clean up my face. "Now that you've felt it, you know it's there. You don't have to be afraid of it anymore."

I look at her, and I know she's right. I have been afraid to let myself feel all that hurt. I've been fearful of letting it out, thinking I wouldn't be able to stop, but now I know I can control it. And I survived it. And will survive it again should it overflow again.

"Thank you." I'm so grateful she showed up just now. "Thank you so much for that."

"You're welcome," she says, sitting on the other side of the table now that I've got myself under some semblance of control.

We talk for almost an hour about Benji's accident, and his current condition and prognosis. Of all the years I've known her, I never spoke to her like this or for this long. It's nice. And unexpected. Then she starts talking about Ryan, and I stiffen at his name.

She notices my reaction and grabs my hand again. "Sarah, believe me, I'm not saying this because he's my only son, but Ryan is a good man." She sees my reactionary frown. "I know. I know. I would have done the same as you, and I even told him so. And regardless of whether anything happened with that la puta in his hotel room, which I've confirmed with two other people, nothing did; Regardless of that, he should never have put himself into that situation for you to see in the first place."

I nod, agreeing with her that he put himself in a bad

situation. Whether or not I believe nothing happened with that girl is another story.

"Did you know he's not had a drop to drink since that night?"

That shocks me, and I shake my head. I can't believe he can do that while on tour with all the temptation surrounding him. That's an amazing and colossal acknowledgment that things had gotten out of control. It's very mature of him to take matters into his own hands and face his problems head-on like that. It's lovely to hear.

"And - they will be opening for some Ink band this summer, which I guess is a big deal. Well, it is to Ryan anyway."

"Incendiary Ink?" I'm amazed. "That is huge. Ryan and the band must be thrilled." I am genuinely so happy for him that he's getting his life together and finally seeing the success he deserves. My heart aches a little, knowing he's now doing all these great things without me, but it's for the best. We were a nice thought, but it could never work. And now, with Benji and his uncertain future, I'm glad Ryan doesn't have to deal with all of this, and can focus on his career as he should. I'm mature enough to want that for him.

"He is happy." She frowns and moves her head from side to side as though he's not happy at all.

"Is he not happy?" I'm confused. "He should be ecstatic. That's a big break for them."

She looks across at me from under her lashes, unsure if she wants to say what she's about to say. "He'd be happier if he had a certain someone to share things with."

Her words hang in the air between us, unsure of where

to land. I glance down at the table, unable to meet her gaze. Admittedly, before Benji's accident, there wasn't a day that passed without me thinking about Ryan. It's hard not to when he's texting and leaving messages every day, even if I don't read or listen to them. But more than that, I missed *him* terribly. I felt like the other half of my soul was missing. Since the accident, that empty feeling has been magnified tenfold, but I don't allow myself to think about Ryan. I have so much more to worry about than my love life right now. I can't even consider anything more than Benji, including myself.

Mrs. Crawford gets up from her chair and puts her coat on, glancing out the frosted window at the snow that piles up outside. She comes over, and I stand to give her a hug. The grip on each other is stronger this time and more meaningful between us. "Just keep your heart open, Sarah." She grabs my cheeks like my grandmother used to do, making me laugh a little. "The heart is the hardest working muscle in the body. You don't have to protect it too much. It can take more than you think. And it can also give. Remember that, okay?"

"Okay," I nod, so thankful she came around when she did. "Be safe driving home."

"I will," she says, and heads out of the cafeteria and into the storm to head home.

It's automatic for me to tell everyone to drive safely now as they leave. Even though Benji was driving perfectly safely when they were hit, I'm compelled to remind everyone. If telling someone to be safe driving is my way of telling someone I care about them, so be it.

I head back up to Benji's room, ruminating on the

discussion with Mrs. Crawford about Ryan, and the steps he's taken to improve since Vegas. It was great to learn how well he and the band are doing. I've been following the success of their first single with not a small amount of pride. They all deserve every success they're achieving. And I admit, it would be nice to dream about a relationship working out with Ryan, but I stop myself before I get too far into it. As much as I still love him, and yes, I still love him, I can't allow myself to wish for things I can't have. Especially now.

33

Break On Me

RYAN

The first leg of the journey goes smoothly and without issue, but I've been stuck in Vegas for six and a half hours as flight after flight to Cleveland gets canceled due to another storm hitting the area with lake effect snow. That means some of the surrounding major cities and airports are getting hit with snow too, so finding alternative routes is extremely difficult.

I don't know what it is about airports that bring out the worst in people, but I can feel some empathy for how it happens. The airline employee behind the ticket counter is trying his best to accommodate all of us stuck in the same situation, with others missing connecting flights to even further destinations. I'm trying to be patient since I know he's just doing his job, but after being stuck here for so long, it's becoming more and more challenging to keep my cool.

"It appears I might be able to get you to Indianapolis with a connecting flight to Columbus, which is still open. That's the closest I'm going to be able to get you for a while. Could you perhaps rent a car in Columbus to travel to your final destination?"

I do some quick math in my head for travel times between cities, but then think, *fuck it.* "That's fine. I'll take that."

"You don't have any checked bags, do you?" he glances around me, suddenly worried.

"No, just this carry-on."

"Let me print your tickets for you." He's moving like molasses. I know he's really not, but now that I have a workable option, I want to be on the move as soon as possible. "Oh, my." He frowns at the ticket.

"What is it? What's wrong?"

"Your flight leaves from gate D54, and we're currently at gate D12." He points to the airport map, showing that these gates are on complete opposite ends of the concourse from each other.

Fuck me. "How much time do I have?" I say a silent prayer that he says something reasonable. But of course, my prayer gets ignored.

The poor guy swallows hard, "It just started boarding...."

I snatch the ticket out of his hand with a muttered "Thanks," and take off running at light speed towards gate D54. I eventually get to the gate by bobbing and weaving between people, and trying to pass on the correct side of the sedentary folks on the people-movers without bowling them over. I'm completely out of breath and have a stitch in my side, but I try to hide all of that as I approach.

An older female airline employee at the door to the gate smiles at me as she puts her hand out to take and scan my ticket. "Are you Mr. Crawford?"

"Yes?"

"They called from the other gate and had us hold the plane for you."

"Seriously?" I'm still breathing heavily from the run and shocked at the generosity. Airlines aren't exactly known as being so accommodating.

"It's only been a few minutes. You must be a fast runner." She hands me back my ticket. "Merry Christmas."

"Damn, I almost felt special for a minute there," I joke.

"Well, we try to make everyone feel special," she winks.

Not sure if she was flirting with me, or pushing their marketing motto, I jog down the gangway to board the plane to Indianapolis.

Once in Indianapolis, I again need to run to the next gate to catch the connecting flight to Columbus, but I make it in time to stand in line with everyone else waiting to board. I've only been able to doze for a few minutes here and there, and between the wait, and the time difference traveling back east, I can't tell if I'm coming or going. Since leaving Las Vegas, I haven't eaten anything but the ginger cookies they give you on the plane. In Columbus, I take a minute to grab some food and then check in with my mother as I walk to the car rental counter.

"So, did you land in Cleveland yet?" my mother asks.

"No, the airport is closed. I'm in Columbus. I'm going to rent a car and drive the rest of the way." I specifically didn't tell her all of my travel plans for this very reason. More often than not, her ignorance is my bliss when it comes to things like this. I knew if there were hiccups, she'd worry even more. Like she's about to.

"Ryan, are you crazy? If the airport is closed, you shouldn't be driving either." And there she is. The overprotective mother.

"I'm coming from the south. There's no lake effect snow down here," I say, trying to appease her worry. "I should be there sometime tonight."

"Still, you're going to drive right into it."

"I don't have a lot of choices right now. I'll be careful, I promise."

"Oof. Dios mío. My son the daredevil," she sighs. "Keep an eye out for Santa Claus, why don't you? He can give you a ride in all this snow. Crazy man."

"I'll be fine." I approach the car rental counter. "I need to go. I'll talk to you later."

"I went and saw your Sarah," she says before I can disconnect, and I stop in my tracks. *She visited Sarah? My Sarah? What's that about?*

"Oh?"

"I went to the bat for you, so you'd better not screw it up again when you get here."

I have a million questions, though I'll be there myself in a few hours. "What did you say to her? What did she say? More importantly, how is Benji doing?"

"Sadly, there's no change with Benji. But she needs you, Ryan. She needs a good man to lean on. That girl has done so much on her own; she needs to share her burden with someone. Do you know what I'm saying?"

"I do. And you're right, she's had to handle too much by herself. But I don't know if she'll let me in after....what happened." I want to be that person for her to lean on, but I'm afraid Sarah built the wall between us too high for me to overcome.

"All you can do is try. I think you're coming to be with her will go a long way towards healing what's broken with you two."

"I hope so." I glance at the clock behind the counter and feel the pressure to get on the road and to Sarah already. I'm going to have a hard enough time keeping to the speed limit as it is, despite the weather. "I'm getting a car now. I'll call you later."

"I love you."

I pull the phone away from my ear and stare at it briefly. My mother doesn't usually say that on the phone. All of this must be affecting her. "...Love you too."

As I start my drive back home, I try to plan what I'll say to Sarah when I see her. But instead, I end up spending the whole time writing another song for her. Inspiration can come out of nowhere and hit when you least expect it. You need to take advantage of it when it strikes or lose it. I use the voice memo app on my phone to record it, so I don't forget it as soon as I step out of the car, which I'm likely to do since I'm so tired. It's not a grand opus or anything, but it's one of the most heartfelt songs I've ever written, outside of 'Almost,' that is.

34

Arms

SARAH

"Here, Lorelai made this for you." Jenny hands me a bag of plastic containers full of food I can't possibly eat all by myself.

I take the bag from her, its weight yanking my arm down. "Tell Lorelai, "Thank you" for thinking of me."

"Any change since I was here yesterday?" She sits beside me and shrugs out of her coat, damp with melted snow.

"His brain swelling is still going down, which is good, but he had another blood pressure crash this morning." I shiver, remembering the doctors and nurses rushing to bring it back up. It's always so scary when you're ordered to leave the room so they can perform some emergency activity with him. "But they might try to bring him out of the coma and off the ventilator as early as tomorrow, so that's encouraging." I've been trying not to raise my hopes up too high about anything, but when they told me, I allowed myself to want to believe something good might happen for a change.

"That's wonderful news." Jenny rubs my arm. "And I heard Joe was released this morning too. So there's good news all over today." She's trying so hard to raise my spirits, but I don't feel it right now. With it being Christmas Eve, and having to spend the holiday here in the hospital while the only family member left to me lies in a coma, my mood is decidedly dark. I love Jenny and my friends, but it's not the same thing.

"Yeah, Joe was able to visit this morning after he got released." I try not to choke up. "It was hard to look at him when he came out of the room. I've never seen Joe so upset."

"I'll bet it was hard on him." Her eyes are misting thinking about it.

"I tried to prepare him before he went in, but there isn't preparing anybody for that initial reaction. He seemed okay by the time he left, though, and his friend Olivia promised to bring him by again tomorrow."

"That's good. And how are you holding up?" She asks me this every time she comes by, and I think she expects me to say something different, but I never do.

"I'm okay," I nod, dragging the hair that's fallen forward behind my ear. Every time I say it, I try to convince myself, but it doesn't work. Not completely anyway. I *want* to be okay, but I want Benji to be okay more than myself.

"Gunner misses you," she chuckles, trying to lighten my mood. "And I think Missy has sworn a blood oath to kill me in my sleep for letting him into our house for so long." Missy is Jenny's thirteen-year-old calico cat. That cat is so mean.

I swear it would kill anyone in their sleep just for the pure fun of it.

"I appreciate you taking care of him for me." I force my lips to smile as I pull the food out of the bag on the low waiting room table.

"I know it's the furthest thing on your mind, but I am sorry your release party isn't going to happen. I know how much you were looking forward to that."

"You're right. It is the last thing on my mind. I actually forgot about it until you just mentioned it. We can have a party later when Benji comes home. It's fine." It really is the last thing on my mind. There's no way I could even think about a party now.

She gives me a look that oozes both empathy and compassion, and not a shred of pity. She gets where I'm coming from. "Can I visit him real quick before I head home?" she asks.

"Of course. Take your time."

Jenny and I have been friends for so long she considers Benji the brother she never had. She's almost as protective of him as I am, and was devastated when she got the news of his accident. I've had to be strong for her, just like I've been strong for everyone who visits, but I don't mind. It's a role I'm familiar with, and I play it well.

I open a couple of the plastic containers to peek and check what Lorelai conjured up for me today. She's a fantastic cook that can give Joe a run for his money, and it all smells delicious, but I know I won't eat it. At least not right away. My appetite has been nonexistent, and I've mainly been subsisting on bitter cafeteria coffee and stale donuts.

While Jenny visits with Benji, I go through my phone, posting updates on my social media to help ward off direct texts and calls. There are a few of those as well I respond to. As I swipe through everything, it strikes me I haven't heard anything from Ryan in almost two days. This is the first real span of time that's passed without at least a quick text. My heart sinks a little, knowing he's most likely given up on me by this point. And I don't blame him. Despite his persistence, I haven't responded to any of his messages in almost a month. I'd give up on me too. I can't expect him to just wait around for me. It's cruel of me to even think he ever should. Whether or not I've been fair to him, he deserves someone who will be straightforward with him. Someone who can let themselves fall completely in love with him. I don't seem to be able to do that. Well, I tried that and got burned. Now I don't think I can do that ever again.

I wipe at the tears starting to fall as I feel sorry for myself. I need to stop that right away. I can't be spending energy on dumb pity parties for myself. I can't be wallowing in my own sorrow here in the middle of the hospital waiting room where everyone can see me. I shut my phone off, deciding not to worry about Ryan anymore tonight, but I can't stop my thoughts from repeating Mrs. Crawford's words: "Just keep your heart open, Sarah," she'd said. I'd love to, but I'm afraid now it's too late for Ryan and me. The door to that particular heart is currently closed to me.

Jenny comes back, wiping away her own tears. She always cries when she leaves Benji's room, she has such a nurturing soul. She grabs her coat, and I walk her to the elevators to see her out. "Please try to eat something." She places her hands on my shoulders and shakes me slightly before hugging me. "You need to keep up your strength."

In more ways than one, I think. "I will. Drive safe, and text me when you get home. Give my love to Luke and your dad. Tell them Merry Christmas for me."

"Will do," she says as the elevator doors open, and she moves to step in but stops abruptly as someone steps out first. We both gape as we look up and find Ryan standing there with his phone in his hand, snow still melting on his hair and shoulders and looking absolutely haggard, but absolutely stunning at the same time. Only he could pull that off. "What the..." Jenny takes a step back and then glances between us. "Did you know he was coming?"

I can't take my eyes off Ryan, who still hasn't said anything, but stares back at me, a look I can't discern on his face. I shake my head in the negative, still unable to say words aloud. I had no idea Ryan was coming back. *Surely his mother would have said something, wouldn't she? What about his tour?* He can't just up and leave...

"What're you...." I start, but as he opens his arms up to me, I can't stop myself from crashing into him. I bury my head in his chest, and as his arms wrap around me and he kisses the top of my head, I instantly feel like I'm home. There are no other words for it. I know this is where I belong. Where I'm safe. I can't believe he's actually here. The tears start, and I hear Jenny get on the elevator silently, leaving us to be alone with each other. He strokes my hair gently while planting kisses on my forehead, then my cheekbones, kissing away my tears, then his lips brush my lips ever so lightly. His hand cups my cheek, and I lean into it, turning to kiss his palm. My god, how I've missed his touch. How I've missed everything about him. How much I've needed him.

"How is he?" he whispers, his voice hoarse. He wipes the hair out of my eyes and studies my face with concern.

"Improving slowly," I nod hopefully, "but improving. Tomorrow might be a big day."

"That's great news." He lifts my chin. "And how are *you* doing, Sarah?" The sound of my name on his lips still makes my skin prickle, and my stomach does a little flip. After everything we've been through, I can't help but feel special when I'm with him.

"I don't know," I say honestly as I meet his gaze and try not to cry again. He'd see right through it if I tried to cover any of my pain up with a lie. He knows me better now than anyone. "I really don't know. To be honest, I think I'm still in shock, even though this happened days ago. I don't know what I'd do if...."

"Shhhh. Don't even go there." He pulls me to him again. His strength, his scent, his soothing words, just his presence makes me feel like a heavy burden is being lifted from my shoulders. I know he would share the difficulty with me if I let him. But I have to let him, and I don't know if I can do that. I've never done that before with anyone, and it scares the shit out of me. He pulls back, "Can I go see him?"

"Of course." I grab his hand, check him in at the nurse's station, and lead him down the hall towards Benji's room.

"He's in room 411 on the left down that way." I stop him before he can go any further. "I should warn you...."

"No, you shouldn't." He kisses me softly again. "If you can handle it, so can I." His sad eyes crinkle in the corners as he gives me a genuine smile that's almost grateful. I stand and hug myself in the middle of the hallway as he goes into Benji's room, still amazed he's here.

I pace a little in front of the nurse's station, garnering strange looks from the now-familiar night nurses coming on duty, trying to gather my scattered thoughts into something resembling sense. After a while, I give up on that impossible task and head back to the waiting room. The shock of seeing Ryan is beginning to wear off, and the reality of what he's done is starting to sink in. He just gave up I don't know how many shows on his tour to be here. *How did he do this? Are Matt and Jude okay with this? His manager? His label? Does he even care?* I don't think he'd be here if it hadn't been worked out, but Ryan can be pretty impulsive. I hope he hasn't done something reckless by coming here to be with me. It dawns on me that it's a relief to have something else to worry about other than Benji's dire circumstances for a minute, even if it is the briefest minute.

When Ryan comes back into the waiting room, his expression is dark and worried, but I can tell he's trying to cover it up for me. He shakes his head at me and covers his eyes with his hands.

"I know," I say and wrap him in my arms this time. He grabs onto me so tightly it's hard to breathe, but I don't mind. I don't mind at all. I know how hard it is to see Benji like this.

Especially the first time. It doesn't get any better, but you do somehow get numb to it after a while. Not entirely, but enough to function. The brain is incredible with what it can adapt to and deal with when it needs to. "C'mon, let's sit for a while."

We sit on the one bench among all the chairs to be closer together, and I snuggle against him with my head on his shoulder, and his arm around me. The waiting room has been empty all evening, and that makes me sad for the other patients on the floor who don't have loved ones to visit with them on Christmas. I'm sure the weather is a huge factor in that.

Ryan gently runs his fingers through my hair as we sit in complete silence for long minutes, listening to the white noise around us, and each others' steady breathing. I feel my eyelids get heavy and stop myself before falling asleep. I don't want to miss a minute with him while I have him here.

"How are you here?" I ask, sitting back to study him more closely. "What about your tour?"

"Family first." He runs a finger along my cheekbone. He looks exhausted. "That's our motto. Everyone was fine with it. I'm yours through New Year." His lips twitch into a smile, and mine do the same. The way he said, "I'm yours," warms me from the inside out.

"Oh, good." I'm relieved. Putting my head back on his shoulder, I say, "I thought you went and did something reckless."

"Well, I did have to take three flights, one with a six and a half hour layover, and then drive all the way here from

Columbus in a blizzard, but no, nothing reckless." His voice is chiding with a hint of a laugh.

I jump back up again and stare at him in disbelief. "You did?" *Did he really do all that just to be with me? Wow. Just wow.*

"Of course I did." His eyes are tired, but with a touch of happiness. "If you hadn't noticed from my daily barrage of texts and voicemails, I didn't give up on us. I wasn't *going* to give up on us. When I heard what happened, I knew I had to be here. For both Benji and for you."

"Yeah, but three flights and driving through a blizzard is a bit extreme...."

"As I told my mom, I would have driven straight across the entire country if I had to. What's the saying? Wild horses couldn't keep me away."

"Did you let your mom know you made it? She's probably worried sick about you."

"I texted her in the elevator before I almost walked right into you and Jenny."

"You're crazy." I shake my head at him. I still can't believe he went through all that just to be here to be with me. Maybe I'm the crazy one for not believing how much he cares for me after all this time.

"Crazy for you," he smirks, sliding a warm hand around my neck and pulling me into a deep kiss. A kiss that reminds me exactly how he feels about me. When he pulls away, he whispers, "Merry Christmas, Sarah."

I glance at the clock over by the nurse's station, and see it is just after midnight. It is Christmas, and I won't have to spend it alone. "Merry Christmas."

We doze on and off throughout the night, with Ryan refusing to go home to sleep in a real bed. He insists on staying by my side as much as possible, which I'm not arguing against. I want him with me too. So, on Christmas Eve night, we hold each other on an uncomfortable hospital bench in a sterile waiting room and sleep better than either of us has slept in a month.

# # #

The following day, Olivia brings Joe to the hospital early, since the doctors will try to take Benji out of the coma and off of the ventilator in the early afternoon. When he arrives, he doesn't give Ryan a second glance, and just greets him as if it's normal for him to be here. I love that, but I can tell his anxiety level is through the roof too. He's as nervous as I am about Benji's response to being brought out of his coma. This is a crucial turning point in his recovery, and if he can climb over this hurdle, we could be on the other side of this.

Jenny and Luke arrive later in the morning, as does Lorelai, who brought Christmas cookies to share with everyone here, including the nurses who need to work on this holiday and be away from their own families. I can always count on Lorelai to bring something to a gathering, no matter what it is. However, I sneak to slide the food Jenny brought me yesterday under the chair behind me, so Lorelai doesn't see I haven't touched it. I don't think she would be offended, but I don't want to hurt her feelings. It was too kind of her to do in the first place.

Around one o'clock, Benji's doctor comes into the waiting

room to tell us that it's time. He pulls me into the hall outside Benji's room to talk to me alone. The severe tone of his voice takes me back to when my mother was in hospice, and I get the same chills I got then down my spine. I wish I had brought Ryan out here with me like he'd wanted to, but like an idiot, I told him I'd be okay. I am *not* okay.

"Does Benjamin have a Living Will? Or an Advanced Directive?" His expression is solemn. He's an older doctor with graying temples and compassionate eyes.

"No," I shake my head and cringe at the use of his full name. It feels so impersonal. "Neither of those."

"You are his next of kin, though, correct?"

"Yes." My throat constricts around the air that is supposed to allow me to breathe. The sharp smell of antiseptic cleaner makes me light-headed. I know what he's going to ask next, and suddenly I *desperately* want Ryan with me. I want him to hold me as I face this, but I need to be strong for Benji.

The doctor pushes on as though this is all business as usual for him. Which, luckily, it probably is. "So, as you know, we chemically induced a coma due to the traumatic brain injury your brother sustained, to allow the brain to rest and not use up the energy it needs to heal. There was also swelling that has fortunately receded enough for us to try to remove the medicine keeping him sedated. When we do that, it will wake him up, and we'll try to take him off the ventilator to see if his brain activity returns to normal, and he takes over his own breathing. Does that all make sense so far?"

It takes me a minute, but I catch up and nod, "Yes. I understand." My palms are sweating, and I wipe them on my jeans nervously. "What happens if he can't? You can just put everything back, right? And wait to see if he improves more later on?"

He rubs his jaw thoughtfully, "Well, that's what we need to know from you. Suppose Benjamin's brain activity is lessened to the point that he can't breathe independently. In that case, it'll be your call as to what we do next. We certainly could put him back into a coma and back on the ventilator, but to be honest with you, the longer we keep him like that, the less likely he'll improve. That's why we try to do this as early in the recovery process as we can. However, if you don't want us to attempt any of that, we can try to make him as comfortable as possible and allow the natural end processes to take their course."

"You mean, let him die?" I want to faint. I want to punch this doctor. I want to scream. I want my fucking brother back. What I do *not* want to do is make this decision on my own. I'm not the only one this decision affects. "Can I bring Benji's significant other into this conversation? I don't want to make this decision without him."

"Of course. I'll be right here." *He's so fucking calm. How can he be so fucking calm when my brother could die soon?*

I somehow make my way to the waiting room, where everyone stops talking to turn to me expectantly. Ryan comes over and takes my hand. "What is it?"

I turn to Joe, an urgency taking over, "I need you to come with me." My voice is shaky. He looks stricken, and the blood drains from his face, but he nods, and Olivia rolls his wheelchair into the hallway. Ryan meets my eyes, awaiting any request I might have. "Can you come too?" I ask, my voice now small.

"Of course." He puts an arm around me as we head back to the doctor, who goes through the steps and options again for Joe and Ryan.

Joe's entire body is crumpled, and he can't hold his emotions for much longer. He glances up at me, a sense of sadness and panic in his eyes that I never want to see again as long as I live. "I can't make this decision, Sarah. I just can't."

I squat down to meet him eye to eye, swallowing my own tears, "I'm not asking you to make the decision. I'll make the decision. But I want your input. Have you and Benji ever talked about stuff like this? Maybe he mentioned something in your support group?"

There's a relief in Joe's shoulders, "Okay. Okay then. Let me think. This is a lot right now."

"Take your time." Ryan's hand is now on my shoulder. I look up at him, thankful for his support. He hasn't broken contact with me since stepping into the hallway.

"I don't think he'd want to be dependent on anyone," Joe says, "if that's even one of the options available."

I nod in agreement. "I agree. He wouldn't want that." I glance up at the doctor to check if that's all he needs to hear.

"So I'm clear, no resuscitation and no heroic efforts, correct?"

I meet Joe's eyes, and we both nod. I can't help but lean in and pull him into a powerful hug. The fear we're both experiencing is something only we can share with each other.

"Okay." The doctor is all business now. "Miss Lawrence,

there's paperwork you'll need to sign, and we'll begin in about an hour so each of you can visit with Benji briefly beforehand if you so choose."

I thank him and turn quickly to bury my face in Ryan's chest, allowing myself to break down for only a minute. I don't want to waste any time I don't have.

Joe asks if he can go in to visit first, and I don't argue as I tearfully review the paperwork and sign all the mortal dotted lines while he's in there. I can barely watch him when he comes out, rolling himself in his wheelchair, battered and bruised. He's completely shattered and looks on the outside how I feel on the inside. Olivia runs out of the waiting room and helps him as he continues to fall apart.

The only other person who wants to see Benji is Jenny, and she goes in for just a couple of minutes, wanting to make sure I have as much time as I need with him. I hug her gratefully as she passes to return to the waiting room.

That leaves just me to go in, but I don't want to go. I don't want to say goodbye. I can't say goodbye. I can't do it. I won't do it.

"I've got you," Ryan whispers in my ear from behind, his hands on my shoulders. "Whatever you need. I've got you."

I glance back at him over my shoulder, trying to find the safety I so desperately need. And there it is, gazing back at me with so much empathy and compassion it would break me if it wasn't what was keeping me together. I put a hand over his and lead him into Benji's room with me, and he never leaves my side. Not when I finally break down and tell my sleeping brother how much I love him and how much I'll miss him if he goes. Not when I gather myself and tell Benji that I will understand if he needs to leave. And not when I eventually say nothing, but just hold my baby brother's hand and cry.

He's still there when the doctor comes back into the waiting room later to tell us Benji's brain responded marvelously, and he's awake and going to be okay. He's still there when I rush to my brother's bedside and hear his first drowsy words, which are "I need to see Joe." He's there for me when everyone leaves to spend their Christmas with their own loved ones, and when his mother shows up with dinner for the two of us. He's there for all of it, being my rock when I need it most. I don't know how I would have gotten through today without him next to me, and no matter what happens between us next, I'll always be eternally grateful to him for going to such lengths to be here for me like he has.

35

All This Time

RYAN

During the week between Christmas and New Year's, Sarah and I spend most of our time at the hospital with Benji, who is recovering so well he's been moved out of the intensive care unit and into a regular room. It will be a hard road for him, but he's expected to make a full recovery. Each day that he improves, I can see it reflected in Sarah's entire demeanor. Every obstacle he overcomes, she's his biggest cheerleader.

But it takes Joe on New Year's Eve to make her take some time to herself, and for us to spend an evening together that's not us just falling exhausted into bed after a full day at the hospital. He spelled it out to her so clearly, and in no uncertain terms that I could have kissed him for it.

"Sarah," he says with so much sass, I almost cringe. "No offense, but you need to go and spend some time with your man, and to be honest, leave Benji and me to spend some time to ourselves. It's flipping New Year's Eve, woman. Go get laid or something. You've earned it. Treat yourself. And your rock star boyfriend."

Of course, the rock star comment makes me shudder, but I appreciate the rest immensely. Sarah's jaw practically unhinges, and her eyes bulge as her cheeks redden with embarrassment at his bawdiness.

"Wow, Joe. Tell me how you really feel," she laughs nervously, purposely avoiding my eyes. We've slept together since I've been back, but we haven't *slept* together yet. I don't want to pressure her, and so far, just holding her every night has been more than enough for me.

My love for Sarah isn't reliant strictly on the physical attraction for her. Don't get me wrong, I have a *lot* of attraction for Sarah, and it nearly kills me every night to not try to touch and kiss her all over. But timing is everything, and the timing just hasn't been right, except for maybe tonight. We might have time enough to build up to something special. It would be the perfect way to ring in the new year and our new future together.

After Joe and Benji kick us out of his hospital room to spend New Year's with each other, we stop by my mother's house for a quick dinner. It's delicious as usual, and she, too, is eager to push us out the door so we can spend time alone with each other. It's starting to feel like a conspiracy. Even if it is, I'm not complaining.

When we get to Sarah's house, we're awkward with each other for a few minutes, anticipation vibrating between us as we orbit each other. As we stand in the kitchen, Sarah pours herself a glass of wine and me a soda. My phone dings with a text message. I glance down to see a goofy picture of Matt and Jude at a New Year's party, wearing 'Happy New Year' tiaras on their heads. I hold my phone up to show Sarah.

"Can you believe I work with these idiots?" I smile to myself, then hold the phone up, grab Sarah to get in the selfie frame, and kiss her cheek as she giggles when I take the picture. It turns out perfect, and I send that back to the guys, wishing them a Happy New Year. That makes my mind drift to music business stuff and reminds me that I wrote a new song for Sarah on my drive here. *How could I have forgotten about that? But should I play it for her now? Or should I wait until we can record it properly?*

"What's the matter?" Sarah asks. "You look upset."

"I'm not. Sorry. I just spaced." I tuck a lock of her dark hair behind her ear. "I think I have something for you."

"You think?" she laughs. "When will you know?"

"I mean, I know I have something for you. I just don't know if now is the right time to give it to you. Shit. This is all coming out wrong." I drag my hands down my face, frustrated with myself.

"Well, what is it?" Her brow furrows with curiosity, making her even more fucking adorable than she already is.

I let out a deep breath, resigned to see this through now. "I wrote you a song...."

"Another one?" She's being sarcastic, and *that* makes her even more fucking *sexy* than she already is.

"Yes, another one." I'm sarcastic right back. "But, it's just my vocals on my voice memo app."

"Well, do you want to use my guitar or something? I want to hear this now."

I think about that. I could use her guitar, but I'd need to work out the chords since I've never played it. "Sure, but I'll need a minute."

We go upstairs to fetch her guitar, and she points to the open door across the hall. "You can practice in there." It's her mother's old room, and I look at her, unsure if she realizes what she's saying. "Go on, make good use of that room for a change." And she heads back downstairs without thinking twice about it.

I close the door quietly behind me, treating the room with reverence and respect, knowing that being allowed here is a big deal. I sit on the foot of the bed with the guitar on my knee, ready to start figuring out the song. I glance around at the framed photos on the dresser of Sarah and her brother together with their mother. "Benji's going to be okay," I say softly to the empty room, not sure what the fuck I'm doing but compelled to do it. "And I've got Sarah covered. But thank you for her. I do love her." I hesitate for a second as if waiting for a sign of some sort, like some sort of musical ghost hunter. Nothing supernatural happens, and I start playing the song.

When I think I have the song figured out, I head back downstairs to play it for Sarah, but find her sitting in front of her laptop with a hand over her mouth, and her eyes wide.

"What's wrong?" I ask, rushing over to her. I glance at the screen but only see her email program. "What is it?"

"Do you know an Ian Summer?" She's still not taking her eyes off her screen.

271

"Yeah, he works for my label," I say, and it hits me. "Did he finally reach out to you?"

"Finally reach out to me? What do you mean?"

"You really didn't read any of my texts, did you?" I ask, shaking my head, not surprised, but still a little hurt.

"What does that have to do with anything?"

"I showed your videos to Ian, and he said he would keep an eye on your socials and stats to maybe sign you to a deal." She blanches. "Is that what he said in his email?"

She nods, unable to say anything; her hand smacks back over her mouth in astonishment.

"I knew it! I fucking knew it." I grab her up into a hug and swing her around the kitchen, making her squeal. When I put her down, I press my mouth to hers, and the next thing I know, I'm pressing her against the counter, and then she's pulling me upstairs by the collar of my shirt, and then we're in bed, and I'm loving her. And she loves me right back. We put the past month of anguish and despair behind us, and rejoice in every inch of each other. Reigniting the flame that never seems to go out entirely between us, and warming each other by its heat. And we keep going until we burn.

# # #

Sometime around midnight, as we're basking in the moonlight coming in through the window, and just reveling in the touch and feel of each other's skin, Sarah smiles at me while running her hand across my abs, "Happy New Year."

"Happy New Year to you too." I can't help but grin, tracing the outline of her dragonfly tattoo on her arm, making goosebumps rise up on her skin, and causing a shiver to run through her. I love when she does that.

"You were saying something about a song you wrote for me?" She bites her bottom lip and looks up at me through her lashes, and I just want to take her all over again. She knows what she's doing, driving me crazy, but I don't mind. I don't mind one single bit.

"Do you want to hear it now?" I ask, my voice huskier than usual as I restrain myself from jumping on top of her.

"Of course." She traces one of the tattoos along my side, making *me* shiver. *Fuck.*

I throw on my boxer briefs, arrange myself so I can walk straight without pain, and go downstairs to grab the guitar. When I get back, I find Sarah sitting up in bed in my t-shirt and nothing else, and she's simply incandescent. My breath catches as I take her in, so grateful that we get this chance again. Just so thankful for everything.

I climb onto the bed and re-tune the guitar that got jostled in all the excitement. I clear my throat several times and look up at Sarah, meeting her eyes. She's gazing back with such intensity that I almost forget what I'm doing until she blinks, and I snap back to the here and now. *Right. Don't fuck this up.*

"Okay, I'm calling this one 'So Close.'"

> *When you left, there was a death*
> *My heart died at your altar*
> *We were so close to heaven*
> *So, so close*

273

When you cried, as you thought I lied
My heart cried along with you
We were so close to heaven
So, so close

I'm heading back to you now
I'm so, so close
I want to hold you in my arms again
So, so close

I can show you that we can be
So, so close
Don't want to let go of this love when we're
So, so close

The verses and chorus repeat, and when I finish, Sarah leans in and kisses me, pulls the guitar out of my hands, and sets it aside. She climbs into my lap, still kissing me, her hands running through my hair. When we come up for air, she strokes the stubble on my chin with the back of her hand and asks, "Is this close enough?"

"Almost," I say, and her laughter echoes around the room as I reclaim my t-shirt, lay her back, and move on top of her, skin to skin. "But I need to be even closer."

EPILOGUE 1
Perfect Duet

After New Year's, I reluctantly leave Sarah's house and return to the tour. We've committed to talking via video at least once each day, no matter our schedules. No more misunderstandings, and no chance for words to be misconstrued. So far, it's working out beautifully. I still miss the ever-loving shit out of her when she's not with me, but I'm confident that we're going to be beyond fine with how things are going.

The biggest surprise has been the success of the song, 'Almost.' The video of Sarah and I singing together that night at the Stout Hideout went viral, and started getting more hits than our regular singles. It's surreal to watch us in our Princess Bride costumes as we performed, then see Sarah get super embarrassed and run off stage as we all chanted her name. It makes me laugh every time I see it.

So, we flew back to Chandler for a weekend, and went

into the studio and recorded it together, with Sarah producing. We then shot an actual video on the Hideout's stage of the two of us singing to each other in a spotlight. It's pretty special, and features actors playing out our napkin passing incident. Since the song wasn't on our album, we released it as a single with Sarah as a 'Featured Artist,' which should start even more buzz for her with the release of her own album soon. I've always known she was super talented, and now the rest of the world gets to find out.

Things aren't always perfect, but nothing in life ever is. I wouldn't trade our relationship for anything. Having my 'Almost Got Away' become my 'Absolutely' is more than I could ever dream of, let alone ask for, and I cherish her every single day. And I'll continue to do so as long as she'll let me.

Epilogue 2
More Than Words

Almost an entire month later, Benji finally gets to come home from the hospital and continues to grow stronger every day. He works his ass off in physical therapy, and regular therapy. He occasionally has slight short-term memory issues, but we're lucky that seems to be the extent of any permanent damage. He's agreed to a monetary settlement with the city that will cover all of his past and future medical bills related to the accident, plus more for punitive damages. When Benji does decide to go back to school, I won't need to worry about paying for it. It's a nice reassurance, but I'd just as soon give every cent back for the accident to never have happened. We get through it day by day. Some days are better than others, but they always are.

Joe comes by every day to visit him and doesn't seem to mind Gunner's shedding hair anymore. He's really grown as a person. The Van Gogh cast Olivia painted for him was indeed a work of art, and it was sad to see it cut off. The two of them are still relationship goals, if not more so now than before the accident, but Ryan and I are giving them a run for their money in that department with our own relationship.

Things with Ryan are going so well. I sometimes wonder if they're going *too* well, if that's even a thing. Sure, there are brush-ups here and there, but nothing like I see other couples doing. We just don't really fight. Not that there isn't intensity between us, because there is plenty of that, but we care about each other so deeply, even when we're disagreeing, we take particular care not to hurt the other person.

That trait is beneficial since we spend every day together on the road. Once 'Almost' took off and my album came out, I joined Indigo King, and Incendiary Ink on their summer shed tour. Every night, either I join Ryan on stage, or he joins my set, and we perform 'Almost.' The crowd goes nuts every time, and I'll never get tired of singing that song with him. We're even considering recording 'So Close' as a duet too, but are still deciding on that one.

Amazingly, I have *two* songs in the top fifty since my own single, 'I'll Never,' currently sits at 32 with a lovely bullet on the streaming charts. My dream of pursuing my own music career, that only a few months ago I thought was completely out of my reach, is actually coming true. I don't think I can be much happier than I am now. And to think, I almost threw it all away over a simple drunken misunderstanding. I'm glad that one was just an a*lmost.*

- THE END -

Almost Playlist

Spotify: https://open.spotify.com/playlist/6BwhtffEfs26M-KQ4kY2gpI?si=dc1bebe4ffc74661

Vance Joy, *From Afar*

OneRepublic, *Come Home*

Lifehouse, *From Where You Are*

Flyleaf, *Traitor*

Penny and Sparrow, *I Fall to Pieces*

Emma Ruth Rundle, *Shadows Of My Name*

FINNEAS, *A Concert Six Months From Now*

Snow Patrol, Martha Wainwright, *Set Fire To The Third Bar*

Ryan Cabrera, *True*

James Arthur, Anne-Marie, *Rewrite The Stars*

Lauv, Julia Michaels, *There's No Way*

Joseph Vincent: *Killing me Softly*

Christina Perri, *the words*

Carolyn Dawn Johnson, *Complicated*

The Smiths, *Please, Please, Please, Let Me Get What I Want*

Toby Keith, *You Shouldn't Kiss Me Like This*

James Arthur, *Say You Won't Let Go*

George Michael, *Kissing A Fool*

Wham!, *Careless Whispers*

Sam Smith, *Too Good At Goodbyes*

Ellie Goulding, *Love Me Like You Do*

Band of Skulls, *Cold Sweat*

Rosi Golan and William Fitzsimmons, *Hazy*

James Bay, *Let It Go*

Sara Bareilles, *1000 Times*

Kelly Clarkson, *Never Again*

Del Amitri, *Tell Her This*

Hailee Steinfeld, *Wrong Direction*

Sam Smith, *Not In That Way*

PJ Harvey, *The River*

Foo Fighters, *Home*

FINNEAS, *Only A Lifetime*

Keith Urban, *Break On Me*

Christina Perri, *arms*

OneRepublic, *All This Time*

    Epilogue 1 Ryan - Ed Sheeran & Beyonce, *Perfect Duet*

    Epilogue 2 Sarah - Extreme, *More Than Words*